THE DANCING DELILAHS

The Dancing Delilahs

Pauline Cushman & Antonia Ford
CIVIL WAR SPIES

Warm Wishes,
Pamela Bauer Mueller

Piñata Publishing

Copyright 2016 Pamela Bauer Mueller

All right reserved. No part of this book may be used or reproduced in any manner whatsoever without prior written permission except in the case of brief quotations embodied in reviews.

Piñata Publishing
626 Old Plantation Road
Jekyll Island, GA 31527
(912) 635-9402
www.pinatapub.com

Library of Congress Cataloging-in-Publication Data

Bauer Mueller, Pamela
  The dancing delilahs : Civil War spies Pauline Cushman and Antonia
Ford / Pamela Bauer Mueller.
    pages cm
  Includes bibliographical references and index.
  Summary: "Through research of primary and secondary sources,
Pamela Bauer Mueller presents the stories of two (one from the North,
one from the South) female Civil war spies in a non-fiction novel—
Provided by publisher.

ISBN 978-0-9809163-4-8 (alk. paper)

    1. United States—History—Civil War, 1861–1865—Women—
Fiction. 2. Women and war—Fiction. 3. Historical fiction. 4. Spy
stories. I. Title.

    PS3602.A93566D36 2016 813'.6--DC23   2015021682

Cover art by Gini Steele
Typeset by Vancouver Desktop Publishing Centre
Printed and bound in the United States by Cushing-Malloy, Inc.

I dedicate this story to the brave women, in times past and present, who fight for their beliefs, even when not politically correct. Thank you for your faith, your courage and your example.

"Oh, what a tangled web we weave,
When first we practice to deceive!"

—Sir Walter Scott, Marmion,
A Tale of Flodden Field, 1808

Author's Note

I feel totally challenged when I begin to write a new book. Will I be able to capture what it is like to live between the years 1861–1864? I know now that writing is an act of faith, and I must believe those details will emerge when I need them.

A writer is more than a scribe. We must preserve the protagonists' stories and, at the same time, embrace the conflict necessary to make the stories believable, and not safe or predictable.

As a writer, I try to flavor each story with the language of my characters. And I try to surprise myself as I write. Sometimes, I feel like I am floating above the story and watching the themes as they arise. That is truly magical!

Character is elemental. Paying attention to people and the language they use to find their voices reveals human behavior. Someone once said, "Writers write; characters row."

This new spy novel came about from my desire to write about our country's history by finding ordinary people thrust into extraordinary circumstances. Writing about famous women is easy—there is a wealth of information available. Writing about the women history has forgotten is more difficult, but they also deserve recognition. And I especially love to present women who are edgy, salty and downright eccentric.

Despite the fact that both were Civil War spies, Antonia Ford's and Pauline Cushman's lives and stories were completely different. Their stories personify Laurel Thatcher Ulrich's famous quotation, "Well-behaved women seldom make history."

My greatest challenge in writing *The Dancing Delilahs* was to factually create both women's viewpoints—by telling each woman's story in the first person. I had never done this before and welcomed the opportunity, allowing me to grow as a writer. I have attempted, in each of their stories, to provide the accurate setting for the women to make difficult decisions in their daily lives. Their choices would reshape their futures.

Another enormous challenge has been to keep the focus of the story personal rather than on the events themselves. I want readers to think about abstract ideas such as their individual relationships, their intimate lives and even their sufferings. This kind of writing can be frustrating and exhausting, but in the end, it is exhilarating.

I have always been captivated by history—its broad sweep and its guarded corners. People make history by keeping diaries, writing letters, or embroidering initials on linens. History is a conversation between the present and the past, and sometimes the voices are barely audible. Through far-ranging research, I hope to uncover these voices and bring them to you. Often I convert their "written words" into conversations, offering you a better understanding of their feelings and beliefs.

Throughout the Civil War, many female spies were slaves, desperate for a Northern victory to secure their freedom. They risked their lives passing information to the Union Army. Spying was also practiced by well-to-do white women, from both the North and the South, who used their large hoop skirts to hide weapons and conceal documents and other contraband.

Both Antonia and Pauline utilized their charm and resilient characters for the foundation of their beloved country. Each woman was an unusual product of 19th Century America, able to influence officers from both sides during the bloody conflict of the Civil War.

In the words of Professor Julius Lester, "History is not just facts and events. History is also a pain in the heart."

Pauline

APRIL 16, 1863

It is so unpleasantly humid behind the garish stage foot-lights. Louisville is under Union control, and the Civil War is in full and deadly swing. Yet inside the theater the loyal Feds and Rebel sympathizers sit shoulder to shoulder, seemingly tolerating each other's company. They have gathered to enjoy our popular musical about seven female demons who rise from hell to go sightseeing in New York City. We actors already know it is a runaway hit.

From the wings, I can see the theater is packed. Word has spread that something unexpected will happen on stage tonight. I am petrified. I sit down and force myself to breathe slowly, even though my heart is racing. After my shoulders untense and my jaw unclenches and my hands unfist, I force myself to stand up leisurely.

Dressed as a gay young blade, I feel a thin worm of perspiration dribbling down my spine. My fingers twitch nervously as they travel over my tight-fitting gentleman's outfit, pulling down my wristbands, flattening the shirt collar and straightening the bow of my polka dot cravat. I breathe in deeply as I was taught to do in my theatrical training.

On my left I see Phillips, the stage manager, signaling me to step forward. I feel dread sliding through my body.

All eyes are riveted on me as I mount the stage at the Wood's Theater, my nerves struggling to hide behind a warm smile. I allow my sense of stage presence to direct me, and I make it effortlessly through the first half of *The Seven Sisters.*

Now the supper scene begins. I step forward and survey the huge audience. Lifting my wine glass, I look into the face of a gentleman up front and make the astounding toast I have been paid to propose. My throat has closed down and I must clear it in order to speak, causing a dramatic pause.

Recovering my distinct, transparent, ringing voice, I pray that my fright will not be perceptible.

"Here's to Jeff Davis and the Southern Confederacy," I intone. "May the South always maintain her honor and her rights!"

Lifting the glass to my lips for a single gulp, the hall is so still I can hear myself swallow. Everyone in the front row must hear it as well.

A shocked silence greets my words, followed closely by shouts of both praise and condemnation. The sentiment falls upon the audience like the explosion of a shell. I knew the theater was packed with paroled Confederate officers and patriotic Unionists. A cacophony of Rebel cheers, mixed with Union yells, boos, and catcalls, depending on their loyalties, fills the air. The Union persons are mortified and indignant, yet the Confederate sympathizers seem delighted. I eventually hear the applause, mingled with the jeers, and become aware that hats are flying through the air.

The stage manager orders the curtain lowered, then rushes to remove me from the stage as fist fights break out in the audience. Fellow actors stare at me in disbelief. I ache to tell them the truth, but I cannot. This burden must be borne for my country's sake.

Having made my decision, I will not go back on it, even when the Union guards arrive to arrest me. This is also part of my agreement. I will be held for one night to fool the

Confederates, then report to the Provost Marshal tomorrow morning at ten o'clock. I sincerely hope I will never regret my decision.

ONE

Pauline

JUNE 1861

I was playing an engagement in Cleveland, Ohio when the war broke out. Charles and I, along with our two small children, were living with his parents. Patriotic fervor in Cleveland was equal to that of any other city, so we were naturally swept up in it also.

General James Garfield, back in Ohio within weeks of the firing on Fort Sumter, was raising a regiment he hoped to lead into battle. Shortly after, Charles and his brothers, Albert and James, joined the Union army as musicians in the 41st Ohio Infantry's band.

Charles Dickinson and I had met nine years earlier in New Orleans, while employed with the same stage company. An excellent theatrical musician, he had been discovered by Thomas Placide, as had I. Our quick and exciting romance led to marriage on December 2, 1853. Charles was just twenty-one and I was twenty. One of Mr. Placide's theater bills might include five or six hours of various entertainments such as farces, a main piece, an afterpiece, musical entertainment, and ballet. He staged several simultaneous productions, and always had work for us. Tragically, his largest theater was destroyed by fire in 1854, so our troupe completed the season in Mobile, Alabama.

Charles and I set out for New York and worked with several musical companies, but not always on the same production. At that point I was using several stage names, including "Asa Cushman," or "Miss A. Cushman."

While pregnant with Charlie, I discontinued all stage work to begin a family. Our son was born on March 9, 1858, in New Haven, Connecticut where Charles taught music. We enjoyed a quiet family life until I became pregnant again six months later.

When Ida Dickinson was born in Cleveland, Ohio on July 7, 1859, we decided to move back to Charles' family home. Then tragedy struck. Charles' youngest brother died on July 28, 1859, at the tender age of three.

Between 1858 and 1861, my life became that of a typical Victorian woman. Charles taught music and played with several local bands. His family provided emotional support, yet I often felt "at loose ends."

Away from the excitement of life in the theater, I spent long lonely months in Cleveland with our children, while Charles followed opportunities in other cities.

I had been brought up in a family where several languages were spoken. Living like a tomboy with seven brothers in the wilds of western Michigan, we became close to the Red Indians living close by. Learning their language made me independent and prepared me for the challenges and social whirl that awaited me as an actress and later as a scout.

Life on the frontier no longer suited me, but it was not easy to adjust to virtual confinement in the Dickinson city home either.

My own family seemed so far away in Michigan, and in any case we were never very close. Upon turning eighteen I had headed straight to the theater district of New York City.

I was born in New Orleans, Louisiana on June 10, 1833. My given name was Harriet Wood. One year later Mama, Papa and I moved to Grand Rapids, Michigan so my father could operate an Indian trading post. My seven younger brothers and I grew up learning Spanish from our father, French from our mother, and some Pottawatomie from the native Red Indians who traded with us. We also rode bareback, shot firearms, tracked animals through the woods and swamps, and navigated canoes over fierce rapids. I grew up strong and independent and quickly developed a lifelong love of nature.

Papa had met Mama in France and they married, despite the objections of her family—respectable wine growers from Bordeaux. They eventually set up their home in New Orleans, which was at the height of rapid prosperity due to the cotton trade. After a few years Papa's trading business failed, so shortly after my first birthday, he took us to Michigan.

Mama was a mild and kind soul who gave each of us her unbounded affection. A strict Catholic, she carefully trained us in all her church's ceremonies and beliefs. My father's rigid nature clashed often with her gentle temperament, so the eight of us were forced to witness their many disagreements. William, my brother closest to me in age, distracted me by challenging me to outdoor competition. He knew my refuge was in the plains and wild companions that surrounded our home.

"Harriet, go get your rifle. Let's ride out to the river and shoot." I'd run on ahead, eager to show how I could best him.

Many days my adolescent Indian girlfriends taught me to braid many little leather objects to sell. The boys would instruct me and my brothers in the warrior preparations. The young braves called me "Laughing Breeze," and each brother also had a nickname. The wigwams of the Red Men were always open to welcome us.

I grew into my teen years, tall and straight as an arrow, my long dark hair streaming behind me as I rode my half-tamed pony over the broad plains. I loved to read and learn, and began dreaming about another world, the big city world of luxury and entertainment. And I yearned to live the romances that I was discovering. My imagination soared as I read about the theater and the female performers leading lives of adventure. Would I ever be able to *live* such fantastic stories?

I was blessed with a decent if uncultivated voice. Mama described my singing as "free and unrestrained," similar to the prairie birds I liked to imitate, and encouraged me to pursue singing. "My love, with your grace, beauty, and tact, you have everything you need to make your mark." And I believed her.

Against my father's wishes, but with Mama's secret encouragement, I left Michigan for New York City shortly after my eighteenth birthday to join the theatrical movement spreading across the nation. I took a few dance and voice lessons with other eager young thespians and made contacts wherever I could.

Providence led me to Mr. Thomas Placide, the manager of the New Orleans "Varieties," who was in New York City recruiting performers for his company. He was so taken by my looks and "spunk" that he promptly offered me an opportunity to appear in a new production at his New Orleans theater.

He helped me choose a stage name as well: *Pauline Cushman*, a name that audiences might easily recognize because the actress Charlotte Cushman was at the height of her popularity as an actress in *The Queen of Tragedy*. This appealed to me, as I was keen to let some of her glory reflect on me.

My exciting new life was tempered by the loss of my dear mother, who passed away shortly after I arrived in New Orleans. This crushing news didn't reach me until it was too late to attend her burial. Then a year later my father died. For months grief lingered in my heart until I met Charles Dickinson, whose attention and love helped to ease my pain.

Suddenly, everything changed again. Charles and the rest of the musicians spent a lot of time with his regiment at Camp

Wood, just a mile from the house. The children and I often took a horse-drawn streetcar to visit him, and I liked to read the news on the way. One day, I chanced upon a most stimulating article in the newspaper.

I hurried to Camp Wood from the street car stop, newspaper in hand, and thrust it into his hands as soon as we saw him.

"Did you know about this, Charles? Have you ever seen her?"

His eyes ran quickly over the words of the story.

A Sensation in Camp Wood—Discovery of a Female Volunteer.

Quite a sensation was occasioned at Camp Wood, where the 41st regiment is encamped, yesterday afternoon, by the discovery that a recruit, recently enlisted in the McClellan Zouaves, is a female. She came from Dayton, as she claims, on Monday last and enlisted at once. She wore men's clothes...She gave the name of MARY SMITH. She has been removed from Camp, furnished with more fitting apparel than a soldier's uniform, and will be sent to Dayton.

Charles raised his eyes to meet mine. "Having heard only gossip, I decided the others were joshing when they talked about it."

I threw my head back and laughed, eyes dancing with excitement. "What an adventure! I believe I should like to do the same."

He placed his hand over mine and spoke somberly. "Dearest, please do not mention this here at camp. The newly-appointed colonel of the 41st would never tolerate such unseemly spectacles here."

I was frustrated, but nodded as if in agreement. However, a seed had been planted.

TWO

Antonia

JULY 1861

I was twenty-three years old the year the war began. Until that time, I had been living a life of quiet comfort. My father, Edward Ford, came from a family long-established in the Old Dominion, and was a prosperous merchant. Of course he was also a staunch Secessionist. Many say he was the foremost citizen of Fairfax Courthouse, Virginia—my home town. We lived in a lovely house on Chain Bridge Road, across from the Fairfax Courthouse and midway between Washington City and Manassas. Our home was called "a cultural and political center" for the burgeoning Southern insurrection. It also provided front-row seats to the comings and goings of Union General McDowell's troops.

Before the Battle of First Manassas on July 18, 1861, we often played host to Southern troops stationed near our village. My cousin Laura Ratcliffe and I became regular visitors to the Southern army camps. It was our only chance to socialize, as most of our local young men had been mobilized. These visits provided stimulating conversation, dances, games, moonlit walks and even carriage and horseback rides.

My younger brother Charlie was already serving in the Confederate Army as 2nd Lieutenant in McGregor's Battery—General Jeb Stuart's famous Horse Artillery. Papa told Lindsay, a young slave of twenty, to accompany Charlie as his manservant. Lindsay said he was eager to go with Charlie.

Charlie wrote that he hoped to send us an albumen silver print carte de visite like that of one captain, which included a photograph taken with his manservant wearing a nine-button shell jacket. Unfortunately, the North's military blockade meant he could only send us an ambrotype cased image of himself and Lindsay.

Late in the evening of June 1st we heard a great commotion outside our home. My sixteen-year-old brother Clanie told Papa he would go outside and investigate.

"No, Clanie. Remain here with the women. I will go." His dark eyes went hard.

As he prepared to leave, a neighbor rapped on the door and I reached out to open it, my father standing close behind me.

The neighbor was very excited and breathing rapidly. "Company B of the Union 2nd Cavalry just attacked us from the Falls Church Road! Lieutenant Charles Tompkins led the men. I think the Warrenton Rifles are holding them off," he gasped.

Mother invited him in and made some tea. We sat and waited, listening to the rapid gunshots. Eventually my father walked out into the street and found Captain William Smith.

"Have you run the Yankees off?" he asked.

"We have, but we've lost track of our commander, John Quincy Marr."

"Are there casualties?"

"One or two are wounded, but no deaths."

The skirmish we had just witnessed happened during the march of Brigadier General Irvin McDowell's Union Army of the Potomac from Washington to Manassas. Their path took them directly through Fairfax Courthouse and close to our home, situated between the capital and the battlefield.

The following day we learned that our commander, John Quincy Marr, had been the first Confederate soldier killed in the war. Governor William "Extra Billy" Smith, who had served as governor in the 1840s, was ordered to take charge of the Warrenton Rifles.

Several days later, the Sanitary Commission was formed in New York. Its purpose was to impartially distribute supplies to both Union and Confederate prisoners. Mother and I gathered up blankets, bed linens, underclothing, pillow covers, and anything else the troops might need. My eleven-year-old sister Pattie helped us make bandages for the wounded.

My father offered our home (where some officers were already paying customers) as the local Confederate soldiers' headquarters. They told Mother that our home was a "refuge from the storm" because of my parents' hospitality and charm. Some evenings we even provided music for the guests, and I played the piano. I enjoyed these soirees for more than their entertainment value. I learned a lot about what was happening by listening to political conversations.

On July 16th, Papa, Clanie and I traveled by carriage to Alexandria. Papa wanted to do his part for the Southern Cause and had been exchanging war information with the village leaders in Alexandria. As we approached the village, but still a distance away, we noticed a young man on horseback riding toward us.

"You'd better turn around," he shouted. "The Yanks are a scant mile away."

Papa asked him how many were nearby. "Don't know, sir. It's the advance troops of Brigadier General McDowell's Army." With that, he hurried away in the direction from which we had come.

My father decided it would be safer for us to stay with his friends who lived nearby. They welcomed us with steaming hot tea and comfortable sofas. Our conversation was interrupted by a loud bang on the door.

A soldier's large frame filled the doorway. "I am Major Wadsworth, General McDowell's aide-de-camp. On behalf of the Union army, I am here to commandeer this house for temporary Union headquarters."

Our host's face paled as he stepped back. "You may come in, sir. I am not happy about this, but I will be accommodating."

Papa and Clanie had remained in a back room and signaled for me to join them. The three of us slipped out to the back porch and conversed in secret.

"Antonia, I will ask my friends to keep you here while Clanie and I go on to Alexandria. Not knowing what lies ahead, your safety is paramount." He pulled me close to whisper, "Perhaps you can learn something about their strategies during your stopover."

I nodded, eager to be included in Papa's plans, and wished them safe travels.

My father's friends courteously invited the three officers, including General McDowell himself, to accompany us at dinner. After a pleasant if constrained meal, we retired to the parlor. Their oldest daughter and I played the piano while the men drank whiskey. I waited for the right moment to gather my information.

"Major Wadsworth, how long will you remain in this area?" I asked demurely, just after General McDowell retired for the evening.

"We're here until the General moves us on," he answered, already on guard.

I noticed another officer's interest in me, made warmer by several whiskies.

"What is such a beautiful young lady doing here alone?" he asked, brazenly sweeping his eyes over my figure.

"Visiting my friends, Major. My father will be here for me shortly."

"Surely you have a husband, Miss Ford. With those full lips, tilted nose, and that mane of beautiful blond hair, you are quite a vision to behold." Although shocked at his boldness, I remained silent.

Changing the subject, I deftly queried him with a disarming smile. "How many men does the General have?"

"More than six thousand, my dear," he answered pompously. "More than enough to clear the Confederates out of their holes with our planned maneuver up the Warrenton Pike." While he grinned and boasted, I took further advantage of his interest.

"Will you travel as far as the Old Stone Bridge?" I asked, batting my lashes and leaning closer.

"Further, my lass. We'll take everything between here and there. It's already in motion, so I do not mind telling you." Leaning toward me and taking my hand, he whispered as if to a co-conspirator. "We are ready for battle, and already have other brigades nearby to assist us. At least three of them," he chuckled.

I discretely withdrew my hand and stood up to excuse myself, and was joined by the hostess and her daughters. At the top of the stairway I thanked them and explained that I would be leaving early the following morning.

"Please tell Papa I could not wait for him to pick me up." Lowering my voice I murmured, "I have acquired important information that I must take to our troops. Might you send me on one of your horses? "

They agreed, although persuading them of my safety took a minute. Awakening early the next morning, I found General McDowell already seated at the breakfast table.

"Oh, General McDowell, I am happy to see you this early," I said with a sweet smile. "I must return immediately to Fairfax Courthouse, as my mother has taken ill and my father is away. Would you be willing to issue me a pass for safe travel?"

He straightened up in his chair and eyed me suspiciously.

I held my breath as he slowly nodded and wrote the note. I had purposely not mentioned the war the evening before, so he probably considered me a fellow Federalist at heart. The pass went into my traveling bag.

The horse was saddled and waiting. My hostess handed me a canteen of water and a small bundle of food.

"Thank you for everything," I said, embracing her. "Please explain to Papa and Clanie the state of affairs, and tell them I'll be home as soon as I can."

"Godspeed, my dear," she whispered. I mounted the borrowed horse and rode off.

THREE

Antonia

JULY 17, 1861

I rode like thunder for hours, pushing the poor horse as much as I dared over the muddy and eroded roads to reach General Beauregard's camp. Hopefully it would be where I expected, based on past conversations between soldiers in our home. I took some alternate routes to avoid Union soldiers on the main roads. Several times they stopped me, and I had to present my pass. The total distance was only about thirteen miles, but with the stops, detours and rain, I didn't reach Bull Run until after four o'clock.

"Please, can you direct me to General Beauregard?" I asked two Confederate artillerymen standing stiffly at attention.

They studied me, visibly surprised to see a lady riding astride a winded horse instead of the usual sidesaddle. I knew my hair was wild, and my face and arms were covered with dirt. I could see the muscles in their forearms flexing nervously.

The soldiers remained silent, staring intently at my strange appearance. I drew in a deep breath, juggling my words awkwardly. "I have very important information about enemy troop movements to share with him."

One of the soldiers answered cynically. "Then follow me to his tent."

He waited outside the tent with me until an officer exited through the flap and, with a disapproving glare, exited into the dusk. Finally, I was ushered inside.

General P.G.T. Beauregard regarded me for a long moment, and then smiled slightly. "Who are you? Why are you here?" he asked quietly.

"Sir, my name is Antonia Ford. I live in Fairfax Courthouse and have firsthand information of battle plans being laid by the Yankees to trap you. They plan to make an attack on Manassas the 18th of July, which is tomorrow!" I shook from exhaustion and the magnitude of my news.

He studied my face and urged me to continue. I told him everything I heard the previous evening.

General Beauregard eventually stood up and extended his hand. "Thank you kindly, Miss Ford. You have brought me useful information. You may now return to your home."

I hurried to my horse grazing nearby, gasping when a strong hand grabbed my arm.

"What are you doing?" I cried out, trying to shake myself free of his grip.

Lieutenant Thomas Rosser of the Washington Artillery from New Orleans introduced himself and explained why he had stopped me. "You are under arrest for suspicions of being a spy and supplying us with misleading intelligence."

I stared at him in shock, shaking my head in disbelief. "You are incorrect, sir. I am a patriotic Southern lady, here to help you."

"You will have to come with me until we clear this up," he snorted, tossing his head disdainfully as his fingers tightened on my arm.

We rode to the village of Brentsville, just south of Manassas. As we reached its jailhouse I was still protesting. "My brother Charlie is with Colonel Kershaw's Infantry. My father is E.R. Ford, a staunch supporter of the South. You can inquire and will learn I am speaking the truth."

They put me in a guarded cell and gave me warm food and

water. I begged the guard to let me out so that I might explain to the authorities, but to no avail. Finally, I tried to sleep, but having never slept on a dirt floor before, my sleep was fitful and sporadic.

The following afternoon, after nearly twenty-four hours of incarceration, a stranger arrived to release me.

"Ma'am, my name is John Burke. I work for Jeb Stuart in Washington," he said in a strong Southern accent. "Allow me to humbly apologize for our mistake. We have confirmed your story and will escort you back to your home," he said gently.

"Confirmed my story? How?" I asked, astonished.

"I also work as a spy and confirmed your story with information from a female spy named Rose Greenhow. Perhaps you know her?" he added.

"No, I do not." Relief flooded through me as I offered him a weak smile. Together, we made our way back to Fairfax Courthouse by a circuitous route. The roads were swarming with Blue Coats, whose arrival I had predicted.

My family had been anxiously watching for me. The door flew open as soon as we turned the corner of my street.

"Dear Lord, Antonia!" My mother burst into tears as she pulled me to her. "How could you have put yourself in such danger? We feared you were dead!"

My father, at her side, brushed away his own tears as I began to explain. "But of course I had to give the information I obtained to General Beauregard. That's where I've been."

As I explained the details of my escapade, I saw anger cross my father's face. "What an outrage that our own Confederate Army would treat you as a Union spy," he sputtered, eyes flashing sparks.

Then Mother calmed him down. "Well, we also have news of our own. The Yankees have begun pouring into town. Pattie and I spent the day together, frightened without news of you or your father or Charlie. Finally, I stood in the doorway and watched the poor Confederates departing, abandoning their heavy knapsacks on the streets. It has been quite a day," she sniffed, still wiping away tears and clinging to my father.

Clanie chimed in. "We had to watch the Confederate flag being lowered from the courthouse pole. But the worst part was seeing the United States flag going up."

I turned to my father, puzzled. "But what about our home? Will they now ransack and loot it?"

He shook his head, his face drained and saddened. "No, my love. They will be using it for their Yankee headquarters."

"What!" I cried, incredulous, stunned beyond speech.

Mother nodded, reaching out for my hand. "General McDowell was here yesterday to send a dispatch to Washington. He spent the night in our home and then left for Sangster's Station. We know not what will transpire tomorrow."

We sat together in strained silence, pondering the future of our family, our community, our very way of life.

Then Octavia, at work in the back room, began the popular Negro spiritual, "Go Down, Moses." The velvet sounds of that familiar melody seemed strong and hopeful, yet came across as a melancholy tune. Coming from the slight woman with such a big heart, the song quickly settled our mood.

As Octavia placed a tea pot and cups on the small living room table, Mother asked her gently, "Octavia, the latest news about Yankee boarders will mean more unhappy chores for you, Adam and Mathilde. What is there for you to sing about in such a situation?"

Pushing her palms across her apron front to dry them, she smiled sweetly and explained.

"Well, ma'am, we all be learnin' how to face dese hardships together. We learn long time ago dat our problems in life cain't stop us if we face dem side by side. 'Tis a blessing to stand beside you and de family."

Three days later, the officers were still using our home as headquarters. We all watched from our front porch as Union soldiers staggered in retreat through Fairfax Courthouse.

That evening I answered a knock at the door.

Before me stood Major Wadsworth—the officer who had told me about their planned strategy. I wondered if he remembered his drunken bravado.

"What an unexpected surprise to see you again," I managed to stammer.

"A pleasure indeed," answered Major Wadsworth. "I've been informed this house is our headquarters, so I will ensure that the stragglers and worn-out soldiers are not left behind."

"Left behind? Where are you going?" I asked, disbelieving my own ears. "Was the battle a Confederate victory?"

"This time, yes. The surprise attack turned out not to be such a surprise," he told me a little bitterly. "We lost 3,000 men versus less than 2,000 on the Rebel side. We are returning to Washington and will be gone by dusk," he said, as if to a child.

I ran to find my father, stacking firewood by the back steps. "Papa, I have achieved my first scouting victory. The Battle of Manassas was won by the Rebels. Did you know?" I found myself laughing wildly.

"First, my dear? What do you mean," he grinned, his eyes playful.

"Well, Papa, military intrigue may get under my skin as it has for you. Let us wait and see."

Later I learned the full story of that historic battle. A brigade of Virginians, under a relatively unknown brigadier general from the Virginia Military Institute named Thomas J. Jackson, stood their ground. During the battle Jackson's bravery earned him the nickname, "Stonewall Jackson."

Following the Confederates' strong counter-offensive, green Union troops had to withdraw under fire. Many panicked, and the retreat turned into a rout. McDowell's 35,000 men frantically scattered in the direction of Washington. Both armies and the public, sobered by the fierce fighting and many casualties, now realized that this war would be much longer and bloodier than either side had anticipated.

Was my timely intervention responsible for that win?

FOUR

Antonia

AUGUST 30, 1861

Jeb Stuart and his scout John Mosby were frequent visitors to our home and friends of the family. John was a slight, handsome twenty-eight-year-old private in the 1st Virginia Cavalry. "The Gray Ghost's" usually smiling blue eyes shone with intelligence and mischief and he smiled often. I was fond of his boisterous laugh.

But on the evening of August 26, his eyes were smarting with pain as he leaned on two soldiers carrying his wiry body across the threshold of our house.

Mother quickly removed John's smashed hat and filthy jacket while Papa covered him with blankets. Reclining on the sofa, he gave us the account of his situation.

"I fell off my horse while I was on the picket at Falls Church. Our orders were to fire on all cavalry that came from the direction of the enemy, so I did. Riding back to the main body of my soldiers, my poor horse slipped and fell on me. Then the frightened steed ran off! I lay senseless in the road for a time, and when I awoke, my comrades had retrieved my horse and brought me here."

"Thank God they did," murmured Mother. "You know we will care for you as family and nurse you back to health." She sent Clanie for the doctor while the rest of us washed and bandaged his cuts and wounds.

Over the next few days, John rested comfortably in Clanie's

room, staying off his feet to heal his bruised ribs and injured muscles. My sister and I engaged him in conversations about his wife Pauline and their two small children. I was touched to hear his loving comments, realizing how much he missed his family.

"I met my beloved Pauline Clarke when her family visited from Kentucky. She was Catholic and I am Methodist," he grinned. "Didn't make no difference to either of us, and we got married in a Nashville hotel on December 23, 1853." Smiling broadly at the memory he added, "Best thing I ever did."

"When will you see them again?" I asked, sympathetic about his separation from them.

"As soon as possible, Antonia. My two little ones need a brother or sister." His laugh rolled over us, rich and contagious.

My father and Clanie spoke with him for hours about the war, secession, and whatever else came to mind.

"I spoke out against secession for a long time," he admitted, "but finally joined the Confederate Army as a private. I first served in William 'Grumble' Jones Washington's Mounted Rifles, but when Jones became a major and was ordered to form a more collective 'Virginia Volunteers,' he called on me for help."

Father asked him what the new unit had included.

"Well, together we created two mounted companies and eight companies of infantry and riflemen, and we included the Washington Mounted Rifles."

"Did you begin gathering intelligence then?" Clanie asked him, his face alight with excitement. John had already told us how much he enjoyed scouting.

"Yes, that was our most interesting task. But disappointed with the Virginia volunteers' lack of congeniality, I wrote to the governor asking to be transferred."

"Were you?" My little brother's eyes widened.

"Nay, my request was not granted. Instead I came here to participate in the Battle of Bull Run, which we Confederates call First Manassas. And a few skirmishes since then," he added, pointing to his sore ribs.

Once he was able to exercise, I took him on short walks to limber up, strengthen his muscles, and continue our fascinating dialogues. The road near our house led up into the mild hills past small white churches and farms, where goats grazed in the fields and patient mules were harnessed to grinding wheels.

I learned he had attended the University of Virginia, where he excelled in the Classics. But before graduation, he was expelled for shooting and wounding another student. He was fined one thousand dollars and the court sentenced him to a year in jail. The Governor of Virginia released him after six months.

"He lent me some law books while I waited for my trial date. After my sentence was annulled, I was admitted to the bar and later opened a law office in Howardsville, Virginia."

I was intrigued by his stories and by his personality. "Did you enjoy law?" I asked.

"Well Antonia, I can't rightly say. So far I've completed a lot of paperwork and prosecuted only a few cases. The war cut short my practice."

"John, what about the war? Do you think it will be over soon?"

He shook his head. "Some say so, but not I. I fear the South is doomed. But I will continue to defend the land that I love so much." His voice dropped to almost a whisper.

"But just days ago we surprised the Union forces at Kessler's Cross Lanes in West Virginia, did we not?" I asked with a slow smile.

Returning my smile, he nodded. "But for every punch, the Feds get back at us. Just today I learned that the Union troops in North Carolina captured Fort Clark and Fort Hatteras, losing only one soldier. I need to get back there to help my unit. I think my body is ready for action once again."

John left us the first of September. It would not be long before we saw him again.

It was not an uncomfortable life for my family. We were able to replenish our stocks of food, medicine, clothing and fuel because we had our own shop. Some nights we entertained ourselves with music and song. Other times we read and discussed books, or played cards and games such as "Cupid's Crossing," "Yes and No," "Blind Man's Bluff" or "Guess My Number." Neighbors and friends from other towns sometimes visited. Womenfolk often gathered to quilt or sew.

Sitting companionably in a friend's home, several of us shared gossip of war and family members.

"Oh, we're so relieved to know that our Charlie survived the Battle of Manassas!" exclaimed Mother. "We've just received a letter, delivered by an officer under General Jeb Stuart." The women expressed their happiness and told us about their own sons.

Mother's quilt stitches were exemplary: six even stitches to the inch, and all by hand. Most of us also sewed on a machine, but Mother found it more calming to sew by hand.

It was an honor when the ladies mentioned my resemblance to her, although my hair was golden, parted down the middle, and gathered in a loose knot at the nape of my neck. My mother was tall and stately, with luminous hazel eyes. Her light brown hair was slicked back in a stylish knot worn high on her head.

I sat silently that day as I turned old clothing into bandages, anxious to finish so Mother could nurse the wounded at Jerusalem Baptist Church right after the dinner meal. The church, also called Payne's Church, had a graveyard quickly filling up with newly-buried soldiers. Little Pattie had wept inconsolably the last time we visited, watching young soldiers shoveling pale reddish mounds of dirt onto the coffins.

"Oh Mama," she wailed. "Please don't bring me here to see these dead people."

I knelt before her, wrapped her in my arms and brushed away her tears. "Come, Pattie, let us say a prayer for these three poor soldiers whose names are carved on their crosses." We never took her again, but Mother and I continued to do what we could for the wounded men once a week.

Some weeks Mother and I rode by carriage to Frying Pan Church and helped my cousin Laura Ratcliffe minister to the soldiers. Her father's forebears had founded Fairfax Courthouse and she was born there, but after her father's death she moved to Frying Pan, just south of Herndon. Laura, her two sisters and I grew up together and formed a strong bond. She was two years older than I, yet we were very similar in disposition and enjoyed our time together.

During the war, we girls visited the troops' camps with other single young ladies. Laura was the most striking, with sparkling dark brown eyes, jet black hair and a lovely figure. She was also refined and gentle. Many young soldiers dreamed of becoming her beau after the war was over.

When I graduated from the Fairfax Ladies Seminary (Coombe Cottage)—my private finishing school—I was ready to leave Fairfax Courthouse and attend university. Coombe was operated by Dr. Frederick Baker, my parents' good friend. It was expensive, but my parents wanted their children to receive the best education possible.

Papa was a successful merchant. His village store carried clothing, farming implements, fabrics, household goods and much more. We enjoyed access to the finer things in life, and our parents were devoted to us and our education. We learned deportment, modesty, guiding principles, and religious training by attending Zion Episcopal Church and reading our Bibles weekly.

I shall never forget my thrilling first day at Buckingham Female Collegiate Institute at Gravel Hill, Virginia in January 1854. It was Virginia's first chartered university for women, founded in 1838. Several relatives had attended and I was eager to expand my horizons there also.

As a lively and independent seventeen-year-old girl, my heart was filled with expectations. Papa sat beside me as we left Fairfax Train Station at seven-thirty in the morning to begin my first great adventure.

On our first train ride together we savored a leisurely breakfast of fruit, bread, cheese and ham, washed down with hot tea. Riding past farmlands, hills and thick woods, we stopped at Sangster's Station and then crossed a wobbly trestle over Bull Run at Union Mills. At Manassas Junction depot we could read the signs and stretch our legs. Finally in Gordonsville, we boarded a crowded stagecoach.

After a bumpy thirteen-hour journey, we finally arrived at the college and were greeted by the Reverend Doctor John Blackwell, president of the collegiate institute. My eyes grew wide as I stood in the walnut-paneled hall, with a ceiling populated by whimsical molded plaster figures. There were also staircases shaped like hourglasses, sidewalls of pine painted in white, and oil paintings illuminated by large candles hanging throughout. It felt like I was in Heaven.

"Oh my. Papa, do you see that engraving of the Pilgrim's landing?"

He nodded, his eyes focused on the steel engraving of John Wesley's death.

Reverend Blackwell cleared his throat. "This is where you will assemble for morning prayers." I giggled at my insight.

There was another young lady, Rose Garnett, who resembled my cousin Laura in looks and temperament. We shared several classes that first semester, and quickly discovered similar backgrounds and competitive natures. Becoming fast friends, we challenged one another to become better students.

"Antonia," Rose surprised me one evening from my doorway. "Your book is open but your thoughts appear to be elsewhere."

"Hmm, I was just thinking for a moment what the future holds for us," I replied, my cheeks flushed.

"Well, if we do not apply ourselves properly that might be decided by someone else, don't you think?" she laughed, chiding me gently.

For the next four years I received instruction in Classical Literature, Drawing, Modern History, Modern Geography, Penmanship, French and Latin, Pianoforte, Intellectual Arithmetic, Science, Painting and Needlework. There were also Bible lessons every Sunday. Of course, I returned to Fairfax Courthouse every summer, relaxing and enjoying my time with family and friends. Rose accompanied me for several weeks each summer, after which I joined her in her lovely home in Gordonsville.

Throughout my college years I strove to be, quite simply, the best. I wanted to be top of my class ranks, and in examination results. Completing the final nerve-wracking peak of examinations was my ultimate goal. This passion was so strong that I was terrified of losing momentum and missing any chance to excel. I never regretted all this extremely hard work, and I never let up.

Those four years also brought sickness and devastating loss to our family. In 1855, Mother gave birth to my baby brother James. Just a few months later, he contracted pneumonia and passed away, bringing my family to its knees. One short letter to my dear friend Rose brought her to my side.

My brother Charlie attended Virginia's first high school, Episcopal, in Alexandria, popularly known as "The High School." Over time school became even dearer to me, and I wondered what I would do when it was over.

Finally graduation day arrived and I received a degree, "Mistress of English Literature." My father and my brother Charlie attended the graduation ceremony. Charlie shouted, "Well done, Antonia!" as they handed me my diploma.

When people asked me about my plans I would answer, "Something significant: a school teacher or tutor perhaps. Yet I feel patriotic towards my country and passionate about living my life as a good person in God's eyes."

My brother Charlie suggested that marriage would be a finer calling for me.

"Charlie, I know you consider marriage and motherhood a wonderful calling for a female. Yet I am searching for my life purpose that will coincide with my faith journey. What would God want me to do?"

My darling father understood my response. "I am still seeking too," he said softly, his arm circling my shoulder as he planted a kiss on my cheek.

experience. My move away from home was prompted in part by a desire to overcome the challenges of a changing society. In a sense, I saw the war as a struggle between an old world and the new one. And as an actress ready to take on new roles, I hoped the Union would prevail and become a dynamic force in the upcoming world. One day I was stunned to find this article in the newspaper:

> *Two females in soldier clothes were detected at Camp Chase (in Columbus, Ohio) on Friday afternoon. They were taken to the city prison to await their transportation to their homes in Cleveland in the charge of a police officer.*

Because of my theatrical experience with cross-dressing roles, this incident and others in a similar vein amused and encouraged me. (Little did I know that I would also be enjoying this type of notoriety myself, when the following news article appeared in late 1864.)

> *Miss Pauline Cushman is a lady who belonged at the beginning of the war to the theatrical profession. She is still on the youthful side of the prime of life. Her features are good, and, above all, expressive. Her eyes are bright and beautiful. In fact, the whole contour of her head is at once heroic, poetical, and feminine. Feminine, there is the charm; for with such adventures as she relates, and with the profession of spy and scout, one would expect to see an Amazon. Miss Pauline Cushman, however, is tall and slight, and with her major's uniform, which she wears with the ease of a soldier, might pass easily for a young man.*

On March 8th, I spotted females in military uniform strolling down the city streets. It turned out they had fought in the Battle of Stones River, and afterward had effectively administered to the needs of wounded and dying soldiers. This did not save them from being taken to the Infirmary Prison.

I heard that General James A. Garfield, who had led the 42nd Ohio Infantry and was a brigade commander in Kentucky, had been promoted to brigadier general. He was then offered the choice of the command of a division in the Army of the Cumberland, or a position as General Rosecrans' chief of staff. Garfield chose the latter. Charles and I had met General Garfield in Ohio, and I believed our paths might cross again one day.

Shortly after my arrival in Louisville, I gained the role of "Plutella" in the production of *The Seven Sisters,* portraying one of the sisters. This relatively new musical burlesque extravaganza had drawn huge crowds in New York. It featured elaborate and expensive scenery, as well as singing and dancing actresses. Our costumes had low-necked dresses and tight-fitting clothing, much to the delight of our mostly male audiences.

For ten days we performed *The Seven Sisters* in both the Louisville Theater and Wood's Theater, and I worked in both. Then we performed only at Wood's Theater. Subsequently, I was given the part of "South Carolina" in an entertainment entitled *Uncle Sam's Magic Lantern:* I was one of thirty-four young ladies representing our glorious Union.

In early April, during this production's run, Louisville welcomed a new provost marshal, Colonel Orlando Hurley Moore of the 25th Michigan Infantry. I met him shortly after that.

Colonel Moore, it turned out, would play a role in my conversion to espionage.

At the time almost all Union spies were men, including freed slaves who took advantage of white southerners' ignorance. No Southerner would expect a Negro, freed or not, to be intelligent enough to be a threat.

Spying is very much like play-acting…until you're caught doing it.

SEVEN

Antonia

SEPTEMBER 1861

N ow that our town was under Southern control again, Generals Beauregard and Johnson made our home their headquarters on September 17. Jeb Stuart and his men came to call, and we entertained John Mosby and his soldiers as well. My friends and cousins enjoyed meeting with the young officers and sharing their company.

We always tried to make the soldiers' free time as pleasant as possible. When they told us they had lost personal Bibles in battle or on the march, we helped them get free copies from the U.S. Christian Commission. My father liked to organize impromptu baseball games. We sewed together soft balls because to get a runner "out," the pitcher had to hit him with the ball.

Laura and I were also very attentive, picking up bits and pieces of news, which we related to Stuart and Mosby. We called this "our intelligence."

One young man in our social group, John Esten Cooke, showed particular interest in me. He had been a suitor for several years. My family liked him and both my parents encouraged him, telling me what a good match he would be. I felt only a strong friendship for him, although I once dreamed that the initials of my true love were "J.C." One thing I liked about John was that he appreciated and encouraged my interest in politics. Still, I never told him my secret desire was to become a spy.

He sent word that he would pay me a social call in late September. I was always happy to see him.

"Antonia, I've come to say goodbye," he told me in a solemn voice as we stood in the entry hall. "I will serve as a sergeant in the Richmond Howitzers 1st Company in Leesburg." Lifting my hand in his, I noticed how intensely his eyes shone.

"I am so proud of you, John. Your patriotism is admirable. Come sit down and warm yourself." I led him across the hall to the parlor. It was cozy and welcoming with the fire burning brightly in the grate.

After several moments, he rose from the wing chair to sit next to me on the sofa. "You do understand my feelings, dear Antonia, that I must fight against tyranny, against a government that imposes its will on its citizens."

"But you are not fighting for slavery, are you?" I looked at him steadily.

"No! I believe that to be an evil institution."

I smiled warmly. "So do I, John. Yet I cannot bear the thought of this war taking away my loved ones."

John's eyes widened as he asked candidly. "Am I one of your loved ones?"

I gave him a sweet smile. "You know my entire family is very fond of you. You mean a great deal to me, and I shall miss you very much."

There was a long pause before he spoke. "Will you write to me?"

"Indeed I will, John. Even with the erratic post, I'll fill my letters with prayers and cheer."

As we stood up together, John pulled me into his arms. "Your kitten eyes are glowing the color of sapphire," he whispered, pulling me closely to him. I was surprised at the pleasure I felt from his passionate farewell kiss. I would miss him, and I told him so.

General McClellan now commanded the Union troops occupying the territory from near Fairfax Courthouse to Leesburg. Our village was the sole Confederate enclave.

I wrote to John Cooke as promised and received encouraging letters in return. Still I never expected to see him so soon, standing in our doorway with General Jeb Stuart.

We had been enjoying the warmth of the fire that October evening when a knock on the door startled us. Expecting no one, my father walked cautiously to the door. The first thing I saw was the black plumed hat of General Jeb Stuart. Then I saw John Cooke, standing smartly at his side.

I hurried to John's side and reached for his hand. "Welcome," I beamed. "Welcome to both of you."

During that delightful evening together I learned that Jeb Stuart's wife Flora was a cousin of John's. I enjoyed watching this handsome leader with auburn hair and bright blue eyes that sparkled when he told us stories of their adventures. With his full beard and handlebar mustache, he carried himself with an officer's bearing.

"Well done, Brigadier General Stuart," my father crowed. "Congratulations are in order. Colonel Early has been heard shouting your praises. He claims your charge on July 21st did as much to save the Battle at Manassas as anyone. Your promotion is well-deserved."

"Thank you, sir. And please join me in applauding our fine young friend, John Esten Cooke, who is now an ordinance officer in my cavalry."

We passed the evening celebrating victories and sharing stories of our families and common friends. I observed the general as he sipped his brandy, knowing that as a devout Christian, he drank only in moderation. John Mosby had once told us that he did not swear (unusual for a soldier) and indeed had no vices. We sang hearty patriotic songs, including "Dixie" and "The Bonnie Blue Flag."

I had not seen Mother this happy for a long time. She and I laughed unreservedly along with the men. As the night wore on, we all offered our opinions on everything from slavery to religion.

John Cooke had been sitting at my side throughout the evening, eagerly showing his tenderness and devotion. I battled a sense of sadness regretting that I didn't reciprocate his feelings.

Finally, he stood and pulled me to my feet. With a crooked smile, he spoke loud enough for everyone to hear.

"Antonia, what a thrill to learn about your part in warning General Beauregard about the advancing Northern troops at Manassas," he said playfully.

I looked over at my parents to see if they had told him. They shook their heads and grinned.

"Did you know that General Ewell came by to thank her personally?" added Mother proudly.

John laughed. "Of course he did. He knew where to find a beautiful face and a musical voice. I'm sure he enjoyed delivering his compliments in person."

Jeb added, lifting his brandy snifter. "To a courageous young lady. Cheers! And permit me to express my irritation about the treatment you received after taking that important message to Beauregard."

My little brother Clanie offered up an idea. "Sir, why don't you put Antonia on your staff?"

Already warmed by the brandy, I felt the affection filling the room. Jeb Stuart had been studying me thoughtfully.

"Mrs. Ford, would you have a pen and paper available?" he asked, turning to Mother.

Once he had them, he sat quietly and wrote for a minute,

then took a small stick of sealing wax from his coat pocket and removed his signet ring. We watched fascinated as he melted a bit of wax onto the document and pushed his ring into it. Rising and approaching me, he gave a courtly bow and handed me the document.

"Please read it, Antonia," he urged.

"Of course," I replied, puzzled yet emotional, as I began reading.

TO ALL WHOM IT MAY CONCERN:

Know ye, that reposing special confidence in the patriotism, fidelity and ability of Miss Antonia Ford, I, James E.B. Stuart, by virtue of the power invested in me, as Brigadier General in the Provisional Army of the Confederate States of America, do hereby appoint and commission her my Honorary Aide-de-Camp, to rank as such from this date. She will be obeyed, respected, and admired by all the lovers of a noble nature.

Given under my hand and seal at the Headquarters Cavalry Brigade, at Camp Beverly, the seventh day of October, A.D. 1861 and the first year of our Independence.

J.E.B Stuart
Brigadier General, CSA

My cheeks reddened and burned hot at this commanding compliment. Everyone was clapping and suddenly, I felt unnerved.

"Thank you, General, for this heartfelt gift you have given me. It will always be one of my most cherished possessions." I had no more words.

Mother came over and put her arms around me. "We are very proud of you, dear girl. Your loyalty to us and to your country is evident," she beamed.

"Yes, it is. And to you, Mr. Ford, I formally thank your family for all your assistance this year. Any further intelligence concerning Yankee troop movements or plans will be appreciated more than you know." Then he grinned, looking my way and winking. "And from you as well, my dear scout."

I took my prize up to the bedroom and re-read it again and again. I finally understood that Brigadier General Stuart had invited me to work for him. Folding the letter in half, I carefully tucked it under my mattress.

EIGHT

Antonia

MARCH 1862

Traveling on the country roads was dangerous as each side became increasingly suspicious of everyone. So during the winter, we didn't venture far. Father, needing to keep his shop stocked with provisions, requested a letter of safe passage from L. Herman Brien, Assistant Adjutant General. Shortly after he received it, a skirmish in Vienna, Virginia—very close to Fairfax Courthouse—persuaded him to wait for a safer time to leave us.

Our Christmas was quiet, but enjoyable. Four days after Christmas we received a letter from Charlie.

> *I think that I have committed myself as regards the artillery and I am not sorry for it, because it is my inclination to go through the war.*

John Cooke visited us over the holiday. He excitedly chatted about the book he wanted to write about my spying adventures: I was to be the model for his heroine. I could see such admiration and love in his eyes that I knew it was time to make my true feelings clear. I asked him to join me in the parlor.

"John dear, your friendship has always been and will always be very important to me. Knowing you so well, I fear you feel more deeply for me than I can give in return."

His eyes declared in silence what he could not say aloud.

"I am hoping that with time, your feelings will change," he answered in a shaky voice.

I lifted his chin gently until I could look directly into his eyes. "Perhaps, my dear, but I feel it would be better for both of us if you thought of me as your loving friend, and continue to look for your beloved."

John seemed to take it well and we parted on good terms. He asked me to write him detailing my emotions during the scouting adventure with General Beauregard. I wondered how serious he was about turning my story into a book.

Meanwhile, my brother Charlie's letters told of his concern about making it home safely. Mother, worried about his mental state, had long discussions with Papa and me, and we prayed more fervently for his return.

When our troops moved further south, many of our villagers felt defenseless and more at risk. I had a feeling that trouble might be coming. Three days later I heard horrifying noises outside. Opening the door a crack to see from whence they came, I witnessed a horrifying brawl in our front yard between a Yankee soldier and a Confederate soldier.

When the Confederate managed to stab the Yankee in the chest with his short dagger, a stream of blood sprayed into the air. I watched in horror as the poor man convulsed, then fell to the ground screaming in misery. Seconds later, he became quiet. When I looked up again, the Confederate soldier had disappeared.

I closed the door when I heard a Yankee officer shout: "Perform a thorough search of all the homes."

Frantically bolting the door, I went in search of my parents and told them what had happened. Papa hurried to his office to gather important papers and hid them under a loose floorboard. Rushing upstairs, I retrieved the aide-de-camp letter from under the mattress, then maps and other incriminating papers from my desk. As I madly sought a hiding place, fists began pounding on the door. It was too late! I flew downstairs to the parlor, where Mother was gathering up the young ones.

Seating myself calmly in a large chair, I secured the papers in my crinoline hoopskirt and picked up my embroidery. Spreading my skirts in a wide circle around the chair, I smiled at Mother, who was now calmly stitching her quilt. Pattie, sitting at her feet, stroked one of the kittens. And Clanie had pulled out his playing cards and started a game with his little brother Frank.

This is the peaceful family scene that greeted two Union soldiers, one tall and rough-looking, the other younger and soft-spoken, when Papa opened the door.

The tall one informed my father imperiously that the search would begin upstairs. While accompanying them, he quietly answered their questions. Each time they pulled something from the drawers and threw it onto the floor *willy nilly,* Papa came up from behind and meekly retrieved it.

"Now we'll search this room, ma'am," the shorter, kinder soldier told my mother politely from the parlor's doorway. She looked up with her warmest, gentlest smile.

The soldier looked at me, nodding as he observed my frightened sister Pattie gripping my right hand in both of hers.

Having found nothing, the frustrated officer in charge brusquely ordered me to "Stand up."

My eyes narrowed, radiating anger and contempt.

"I thought not even a Yankee would expect a Southern woman to rise for him!"

Thoroughly humiliated and shocked, he bowed stiffly and retreated, slamming the door behind him. The dismayed younger officer who was left behind stared in surprise.

Little Clanie could not contain his glee. "Antonia, you showed him up," he giggled.

Then the junior officer apologized and left. Sinking deeper into my chair, I attempted to console Pattie as Mother rocked a sobbing Frank. Glancing down, I realized one document had fallen from my hoopskirt and lay on the floor. How had they not seen it?

Papa asked me what it was.

"Oh Papa, it is a map of shortcuts I drew for Mosby."

Dark tension carved into his features. "Do you not realize the danger you've caused us? Had they seen it, we would have been taken into custody." He slumped bonelessly onto the sofa.

"I'm sorry, Papa. You are right. But the Lord arranged for them not to see it, and now they are gone. I promise to be more careful in the future."

As I climbed the stairs to replace the papers in my room, I heard shots ringing out in the distance. The danger was far from over.

NINE

Pauline

APRIL 15, 1863

The "Rebel toast" was born in the Louisville boarding-house where I rented a room. This delightful city had become headquarters of Rebel sympathizers in the region, so several Confederate soldiers also lived there as well as the Confederate woman who owned the home. Colonel Spear and Captain J.H. Blincoe, two paroled Confederate officers awaiting their exchange, were unfailingly courteous and kind.

One evening after supper Colonel Spear asked if they might speak with me, so we retired to the small front parlor.

"Miss Cushman," he began with a conspiratorial grin. "Please permit me to request your assistance with a plan the captain and I have concocted."

"And what would that be?" I said. "Do tell."

The colonel continued with a self-deprecating chuckle. "Pray do not think this a joke, although it does sound quite far-fetched. To show you our good faith, allow me to offer you $300 in greenbacks for your participation."

Suddenly alert, I felt certain that my face revealed my curiosity. "Does it have anything to do with a stage performance?"

They both nodded, and this time the captain spoke. "Indeed it does. We would like you to propose a toast to the Confederacy during tomorrow's performance of *The Seven Sisters*. We are prepared to pay you well."

"But good gracious, gentlemen! I should be locked up in jail if I were to attempt anything of that kind." I blinked several times, not certain I had heard them correctly. My expression must have registered the shock I felt.

"Do not be offended, Miss Cushman," Colonel Spear's voice was level, but seemed 'tight' in his throat as though he were forcing it out. "You are the perfect actress to do this, since as Plutella, you are required to assume many characters. When you become the fine gentleman of fashion, we know you drink wine with a friend. We've been watching you and believe you can carry out your part very well."

"But surely you must know how angry Mr. Wood would be with me if I did such a thing," I responded, my voice growing thick with the comprehension of their request.

"Never fear," the captain continued, leaning forward onto his knees. "They would certainly not lock up so charming a lady in a prison. We will take care of everything."

My eyes flashed indignation. "Clearly you do not speak in earnest, gentlemen."

"We most assuredly do, fair lady. We have never been more earnest in our lives."

I swallowed hard and thought about this. Then I decided to feign my assent. "Who will prepare the toast?"

"We will see to all the details," they answered quickly, cutting me off. "Simply consent and we will make the rest all right."

I lowered my eyes in concentration, dropping my lashes quite deliberately. "Allow me time to think it over, and I shall have an answer for you by tomorrow."

They stood together and extended their hands to me before making their way out the front door. Once I was certain they had departed, I set out for the Federal Provost-Marshal's office, half running in my excitement. My cheeks were burning as I stepped into Colonel Moore's office.

He scarcely knew me, since I had met him only a few days before, but he seemed to be very much a gentleman. I was determined to share with him this proposed outrage against the loyal people of Louisville and direct insult to me.

I found Provost-Marshal Moore as kind and courteous as ever. He looked up with surprise and a hint of pleasure as I approached his desk.

Slim, with a square face and small, beautifully-shaped hands, he possessed a countenance which immediately inspired me with confidence. His peculiar smile lit up his face and added good humor to every feature.

"Please sit down," he offered, indicating the chair opposite him. As I sat I felt the fire's warmth creep over me like intense satisfaction.

I stated my case and observed gentleness radiating from his eyes as he absorbed my words. His reception to my confidential inquiry assured me that he had no misgivings as to the prudence of my course.

"Miss Cushman, you have assured me of your love for the Union, and your earnest wish to do nothing but what is loyal and just."

I smiled my gratitude, but remained speechless.

"Nor do I have any doubt of your patriotism. But allow me to remark on one thing. We are often compelled to do things that are repulsive in order to further our beloved cause." He said this quietly, searching my face as he spoke.

After a few moments, I responded. "Well, sir?"

He crossed his legs and rested his elbows on the arms of his chair, his fingers forming a steeple. "I advise that you drink this Rebel toast as proposed."

I could not believe my ears. "Drink to Jeff Davis and the Southern Confederacy?" My voice had risen to a screech. "Oh, Colonel, you surely cannot mean this!"

"Miss Cushman, you love the Union and our country, do you not?" he asked thoughtfully and with a certain gravity, almost sadness.

"More than I do life itself," I responded honestly.

"Then do my bidding. If you were not perfectly loyal I should at once arrest you at even the briefest mention of such treason; as it is, I request you, in the name of that country which you love so dearly, to propose this toast from the stage."

I felt a quick flash of anger burning in my eyes. My breath caught in my throat. My eyes smarted with brimming tears as images of my small children came to mind. What would become of them if I were condemned for treason?

"Moreover," he added, "I promise you that I will be present at the theater when the event comes off." He smiled briefly. "When will that be, do you know?"

I could barely answer. In a small careful voice, I said, "Possibly tomorrow, sir. I must arrange it with the Rebel officers."

"Go to them, young lady. And when it is finished, I will speak with you about being a detective for me in the business of the Army Secret Service. I believe you have the strength and the nerve to carry this out for our country." Leaning forward, he awaited my response.

I stood slowly, stunned by the magnitude of his offer. I felt a shiver dance up my spine. This exchange from this man, Colonel Moore, who had executed that gallant exploit at Milliken's Bend, where with only one hundred men he was able to repulse nearly thirty thousand Rebels under General John Morgan, was incredible. This great man was discussing detective work with me!

"Fear nothing," he assured me. "It is for a deeper reason than you think that I beg of you to do this. More good to your country may come of it than you can imagine."

Later that evening I informed Officers Spear and Blincoe

that I would do as they requested. There were apparently few secrets in the Secessionist community. By the following morning, the word of a significant surprise at the theater that evening was everywhere. Later I learned that flyers had been distributed to Secesh circles about the special event planned for that night. Every seat was sold and as soon as the doors were opened, the crowd overflowed the house.

TEN

Antonia

APRIL 9, 1862

After a cold, wet winter, we were enjoying several days of beautiful spring weather in our village. Locust tree flowers infused the air like airborne honey. Maple trees shone reddish bronze in the sun. Lilacs emerged in bursts of purple and white, while the azaleas flaunted their brilliant scarlet blossoms. The broad sky's lucid blue was punctuated here and there with rainless white clouds.

However hard I tried to forget that the Union soldiers had again overtaken us, the fact was that our village was at their mercy as a military outpost. During the cold month of March, soldiers had methodically destroyed the old Zion Church and turned its venerable wooden interior into firewood, reducing our haven to a cheerless empty shell. I turned my head away from the devastation, only to find myself staring at the ruined building that was my Uncle Brower's newspaper office.

I hated this shameful war! I detested what it was doing to families, to young soldiers, and to those of us suffering with daily loss. Approaching my house, hot tears spilled over and rolled down my cheeks. Half-blind, I nearly ran into two men standing on the corner. One was in uniform and the other one held the reins of two horses.

"Excuse me, young lady," said the Union officer. "Where is the Ford residence located?"

Wiping away the traitorous tears, I saw that the soldier

avoided looking directly at me, allowing me to compose myself. Grateful for his thoughtfulness, I took a moment before I answered. "What is the nature of your business, sir?"

He replied in a distinguished baritone voice. "Allow me to present myself. My name is Captain Willard and I am a staff officer for General McDowell. He has requested that the Ford home become our headquarters in this village," he stated, somewhat uncomfortably. Then he smiled at me. "What is your name, miss?"

I returned his smile. "I am Antonia Ford, whose father owns the house you are seeking. It is the one over there," I pointed, "the Georgian Revival home with four stories. I will take you there."

The Captain laughed lightly. "I was hoping it was. You have a lovely home, Miss Antonia."

"Yes, it has been a popular stop for many of your officers and troops."

He turned his horse over to his servant and followed me into the parlor of our home. I asked him to wait while I went to find my mother.

I loved our parlor and was proud of the solid furniture with its elegant upholstery and hand-crafted woodwork. The gas mantles on the plaster walls were immaculate. The red-and-cream Turkish carpet was only slightly worn in the passage from doorway to hearth, and Mother had decided it would be removed, because the muddy boots of the soldiers were ruining it.

I found Mother in the kitchen assisting Mathilde with supper preparations. A pot of chicken soup simmered and the kettle sang. After a few words with her, she removed her apron and preceded me to meet Captain Willard.

Rising to his feet, he extended his hand to her. "Good day, madam. I am Captain Joseph Willard. General McDowell has requested your hospitality and the use of your house as his headquarters for the next few weeks. The general, Colonel Schriner, and some of his staff would like to stay here, if we may." He spoke softly, yet decisively.

Mother nodded and gave him a halfhearted smile. "Yes, you may use our home. I have a son fighting for the South, so you can understand how I cannot be as welcoming as I would like." She explained her husband was away on business and that I would help him organize the sleeping arrangements for the men. She excused herself and returned to the kitchen.

"I would feel the same way if I were you," he said thoughtfully as she left the room.

"We are a family of seven—ten including our slaves, so we need most of the bedrooms. We have two rooms upstairs for your men, and space in the back for others to lay down their bedding. Mother and Mathilde will serve you breakfast at the time you establish." I was keenly aware of this handsome officer studying my face as we discussed the sleeping plans.

With a wry smile, I asked him how long he had been away from his family. Although I saw no wedding ring on his finger, I was curious.

"I see two of my brothers, Henry and Caleb, quite often. We work in the hotel business and own Willard's Hotel on Fourteenth Street in Washington City. Henry has been running it since I was commissioned, but now he and his wife are moving back to Hudson, New York, to escape the war danger. My oldest brother Edwin is a soldier, and my youngest, Cyprian, is a farmer in Vermont. We see each other infrequently."

"How do you manage the hotel? I believe it is the Union headquarters, correct? My family and I have dined there, and we truly appreciated the fine cuisine."

Captain Willard laughed. "We have a good overseer managing it, and although it is hard to believe during times of war, the business is booming. Sometimes we have over one thousand guests, with three or four to a room. Everyone understands that it must be so for now." Throwing me a mischievous grin, he added, "But naturally we continue to maintain our usual high standards."

I liked this soft-spoken, refined soldier. With his brown curly hair and mutton-chop sideburns framing his cheeks, he exuded confidence. He wore his blue uniform well and looked the part of a dignified officer. I wondered if I would be able to retrieve some intelligence from him.

We sat down and continued our conversation. I considered asking Mother to send Mathilde in with tea, but found I was more interested in asking him questions.

"Are you stationed with General McDowell in Arlington?"

"At times I stay with him, but I often spend nights in my own home, one block north of the hotel."

"How do you travel from here to Fourteenth Street, sir?" *Perhaps I could learn more about their routes.*

"Generally we go across the Long Bridge over the Potomac. I have noticed that your village's plank roads are alarmingly bad. Those rotted wooden planks have most likely maimed good horses."

I nodded, and continued. "Mother and I used to shop in Washington City before the war, and are familiar with the Long and Chain Bridges. Word has reached us that the Aqueduct Bridge is being used to transport supplies and troops from Georgetown to Alexandria."

To my surprise, he laughed. "You know a great deal, Miss Antonia. And surely you are aware that I am not at liberty to comment on your inquiry."

My eyes flashed. "It was not an inquiry, Captain. I am an educated woman who reads the papers. That is common knowledge, I am certain."

Taking in a deep breath, I changed the subject and asked about the dereliction in Washington City.

"We now avoid the south side of Pennsylvania Avenue because of the pickpockets, prostitutes and beggars. I would not advise traveling to the city at this time."

Lowering my lashes, I tried another tactic. "Forgive me for not remembering my manners. May I offer you some tea?"

"That would be thoughtful of you," he answered, lifting the corners of his mouth.

Mother and Mathilde accosted me in the kitchen, apparently having heard our exchange.

"Antonia, you do not have to serve the enemy. Why are you asking me to make tea?" Mathilde frowned in disapproval.

"Daughter, you know how we go out of our way to allow them to relax in our parlor and drink whisky in our home. I serve them breakfast each morning. How the neighbors must gossip about how sociable we are!" She shook her head in displeasure as she and Mathilde began setting up the tray.

"Thank you both for helping me out. I am trying to get valuable information for our officers," I whispered discretely.

"The rain has picked up outside. I can feel the temperature dropping. Perhaps you should inform the captain to be cautious on his return," suggested Mother, as I carried the tray to the parlor.

I found Captain Willard regarding tin-plate daguerreotypes of my family. He pointed to Charlie's picture with raised brows.

I set the tray down and explained, "That one is my favorite brother, serving for the South."

A gust of wind roared down the chimney, causing the fire to dance and spin wildly. It cast a yellow glow on us. He stared down at me.

"Then your family is firmly Confederate-minded, I would imagine."

"Indeed we are. I am a Southern girl, and glory in the name…"

He finished the poem. "And boast it with far greater pride, than glittering wealth and fame."

My mouth fell open. Finally, I recovered my voice. "So you are a man of poetry as well?"

He burst out laughing. "Like you, I read the newspaper every day, and I have seen that poem. It has become quite admired, even in the North."

I chanced returning the conversation to war. "Tell me, is the Star Fort in Vienna being occupied at this time by the North or the South?"

A brief smile crossed over his features as he answered me with a straight face. "My dear, you are a tenacious lass. Yet I am certain you understand that I am not at liberty to include you in the details of our war preparation."

Now it was my turn to laugh out loud. I realized that no slip of the tongue would emerge from his mouth. I had found my match in Captain Willard, and to finish the afternoon in a challenge, I played a Southern patriotic tune for him on the piano.

"I must go now, Miss Antonia. I fear the weather has turned, and I'm not prepared for the cold and wet." He took my hand between his for just a moment. "I thank you kindly for our inspiring conversation and your delicious tea."

"Adieu, Captain Willard. I am certain we'll be seeing you and your soldiers shortly," I smiled, as we walked to the door. To our amazement, the temperature had dropped considerably. A cold wind was blowing, rustling the trees like living things, and bringing with it moist snowflakes that fell in a horizontal blur.

Captain Willard and I stared in wonder at the luscious pure surface of drifted new snow, covering everything in sight. Our eyes met so I smiled sweetly. "Be safe, Captain," I murmured, silently closing the front door.

ELEVEN

Antonia

OCTOBER 1862

Soldiers wounded in Manassas and Chantilly lay dying in our village and required nursing. Mother insisted that Pattie and I accompany her, despite the nauseating smells that assaulted us all around the makeshift hospitals. She reminded us of how we should hope compassionate women would tend to our Charlie, and bring him relief if need be. So we overcame our weaknesses and served, along with many other women from the village, young and old alike.

Although not trained nurses, we were often forced to take their roles. I helped one doctor hold an injured man down while another amputated his leg below the knee, after which I poured whiskey over his ghastly wound. Through sobs of pity for the poor soldier, I soon discovered he had lost consciousness.

All three of us wrote last letters home for soldiers who weren't expected to survive the night. Our cheeks were damp as we wrote:

Dear Mother,

I am in good hands. Please worry not for me. If I do not see you soon, I will meet you at the pearly gates. You have always been a good mother and I love you.

Your son, Johnny

Laura shrugged. "I respect him and find him very interesting. And he is a handsome man, don't you think?"

Two days later another letter arrived for her, this one written on January 6th. She read it to me and added, "He's sending a friend of yours, Captain Rosser, to escort me to camp for dinner and then will take me to your home."

I laughed. "Let me see that," I joked. "Does he even mention me?" I read it quickly and teased her lightly. "Then he ends his letter with the words: *Be assured that I sacrifice a great personal pleasure in forgoing this visit.*" Was he jealous of Rosser?

Laura seemed amused by his interest, but we had soon changed the topic. The many small skirmishes, midnight raids and daytime maneuvers in the area forced us to spend our time nursing the profoundly wounded soldiers who needed our care. In addition, Stuart requested that we make ourselves available as couriers for Rose Greenhow, who was very successful in delivering intelligence to the Confederate troops. We were anxious and excited to help her in any way we could.

We received word that Jeb Stuart would visit us before I returned home, and possibly escort me back to Fairfax Courthouse. I planned to find out if he was still married, because my cousin hadn't even thought to do so. Then we received another note, saying: *My Dear Ladies, It is such a muddy day that I refrain from visiting you because I would dislike to appear in such an un-presentable costume as the roads would give me. Nevertheless, you may expect me soon, rain or shine.*

The Ratcliffes, like my family, chose to walk the tightrope of pragmatism in Virginia. We were loyal to the South, but not averse to selling food and supplies to the Union troops controlling the area. This was also an effective way to gather information.

Then in late August, my dear Auntie Augusta Brower came

to visit. We were happy to have her, since both Father and Clanie were away in Richmond. The weather was wet, soggy and very muddy, and she arrived with her deep lavender traveling dress covered with mud clusters.

Mathilde, resourceful as always, assured her she would get it looking like new in no time.

The next night I heard a conversation through my bedroom window.

"Guess we're headed to Thoroughfare Gap, west of Gainesville and Manassas," grumbled one Union soldier, standing in the street by our front gate.

"How'd you know that?" questioned another soldier.

"Heard a captain telling another officer that Pope needs reinforcements there."

My eyes widening with excitement, I turned to Auntie Augusta. "What can we do?"

"Can anyone else carry the message to Jeb Stuart?" she asked me.

I shook my head. We knew we had to go. Despite the terrible weather and Mother's protests, we quickly hitched up our two-horse carriage and set off through the downpour, thunder rumbling through the heavens.

After a few miles, Aunt Augusta begged me to slow down and avoid the deep ruts. "We cannot lose a wheel here, because it's almost dark. We're already making good time, are we not?" she asked nervously, clutching my arm.

"With only twenty miles to go, we cannot afford to slow down. Besides, God is with us and will protect us."

Aunt Augusta nodded glumly.

Twice we were stopped by Union roadblocks, and twice we convinced them we were innocent ladies going to see family.

Finally, drenched with rain and cold to the bone, we reached Gainesville. Escorted directly to Jeb's tent, we were met by his angry greeting: "Dear Lord, are you trying to get yourselves killed?"

I let out a long, weary sigh before answering him. "Sir, we had to come. I heard Union soldiers talking. We have important information for you."

He was suddenly all ears. "Go on then, Miss Antonia."

"Pope needs reinforcements at his right flank near Thoroughfare Gap. They plan to go there momentarily."

After a long thoughtful silence, he smiled slowly. "Then you were right to take these risks, and I thank you both fervently. However, it is not safe to stay in camp with us. I will have one of my officers escort you back at early dawn."

"Oh no, sir. That would only draw attention to us. We can do it on our own, with God's help." I lowered my eyes modestly.

We made it back safely, and several days later, all the Union sympathizers left and the Confederates once again controlled our village. I read the following in *The Local News*:

> On the evening of August 26, after passing around Pope's right flank via Thoroughfare Gap, Jackson's wing of the army, along with Stuart's cavalry on the extreme right, struck the Orange & Alexandria Railroad at Bristoe Station and before daybreak August 27, marched to capture and destroy the massive Union supply depot at Manassas Junction. This surprise movement forced Pope into an abrupt retreat from his defensive line along the Rappahannock River. This seemingly inconsequential action virtually ensured Pope's defeat during the battles of August 29-30 at Manassas because it allowed the two wings of Lee's army to unite on the Manassas battlefield.

This had been the Union's bloodiest loss so far: 16,000 casualties and 8,500 wounded. I shuddered as I realized the vital part my aunt and I had played.

General Stuart visited us several days later.

"Our mutual friend, John Mosby, provided service that exhibited his daring and usefulness," he announced. Continuing, he searched the faces of my parents and my aunt. "However, I lost my plumed hat and cloak chasing the Federals at Manassas."

Chuckling, I added," Yet you haven't lost your life."

"Thanks be to you and your aunt." He sent me a fond smile. "I wonder how the Southerners would react if they learned that they owe their lives to you two."

Joseph Willard, recently promoted to Major, made several stops at our home after we met, but stayed for only a few hours each time. We were unable to spend any time alone together. He haunted my thoughts, and I could not understand why I felt so attracted to him.

One evening he simply appeared at the door. Mathilde led him into the parlor, where Mother and I were sitting around a cozy fire reading our books. It was September 1st.

"Good evening, Mrs. Ford and Miss Antonia." He seemed nervous as his eyes remained on mine. "General Ricketts and his staff are outside and have asked me to request the use of your home once again. We've just fought a horrid battle at Chantilly."

Father entered just then, so Major Willard repeated the request.

"I grant you permission, sir, but know that it is certainly dangerous, given the number of Confederate soldiers passing by."

General Pope arrived in the middle of the night. Once again, Mother and Mathilde prepared food for the "enemy." After eating, General Pope asked General Ricketts and Major Willard to join him in the parlor, still within earshot.

"I am sorry to inform you that we have lost Generals Steven and Kearny today; I've ordered my army to retreat all the way to Washington. My belief is that we lost thirteen hundred men today; more than the Rebels. We'll bring some men to the old hotel here."

Joseph Willard's response was heartbreaking. "I am sick to see innocent lives wasted. I hear them cry out to their mothers in their last breaths and pray the end will come soon."

The following morning Major Willard sat beside me at the breakfast table. "I know you minister to the sick and wounded on both sides, and I thank God for people like you."

"I have many loved ones and family fighting, but I sympathize with both sides." I gave him what I hoped was an innocent smile. "Do you truly thank God for me?"

He regarded me steadily. "You are surely an angel, sent to me from Heaven."

With that simple statement, he drew me into his magic circle.

Later that day, before pulling out his troops, General Pope gave Papa a letter of protection for my family's home. This would also prevent the looting of our stores and ensure us free movement about the area without harm.

"Thank you for providing the letter," my father said gratefully.

"That is the least I can do for you after your kindness to me and the officers," he responded.

I told Major Willard I would pray for him, and if he were taken prisoner, he must come to my house. He lightly brushed his lips over my fingers, and then he was gone.

Just a few hours later, our house was filled with joy as my brother Charlie stepped through the doorway with a friend, Sergeant George Shreve. They could only stay for one night, but it felt like a homecoming to us.

In December of 1862, Jeb Stuart led his cavalry troops on several raids against the federal forces in Fairfax County. He also visited Laura at home on several occasions. According to several reports, during one of those visits Mosby asked Stuart if he could be left behind with a small detachment of partisan rangers and continue operations around that area. He saw no benefit from going into winter quarters in Fredericksburg, and Jeb agreed. So when Stuart left on December 30, 1862, Mosby stayed behind with nine soldiers from the 1st Virginia Cavalry. Their mission was to launch raids to impede and disrupt Union operations, weakening the armies invading Virginia from their rear.

During Jeb Stuart's many visits to Laura, he took her horseback riding, sleighing, and even composed moonstruck poetry. He gave her a leather-bound, gold-embossed album with a pre-printed inscription: *Presented to Miss Laura Ratcliffe by her soldier-friend as a token of his high appreciation of her patriotism, admiration of her virtues, and pledge of his lasting esteem.*

The album was ten and a half inches high, eight inches wide, and one and a half inches thick. Its pages were blank except for Stuart's poem and two others on the life of soldiers, written by Scottish poets Thomas Campbell and Lord Byron. Stuart also gifted her a watch chain with a gold dollar attached. I wondered if in addition to impressing her, he hoped she would gather information for him.

Laura brought this beautiful album the next time she visited Fairfax Courthouse. She showed me how she had drawn lines for calling cards on the album's blank pages and collected signatures on them—her way of gathering autographs of important people. Within a year, she would have signatures of Stuart, Mosby, Fitzhugh Lee, and some of the soldiers who fought for them.

Jeb's poem to Laura included these lines:

To Laura—we met by chance; yet in that 'ventful chance
The mystic web of destiny was woven;
I saw thy beauteous image bending o'er
The prostrate form of one that day had proven
A hero fully nerved to deal
To tyrant hordes—the south avenging steel…
I saw thee soothe the soldier's aching brow
And ardently wished his lot were mine
To be caressed with care like thine…
And when this page shall meet your glance
Forget not him you met by chance.

By this time, Laura had learned that Jeb was still married with small children. Still claiming she had no romantic interest in him, she was amused at his obvious infatuation. I wondered where it might lead, but held my tongue throughout her idealistic interlude.

On March 17, Jeb penned this tender letter to Laura.

My Dear Laura,
*   I have thought of you long and anxiously since my last tidings from you … You no doubt will find opportunities to send me an occasional note. I need not say how much it will be prized. Have it well secreted and let it tell me your thoughts, freely and without reserve. Can I ever forget that never-to-be forgotten good-bye? Will you forget it? Will you forget me? I am vain enough, Laura, to be flattered with the hope that you are among the few of mankind that neither time, place, or circumstance can alter—that your regard, which I dearly prize, will not wane with yon moon that saw our last parting, but endure to the end. That whatever betides … you will in the corner of your heart find a place in which to stow away from worldly view the 'young Brigadier' … If you know how*

I would prize a letter, you would write me every opportunity. Have you forgotten?

Laura showed me a letter dated December 28, while Jeb was visiting her and her mother. In this letter, he presented her with his second poem, entitled "To Laura." The last two lines were: *When friends are false save one whose heart beats constantly for thee/Tis then I ask that thee would turn confidingly to me.*

I felt sad; this attention could not bode well for my cousin after the war.

In December, the Federals changed forces at Fairfax Courthouse once again. They brought in Brigadier General Edwin Stoughton and his 2nd Vermont Brigade to protect and defend the area. Stoughton, a twenty-four-year-old West Point graduate, was the youngest general in the Federal Army. He set up his headquarters at the residence of Dr. William Gunnell, only yards from our home.

THIRTEEN

Pauline

APRIL 16, 1863

Despite the feeling that the afternoon would never end, the sun's slanting rays announced the inexorable approach of evening—one fraught with danger. My heart beat ever more loudly as the hour drew near for me to depart for the theater.

I stepped inside the building and inhaled sharply. Not even standing room was to be had for love or money, even one hour before the curtain's rise. It seemed that every Rebel sympathizer in the place knew about the surprise and had flocked in to enjoy it.

My body was burning, shivering—my clothes sodden with perspiration. When I let out my breath, my face felt stricken.

The big fiddles began tuning up in the orchestra pit. Ushers in maroon jackets called out seat numbers. The "call boy" flew here and there, encouraging everyone to take their seats. At last, in obedience to the prompter's final bell, the curtain lifted on Mr. Pluto eating breakfast, within the shades of Hades.

The jokes and mirth of *The Seven Sisters* were, as always, relished by the spectators. Giddy good humor radiated throughout the theater like lantern smoke, to the great delight of the actors. Perhaps the Confederates were thrilled at the rumors of Federal authorities being shamefully insulted in public. The mood spread like ague among the unsuspecting Union sympathizers. Everything happening on stage brought forth storms of applause.

At last the momentous hour arrived, and I made my way to the footlights, goblet in hand. I stopped suddenly and swung around, my eyes wide and dancing with excitement. At that final moment, I found my clear, ringing voice and made the toast.

"Here's to Jeff Davis and the Southern Confederacy. May the South always maintain her honor and her rights!" I knew my face had paled, yet I stood straight and looked directly into the audience.

For a moment the hearts of the spectators seemed to stop beating. Then, total chaos. The Union portion of the audience, sitting spell-bound until now, convulsed in horror at the fearful treason. And the Secesh were frozen with the audacity of the act, even though they had suspected something historic. Finally, a tangled storm of applause and condemnation, fierce and tumultuous, erupted.

Mr. McDonough, the company manager, stormed onto stage and demanded in his most sepulchral tone, "Pauline, what do you mean by such conduct?" Like a kick in the stomach, his words twisted up my insides. The curtain quickly dropped.

My fellow actors avoided me as though I had suddenly been stricken with some fearfully contagious disease. I felt like a ghost, suddenly thinner and sadder as my brave arrogance trickled away.

Finding my voice, I answered him. "I am not afraid of the whole Yankee crew, and I would do this again." My breath constricted.

Later I was assured that I had carried out my part so well that no one doubted for a moment that I was a most virulent Secessionist. I had even managed to deceive my fellow actors.

Stage manager Phillips grabbed my arm and led me backstage. Standing in the dark, I knew I would be fired immediately. I thought of Joan of Arc and prayed that her brave spirit would awaken in my heart.

My position was anything but agreeable. It pained me that my stage companions had turned away from me, and I would have given anything to throw my arms around their necks and enlighten them. I had total confidence in Colonel Moore, but did not yet know what his plans were for me.

As I stepped outside the theater door, I saw the guards waiting to arrest me. But the theater proprietor, Mr. Wood, dismissed them after I agreed to report to headquarters the next morning.

It was a long, sleepless night. Colonel Moore and General Boyle were on hand to greet me the following morning.

"By Jove, that was capitally done!" exclaimed the provost marshal, his face wide with glee. "You acquitted yourself famously, Miss Cushman. You deserve our thanks, and that of our government. Rest assured you shall receive them. You have sown the seed; now you must be prepared to reap the harvest."

General Boyle nodded in agreement. "You must enter the Secret Service, which will be easily accomplished now that you will surely find your discharge from the theater awaiting you this morning." He and Colonel Moore exchanged somber glances.

Provost Marshal Moore cleared his throat. "Miss Cushman, from this day on I advise you not to talk quite so Secesh, but rather moderate yourself in this respect, especially in public. Speak and act as if you had received a severe reprimand from General Boyle and myself."

I listened attentively without interrupting. "Because of what you said last evening, you will be believed and will inspire confidence within the Confederate community. And you shall be of incalculable use to your country and ourselves. Expect to hear from me soon in relation to this. Until then, adieu."

My dismissal note was awaiting me at the boarding house.

Miss Cushman:

By order of the management, I am requested to inform you that your services are no longer required in this establishment, it being inferred that you will be unable to continue your present role for some time to come.

Regretting that it is my unpleasant duty,
For the Management,
H.B. Phillips, Stage Manager for Mr. George Wood,
Proprietor of Wood's Theater

I was discharged, but Mr. Wood, fearing that I would find myself without money and distressed, was thoughtful enough to send me a half-week's salary. I never forgot his kindness.

disposition of his command, and even the countersign currently being used.

In February, Mosby rode into Union-occupied Fairfax Courthouse alone and dressed as a raw, green countryman. Coming directly to my house, he spent three days and nights as our guest. This was truly inconceivable because Federal officers were also housed there.

I gave him a tour of the town, pointing out locations where Federal officers resided and showing him the Union cavalry stables and the picket's hiding places. I furnished him with names and descriptions of the officers, the exact points where the pickets hid, the strength of the outposts, the position of enemy forces and the location of depots where supplies were stored.

Mosby was gathering intelligence for a daring raid that would make him a legend across the South. He was determined to capture Sir Percy Wyndham—a Union cavalry colonel quartered at Fairfax Courthouse—whom he had loathed since Wyndham had called him a "horse thief." Mosby was also offended that a British chap had been given command of the Federal cavalry in the area. The hatred was mutual.

"John, I also have a new friend who works in the hospital with me, another courier of Rose Greenhow, who took some of my information to Rose. She tells me that Brigadier General Stoughton's family will be arriving soon, and will stay with us, because Dr. Gunnell's house has reached capacity."

"Must you feed them as well?" he asked in distaste, rolling his eyes.

"Only breakfast. And he has invited them and all of us to a big party at Dr. Gunnell's home this Sunday. Of course my family will not be attending, nor do I imagine the other Secessionists will," I sighed. "Although I wouldn't mind joining them since there will be a regimental band for dancing."

"You and my friend Sergeant James Ames, a Federal deserter, are providing a great deal of constructive information for the Southern cause. Pray remember that even details you think harmless and insignificant could prove to be vital." He saluted me good-naturedly and took his leave to work on the raid.

SIXTEEN

Antonia

MARCH 8, 1863

On Sunday, March 8, General Stoughton's mother Laura and his sister Susan arrived from Washington to spend the night with us. They were excited to attend the dinner party at Dr. Gunnell's residence, where General Stoughton was quartered.

"May I persuade you lovely people to join us in an evening of merriment?" Laura Stoughton asked my parents. She and Susan had rested and now descended the stairs, elegantly attired for the party at Dr. Gunnell's.

"You must excuse our absence, ma'am," Papa responded carefully. "Please enjoy yourselves and return safely." The night was cold and the rain fell in torrents as they boarded the awaiting carriage.

We all retired around 10 p.m. and slept soundly.

John Mosby and the twenty-nine men he had chosen for his night raid disguised themselves in Federal-issued ponchos that also protected them from the elements. Inconceivably, they managed to snake their way past three thousand Yankee troops and sleeping pickets. Inside the Federal lines, they stole into the Gunnell House at about 2:00 a.m.

Mosby told me afterward that his fate was quivering by a thread. "Getting caught would have ended my career as a supporter of our cause. Everyone would dismiss me as someone foolish enough to try and do what I should have known to be impossible."

As they approached the courthouse yard, a picket called out: "Who goes there?" One of Mosby's rangers silenced him by tossing a coat over the soldier's head and pulling it tightly around his neck.

Then they captured the telegraph operator and cut the wires. Mosby also learned from him that Colonel Wyndham had left for Washington, but General Stoughton was still in the Federal camp.

Mosby was furious. "I wanted Wyndham badly," he told me. "But I'd come so far, I could not back off. So onward we went."

He sent one squad of four men to collect the horses and another squad to capture the guards and any army officers in their surrounding homes. He kept the last five men with him to seize Stoughton from the house where he slept.

Mosby banged on the door of the Gunnell home. A sleepy aide asked what he wanted.

"Fifth New York Cavalry bearing dispatches for the general," Mosby barked. He was glad to have been coached by James "Big Yankee" Ames, a Fifth New York Cavalry deserter who was very knowledgeable about the Union encampments and served as their guide during this raid.

When a guard opened the door, he found himself looking into a Colt revolver's barrel, a hand clapped over his mouth.

Mosby whispered to the guard. "Take me to the general's bedroom. Now."

General Stoughton was snoring loudly in an upstairs room littered with champagne bottles. Pulling back the covers, Mosby slapped him hard on the buttocks.

What is going on?" Stoughton grunted. Opening his eyes to find several pistols pointed at him, he instantly awoke.

"General Stoughton?" asked Mosby.

"Yes. What do you want?"

"The Confederate cavalry under General Stuart has sur-rounded the courthouse," Mosby bluffed.

Stoughton blinked rapidly and tried to process the news. "In that case, kindly escort me to my friend and classmate, General Fitzhugh Lee."

Mosby nodded his agreement, knowing full well that General Lee was with Stuart miles away in Culpeper.

"Have you ever heard of Mosby?" Mosby asked calmly, a sardonic smile flickering across his face.

"Indeed!" exclaimed Stoughton, still thinking he was speaking to a Union man. "Have you caught the son of a bitch?"

"No, but he has caught you!" grinned Mosby. "I am Mosby, and you are my prisoner. Get dressed!"

Mosby was so delighted by the outcome that he used a piece of coal from the hearth to write his name on the wall above the mantelpiece. He took Stoughton outside to join the other prisoners and his rangers.

"I have captured a brigadier general, two captains, thirty enlisted men, and fifty-eight horses. All this without firing a shot or losing a man," he gloated.

As they were riding out at 3:30 a.m., a lone voice shouted from an upstairs window. "Halt, the horses need rest. I will not allow them to be taken."

It was Colonel Robert Johnstone, interim commander of Wyndham's cavalry brigade.

As he repeated the order, Mosby ordered two men to take him prisoner. But the colonel's wife met them at the front door, fighting, scratching and even biting them. Clad only in his nightshirt, Johnstone had escaped through the back door and hidden beneath the outhouse. Somehow he lost his night-shirt enroute. He stayed under the outhouse, naked, for several hours. This earned him the sobriquet "Outhouse Johnstone" from his troops. The poor man was so mortified that he left the service several months later.

The rangers returned to their camp, riding in a column of fours, pretending again to be Union cavalry. A very distraught Stoughton was handed over to his friend Brigadier General Fitzhugh Lee, who seemed unimpressed by Mosby's feat.

In Richmond's Libby Prison, Brigadier General Stoughton had time to follow newspaper accounts of his capture. *The New York Times* called it "utterly disgraceful." *The Baltimore American* called him "the luckless sleeper at Fairfax who was caught napping." *The Washington Star* said: "There is a screw loose somewhere."

Lincoln joked with reporters that he did not mind losing the general, since he could create another one with the stroke of a pen. He hated to lose the horses, which "cost a hundred and twenty-five dollars apiece."

Just two months later, the young Stoughton was exchanged for a Confederate general, but his career was ruined. His health had also suffered from the imprisonment, but more from the humiliation. He died five years later.

Jeb Stuart commended Mosby for the "daring enterprise and dashing heroism of accomplishing a feat almost unparalleled in the war, performed in the midst of enemy troops."

Mosby was making quite a name for himself. After Stoughton's capture, planks were removed every night from some Washington bridges to prevent Mosby from sneaking into the city and kidnapping Lincoln.

SEVENTEEN

Antonia

MARCH 11, 1863

The eccentrically-dressed woman descending from a carriage in front of our home was poorly groomed: her faded calico gown had been out of style for years. She carried herself proudly, yet timidly.

"Is this the Ford residence?" she asked me in a clear and decisive voice.

I nodded. "Who might you be ma'am, and what brings you here?"

"I seek temporary lodging in your home, as I am going to Culpeper Courthouse to see General Fitzhugh Lee and deliver some dispatches to him."

Mother came out to the porch when she heard our voices.

"What is your name, dear?" she asked kindly.

"My name is Frances Abel, but people call me Frankie," the stranger answered with a shy smile.

"It is not safe for young ladies to travel unattended around the Virginia countryside," Mother gently chided her. "Are you requesting lodging with us?"

"Yes, ma'am, but only until meeting with General Lee in two nights. You see, my views are Secesh, and I've been living with cousins in Union-occupied Maryland. It became too uncomfortable, so I'm hoping this meeting will give me a way out."

Mother took her hand and led her to our front parlor. "You may stay in Pattie and Antonia's room." I motioned that she follow me upstairs and I introduced her to Pattie. "Would you like to unpack your bag and hang your clothes?" suggested my nosy sister.

Frankie hesitated for a moment before removing her garments from the bag. Along with dresses, chemises and personal items, she pulled out a coat, a vest and trousers.

"Those are men's clothing," exclaimed Pattie. "Whose are they?"

Frankie lowered her eyes. "Having fallen on hard times, I often wear more durable clothing."

Pattie and I exchanged puzzled glances. She had money for lodging and a carriage, yet resorted to men's clothing. Was she posing as a man to serve in the army?

Or was my own avocation making me overly suspicious of other women?

During dinner, her refined manners became more evident as she laughed and conversed easily with Papa and Mother. Pattie and I found her amusing company when she commented on Mathilde's delicious corn muffins, saying how much she missed Southern food.

Later, under the creepy flickering candlelight, Frankie captivated us by reading Edgar Allen Poe's poem, "The Raven," and telling us how he had lived in Baltimore in the 1830s before dying alone on a Baltimore street.

She was curious about wartime adventures in Fairfax Courthouse, so we shared a few. In turn, Frankie spoke proudly about working for the Confederacy.

The next day I decided to gift her some of my accessories and two gowns, which she gladly accepted.

"I appreciate the fact that you have done much for the Confederacy," I confided at breakfast. "I have worked closely with

Mosby and Stuart, and have some stories of my own," I commented, carefully.

"Oh, do tell," she coaxed, regarding me steadily with glowing eyes.

"Perhaps later," I replied. "Now I must accompany Mother to the hospital. Would you care to join us?"

We spent the afternoon caring for soldiers at the brigade hospital in the Willcoxen Tavern. There was no more war talk until after dinner, in the privacy of our room.

After Pattie fell asleep, Frankie and I continued to relate stories of our lives, our parties, and the men we admired.

"Antonia, do you think you can match my work for the Confederacy?" asked Frankie, a new glint in her eyes.

"Well, I do have a prized possession," I confided, lifting my chin. From under the mattress I pulled out a ribbon-bound pile of letters and keepsakes, including Stuart's testament to my *patriotism and fidelity.*

Frankie read it with astonishment. "How did you get this, Antonia?"

Trying to remain modest, I recounted my unforgettable adventure of a few months back as a playful, not a serious, commission. I began to wonder if I should disclose so much of my covert scout life with this woman.

"I imagine the other papers are equally impressive, "she said, reaching out her hand to see more.

I gave her what I hoped was an innocent smile as I re-tied them together, returning the commission document to the center of the pile. "Not important. Just love letters, drawings, and some maps I drew for entertainment."

"Tell me about your romance with Stoughton," she urged, eyes narrowing in caginess.

"There was no romance," I assured her. "I simply pretended, looking for information. I'm certain you would have done the same." I yawned, bringing our conversation to an end.

We extinguished the lamp and fell into bed. For some reason, sleep was a long time coming.

The following morning Frankie asked me to secure a carriage for her, as it was time to leave for Culpeper Courthouse.

"I shall never forget you, Antonia. In just two days I feel I have found another sister," she said, with a smile that touched not only her lips but also her eyes. She looked much more stylish in my clothes.

"Likewise," I responded. We embraced and kissed each other's cheek. Then she stepped into the carriage, leaving me with a tearful goodbye.

As I spent the afternoon quilting, a strange uneasy restlessness overcame me. The day was warm enough for me to go to the stable and prepare my horse for a ride.

My horse and I had just entered the pasture when I saw a familiar face: Major Joseph Willard.

Our eyes met and lingered on each other's face.

"What brings you here?" I blurted out, feeling my breath catch in my throat. "Won't you join me for a ride?" I finally asked. Suddenly my afternoon was looking better.

"I had business in town and wanted to see you," he smiled slowly, warmth in his eyes.

We cantered easily until we reached the grassy road, and then urged our horses on to the freedom and thrill of a wind-blown ride. The river flowed deep and narrow between high banks so we followed it downstream, through a peaceful arch of willows overlooking wide meadows filled with grazing cattle. The upland pastures were flecked with sheep.

Rounding the bend, we almost ran into a civilian on a beautiful thoroughbred horse. It was Captain Mosby.

It was difficult to maintain my composure when I realized Mosby would greet me.

"Good evening, Miss Ford," he said with his crooked grin.

"It is a pleasure to see you again, Mr. Johnson," I answered civilly. "Do you know Major Willard, of the Union Army?"

Major Willard spoke respectfully. "What a fine evening for a ride, sir. What brings you out on such an evening? Do you not fear Mosby's Rangers, always ready to harass you for your fine horse?" He lifted an eyebrow and studied Mosby's face.

Mosby was enjoying this. "Like you, I enjoy the refreshing evening. However, you are more fortunate than I, having a lovely companion to accompany you."

Following a brief conversation, the Major and I finished our ride and took refreshments with my parents. The subject of the unexpected encounter never came up. But after Major Willard departed for Washington, I told my parents about the narrow escape with Mosby. Beneath our laughter about the surprise encounter some apprehension remained.

"Oh darling," my Papa said as I was going to bed, "I almost forgot. Today we received a letter from Charlie about his promotion. As of February 15, 1863, he is Full Lieutenant 1st Class."

"How wonderful for him," I said, delighted with the news.

It seemed the day had ended well after all.

Soon I would discover just how mistaken I had been.

EIGHTEEN

Antonia

MARCH 18, 1863

We were startled by a loud rap on the door at a most inconvenient hour. Papa opened up to find several soldiers standing on our front porch.

"What is the occasion of this late visit?" he asked them politely.

"I am Sergeant John Odell, and we are here to search your house."

Papa's eyes widened indignantly. "By the authority of whom, may I ask?"

"Lafayette Baker, head of the Secret Service division," answered Sergeant Odell. Then he turned to face me. "Antonia Ford, will you take the Oath of Allegiance?"

"No, sir, I won't," I answered.

He asked the same question to my parents, who also declined. Turning, he motioned his men to enter the house. "Then I have no choice but to search your home," he announced.

We escorted two of them up the stairs to my bedroom, and watched as they searched through my dresser drawers and closet. Sergeant Odell walked directly to my bed and lifted the mattress, where he found the bundle of letters. *He knew just where to look!* I realized. I felt weak as the truth dawned on me. *Frankie Abel.*

"This appears to be a military commission from General Stuart," he announced, lifting the document from the middle.

"It is a compliment from a friend; nothing more," I replied in a cool voice.

"And all these letters and maps?"

My eyes blazed. "Those are letters from my brother and other soldiers who are precious to me. Kindly return them at once."

"They will be used as evidence," he retorted, as he yanked eighty-seven dollars in Southern bank bills and Confederate notes from the pack.

The soldiers had finished their search downstairs. "What did you find?" Odell asked them.

"A great deal of Confederate money and debts amounting to $5,765.00."

My father broke in. "You know that money is worth nothing. Why are you taking it?"

The sergeant turned to face him. "It is evidence, sir, that you are Secessionists." He pulled out some papers. "Mr. Ford, I have an arrest warrant for you and your daughter. The charges are for providing information leading to the Confederate raid on the courthouse. You are also charged for being Secessionists."

Papa was outraged. He lunged at the sergeant. "This is an unpardonable offense! We have housed many of your officers here, and even cared for your sick and wounded. My wife and daughter were even performing such acts of kindness today." His face had turned a dark shade of red.

I ran to Mother, her eyes filled with misery and floating in tears. I wanted to hold her in my arms and console her.

My father decided that was enough. "I will go peacefully with you, but leave her home with her mother," he implored.

"That we cannot do, sir. Miss Ford is also charged with being a commissioned Southern officer, and here is the proof," he attested, waving the document of my commission in front of my father.

"You two have ten minutes to gather up some personal items, and then we must leave." Sergeant Odell turned to give the others their travel instructions.

"Old Capitol Prison? Did I hear you correctly?" asked Mother, finding her voice. Her expression was filled with grave concern.

"Yes, ma'am, you did. Your husband will be incarcerated there and your daughter will go to Carroll, which is the women's wing." He paused. "At least they will be close to each other."

Mother refused to accept his words. "Take me in her place, please. She is of delicate health and will not fare well in a cold damp institution." She reached out for his arm as I turned away, unable to watch. Even at a distance, I could feel the ache in her heart.

I disappeared upstairs to pack my bag. Along with extra clothing I took my Bible, stationery and ink pen, embroidery materials, Federal currency and my copy of *Leaves of Grass*. Mother entered the room and sat on the bed, weeping quietly, letting loose the pressure that had built up inside her.

"Mother, please get word to Major Willard, if you can. I think he alone can help me. I will write, and we must all pray that Papa and I will be released soon." Pulling her to me, I held her tightly.

"Yes, darling, I will. And I shall let Mosby and John Esten Cooke know, as well as General Stuart. We will resolve this." She courageously sent me one of her sweet-eyed smiles.

As we drove away in separate ambulances, Mother shouted out to Sergeant Odell. "Can you not see how pale and sick she is? The jostling in the ambulance will harm her. Have pity!"

I heard his curt answer, "Good evening, madam."

I vomited three times during my transfer to Old Capitol Prison. Old Capitol Prison and Carroll Prison, the women's wing, adjoined each other. The two-story building had windows with iron bars and no glass, as in any jail. Two armed guards patrolled the building's perimeter.

At Carroll Prison, I entered a large hall with benches on both sides of the corridor. I did not see my father or the other nine men of Fairfax who had traveled with him; they were also charged with spying and disloyalty.

Sergeant Odell nudged me into a large room with only a desk and several chairs. Two men sat behind the desk.

"Mr. Wood, prisoner Antonia Ford." He bowed and left.

Mr. Wood's gray eyes looked me over curiously. Then he asked me to take a seat.

"Miss Ford, I know your family. We met last summer. Regretfully, I must incarcerate you, but hopefully not for long." He ventured a kind smile. "You will find that prison is not as comfortable as home, but we will do our best to see that your needs are met."

The other man, still seated, finally spoke. "I am Lafayette Baker, head of the Secret Service." He rose from his chair. I was surprised to see a strong resemblance to Abraham Lincoln, with his tall, thin frame, beard and mustache. But he was a redhead.

"You showed Frankie Abel the document from General Stuart and bragged that you were one of his commissioned officers," he said, with an impassive face.

"That...that was simply a foolish joke," I stuttered.

"Why have you often pretended to be a Unionist?" he asked.

I stared at him. "My family and I had to survive. The Union army commandeered our home many times against our wishes. My brother fights for the South. I am certain that you, sir, would have done the same thing."

He rubbed his beard pensively. "Yes, your family …let us speak of them."

"Leave them out of this! I am physically unable to travel around as you have learned. I have done no spying for either side. My only assistance to both sides is working as a nurse."

Lafayette Baker continued. "I formally charge you with holding a commission as an officer of the Confederate Army and sharing information that resulted in the recent capture of General Stoughton."

"You have no evidence!" I shouted. "I deserve a trial and a lawyer!"

Baker turned to look at Mr. Wood, who shook his head. "It is unconventional for anyone here to be granted legal advice. I must deny your request."

"Then I want to see my father," I whimpered, emotion flooding through me, leaving me trembling.

"We can arrange that tomorrow. Now we must record your arrest. Then you will be taken to your room and the procedures will be explained to you." After he wrote everything on paper, I asked permission to read my arrest sheet.

Antonia Ford is a native of Virginia—aged twenty—resident of Fairfax C.H. VA. She is rather delicate in appearance and a defiant Rebel. She pleads especially for her family, and says she alone is responsible for her sentiments and actions. She has a Rebel Commission from Rebel General Stuart, which she claims he gave her as a compliment and as a personal acquaintance. She acknowledges the will but asserts her physical inability to participate in any manner in this national strife, and positively denies having done a single act for or against either part, but maintains having assisted the sick and wounded of both sides.

After reading the report, I told them my age was incorrect. I have no idea whether they changed it, for I never saw it again.

A guard escorted me through a dark passageway, into the large yard and through another passage. Midway down the hallway he stopped, asking another guard to open the door.

"This is your room, and here is a list of the rules." He left, leaving the door ajar.

My room was cold, with dust and spider webs in all four corners and on the small barred window. The smell of mold and a sour place deprived of fresh air hung like fog. I heard the creaking of the doors and stairways as other prisoners moved through the rambling passages on their way to the courtyard. I could taste despair.

Peering from the window I saw coal and lumber, and considered asking the guard for some to use in the small stove.

I walked to the door and called the guard. "I see a sutler's store near the courtyard. I would like to purchase some essentials there, and I have money." Unsure if they sold newspapers, I was eager to see if news of my arrest had been published. "And please sir, be kind enough to bring coal or lumber for my stove."

He allowed me to go alone, and I returned with a copy of *The Washington Star* and a few toiletries. Straightaway I saw an article written by a soldier at Fairfax to a friend in Vermont. The words brought me goose bumps.

> *There is a woman living in the town by the name of Ford, not married, who has been of great service to General Stuart in giving information, etc.—so much so that Stuart has conferred on her the rank of major in the Rebel Army. She belongs to his staff. Why our people do not send her beyond the lines is another question. I understand that she and Stoughton are very intimate. If he gets picked up some night he may thank her for it. Her father lives here, and is known to harbor and give all the aid he can to the Rebs, and this in the little hole of Fairfax, under the nose of the provost-marshal, who is always full of bad whiskey.*

The article had been written in early March, but printed merely two days ago. The Vermonter who had received the letter from the soldier sent it to the newspaper, along with his own criticism. He added:

> *The Belle Boyds and Antonia Fords have more to do with these Stuart raids than the government is aware of. They are Rebel majors in disguise.*

Tomorrow I would show this to Papa, and we would devise a plan. I could not let this defeat me. There had to be a way to overcome our terrible fate. Gratefully, I looked across the room and saw a small pile of lumber stacked before my stove.

NINETEEN

Pauline

LATE MAY 1863

I live in Nashville now, after departing from Louisville unexpectedly, due to several upsetting occurrences. First came the unsettling arrest of the boardinghouse woman, Mrs. Long. Then my great love of the theater almost proved the end for me.

I had secured star billing in a benefit performance on May 12 at the Louisville Theater, playing the role of Mrs. Trictrac in *The Married Rake*. Although it was only a single performance, I was keen to do it because I would sing and dance, and felt well-fitted for the role.

After the show, a Confederate gentleman stood in line with other audience members at my dressing room door. Unlike the others, he looked quite serious.

"Miss Cushman, it has come to my attention that you are employing your acting career as a means of gathering intelligence for the Union." His quiet words sent a shiver through me, and tension snaked inside my stomach as I glanced over his shoulder to see if anyone else might be listening.

"Such nonsense, sir," I managed to murmur through a calm smile.

His dark, wary eyes seemed to bore into me as I composed myself and continued.

"You are certainly kind to compliment my thespian ability. I am so pleased I am able to convey such an impression."

The gentleman hesitated, took my gloved hand in his, and bowed over it. "Merely be advised, madam, that this gossip is circulating." Then with an abrupt nod, he melted into the crowd. Before receiving the next person in line, I allowed myself an audible sigh.

Colonel Moore and General Boyle continued to encourage my surveillance undertakings. One afternoon a few days later I approached a suspicious-looking woman who had been pointed out to me as "Mrs. Ford."

While dressed in male attire, I finally engaged her in conversation.

"Pardon me for the intrusion, madam, for we have not been properly introduced. An acquaintance happened to mention several visits you paid to General Boyle's headquarters."

Smiling warmly, the attractive woman replied that she had been seeking permission from the Federal authorities to travel southward beyond the lines to join her husband.

"Indeed? Why is he in the South?" I asked, in my coolest masculine voice.

"My dear man is a Baptist clergyman, a representative of the Confederate Congress from Kentucky, and he has, sad to say, been exiled. As a fugitive, he cannot return; therefore, I must go to him," she explained.

"Kindly allow me to help you if I can, madam. My name is Captain Denver, of the Confederate Army. I am visiting Louisville as a spy surveying the movements of the Federal Army. Perhaps I can be of assistance to you."

Her eyes widened as she took in my candid affirmation. She handed me her card and invited me to her home the following afternoon.

I was cordially received by her family, whom I found to have a very strong sympathy for the Southern cause. Naturally, the conversation turned to the war. When the time was right, I revealed my "true intention."

"My goal is to escape through the Federal lines to the nearest Confederate command, carrying as large an amount of quinine, morphine and other medicines as I can safely carry." I spoke in a level, careful voice.

I watched her nod her appreciation of my plan. Then she replied with her proposal.

"I, too, wish to cross the lines and join my husband. I also want to carry contraband goods through the lines. I recognize this is neither safe nor wise, but perchance by working together, we might prevail."

"I only wish I had sufficient money to make extensive purchases, but I do not. I seek assistance from friends of the cause in Louisville," my alter-ego Captain Denver replied.

"Please do not be troubled," she answered. "I shall request an interview with General Boyle for tomorrow morning to report the complete success of my efforts."

After her report Mrs. Ford stated that, even though an enemy of the government, she was an honorable enemy, and would engage in no enterprise which the military authorities would refuse to fully support.

I was ordered to accompany her to Vicksburg in my present disguise. Passes were obtained, tickets bought, trunks checked, and sleeping car berths secured. The night passed comfortably in sleep. Upon our arrival in Cairo, she and her party found themselves under arrest. Mrs. Ford could not have been more astonished and horrified as she was led away in silence.

She was carrying a number of letters and a large quantity of quinine concealed in her clothing. Her trunks were found to contain similar illegal imports and a great deal of information valuable to the Rebels.

After a protracted investigation, Mrs. Ford was sent South. I now worked in the Secret Service, under General Boyd and Colonel Moore. They instructed me to travel from Louisville to Nashville disguised as a Secesh, and to expect my pass to be refused by officials at the station. I would plead to get onto the train for "only a moment" but not get back off. When questioned on the train, I would show my stage manager's order to report to work so I could continue the journey.

With the help of a few womanly tears of regret about leaving Louisville, I made it through to Nashville and took a room in the City Hotel.

It was amusing to see how I captivated both Union and Secessionist sympathizers. Reviewers called me "fairy-like and beautiful." Federal soldiers admired me as a "magnificent specimen of a woman—Rebel or not." And the Rebels said they liked me because I was one of their "own mongrel party."

By the spring of 1863, Federal control had turned the city into an occupied Union enclave.

One day after rehearsal, I received a letter from the Chief of Army Police William Truesdail, ordering me to report to his office. I had heard about Truesdail, who had served under Union General Jefferson C. David and General John Pope. He styled himself a General, and made his reputation pursuing "traitorous" citizens under Rosecrans for the Department of the Cumberland. I wondered why he had summoned me.

"Miss Cushman, please be seated." He stood as I entered the room and gestured to a nearby chair.

"Thank you, General Truesdail," I answered politely.

"Let me congratulate you on your patriotic services to the government of Louisville. I have received good references of your activities there."

I nodded and he continued. "Would you be interested in continuing to serve your country?"

"Oh yes, sir. Indeed."

"I want you to travel to General Bragg's headquarters, and if you agree to do so, I shall give you instructions on how to proceed. It will be a journey of three hundred miles or so, and could be quite dangerous."

"Sharp" Bragg was famous for his temper and use of hangings to enforce discipline. He had reportedly written to General Joseph Wheeler about the presence of refugee spies from Nashville. How could I possibly get near him?

As if reading my mind, Truesdail explained.

"My plan for you is to go in search of your brother, Colonel Asa A. Cushman, who is fighting in the Confederate Army. Your search for him would be a plausible cause for your presence behind Confederate lines." He searched my face, looking for discomfort or fear.

"I do indeed have a brother fighting for the Rebels. I commend you for the quality of your intelligence, and will agree to go in search of him, although we have had no contact for years," I said, adjusting my posture on the seat.

"Good enough. That is settled then. Tell everyone how desperate you are to find him. Confederate armies are now located at Columbia, Shelbyville, Wartrace, Tullahoma and Manchester. If possible, visit all those military bases under the pretense of searching for your brother."

After a deep breath, he continued. "Casually allude to the ill treatment you have received from Federal officers in Nashville, who threw you out of the city, alone and unprotected, without even time to procure your baggage. Do you understand, Miss Cushman?" Again I nodded, feeling my heart skip a beat.

"This dangerous assignment is a great responsibility. Its risks may possibly include life and limb."

He fixed a baleful stare on me from across the table before going through a lengthy list of information they needed.

Despite the obvious danger, the prospect of doing so much for my country filled me with elation.

"You will assume all the sentiments and character of a Rebel lady. You shall not talk or say too much, merely answering any questions in a modest and intelligent manner. Your responses will be consistent to all parties. And you shall make no direct inquiries about the disposition, strength or condition of Confederate forces, or ask about any officer except your brother."

Finally he smiled, and his smile spread from his lips to his eyes. "Are you willing to risk your life to do this type of work, Miss Cushman?"

"I am anxious to do this, General Truesdail. You will not be dissatisfied with my work."

His gaze slid uneasily away. "There is one more important piece of advice. Due to your attractive appearance and modest demeanor, you will have many attentions paid to you by generals and staff officers. You will be invited to ride out through their camps and visit their fortifications. Accept all invitations, but with some hesitancy expressing caution as to the propriety of such excursions. While riding with them, ask to visit the sick and wounded soldiers in the hospitals. There you will inquire about medicines and supplies, where the supplies come from, and how many sick and wounded are housed within."

He rose and approached my chair. Leaning over me, he continued. "Miss Cushman, I do not doubt your sincerity to our cause. However, there are several formalities with which I dare not dispense."

"Do continue, sir," I suggested.

"I will ask you to take an Oath of Allegiance here and now."

Once again, he pursued my reaction. I felt my face go pale. Then I nodded to him, raised my hand and accepted the small American flag he handed me. After repeating the words he spoke, I kissed the folds of the flag and echoed his words, "So help me God."

But he was not finished. "It is imperative that you make no memoranda or tracings of any kind. Only note your expenses by location and date. Equally important, tell no one that you are anything but a refugee and a victim."

"I understand, General Truesdail," I answered, my heart swelling with excitement.

He smiled. "I believe you will be an asset. One final word to you. Upon reaching Confederate pickets, show your papers and request to be taken to the headquarters of the commanding officer. Expressing your desire to find your brother, ask the officer for protection and aid. And at every headquarters you visit, ask for a letter of introduction to the next officer in the chain of command."

My head was spinning with so much information. I felt numb, yet exhilarated.

General Truesdail sent me in his carriage three miles outside the city limits, close to the outer line of Union pickets. His own servant waited there with a magnificent bay horse, impatiently pawing the ground. I mounted, ready to begin my journey.

A young servant boy standing nearby watched me mount the horse. He approached me with his hand out and a reassuring smile. I leaned over in my saddle in case he wanted to speak to me. Grasping my hand in his, he said softly and simply, "God speed."

It was early afternoon when I galloped away down the Hardin Pike toward the biggest challenge of my life.

TWENTY

Pauline

EARLY JUNE 1863

Flying over the hard ground atop a fine horse, I gave in to the sense of freedom. Then I felt my heart crack as I realized I might never again see my loved ones. Thoughts of my children brought tears to my eyes, and I let the fraying ends of control slip through my fingers. Visualizing their small faces always brought me pain, but this evening it splintered in many directions. I pulled my horse to a halt as the sobs overcame me.

Gaining control again, I turned my thoughts toward what lay ahead for me. I realized that my immediate future would be spent on "neutral ground"—a licensed place for *desperados* of both armies; fearful gangs of desperate men who would murder just for the fun of it.

Fortunately, General Truesdail had given me a fine six-shooter with everything I needed to use it. And I was well prepared to use it if necessary.

The eleven miles between me and my destination flew by, until I was watching the setting sun's crimson waves from atop my steed, on the banks of the Big Harpeth River. Grand looming trees arching over the road produced a gloom as dismal as the broken countryside.

A turnpike bridge was almost impassable, having been ruined by the Rebels. My horse and I shuddered, contemplating its few remaining planks, carelessly and insecurely laid across charred, blackened rafters. Just then I spotted a small pathway in the distance that seemed to run along the river bank, probably to a ford further downstream.

"Let's keep walking," I urged my steed, whom I had named Soldier. "I won't ask you to step onto those planks." I walked beside him until he calmed down, holding his reins and murmuring in a soothing voice. After a short walk, we saw a nice-looking dwelling in the distance.

I decided to ask the person in the house if the road led to a ford.

"Greetings," I smiled, as the door was opened by a "Secesh" woman. Before she could speak, I introduced myself.

"I am a hapless refugee recently driven from Nashville for sympathizing with the South. All I have in the world I carry on my back—for they stripped me of everything—my wardrobe, my jewels—everything."

She peered at me and replied in a familiar drawl. "What, the Federals? They drove you outta Nashville? Is that what you said, stranger?"

I lowered my eyes and nodded submissively. "Indeed they have. I told them what I thought—that they were tyrants. My only hope was to find my brother, an officer in the Confederate army. If therefore you could guide me to the closest ford, I will be truly grateful."

She smiled at me. "As for helpin' you, I'd do that right smart," she said. "Especially since you're of the right stripe, and ain't one of them darned 'Yanks.' But I must tell you aforehand that your ford is rather dangerous jist now, and I reckon you best put up here for the night. I'll get my old man to guide you over in the morning. He's gone to Nashville to git goods."

I was surprised. "But how does he get into Nashville without taking the oath?"

She laughed. "Oh Lord, bless you. He thinks no more of

takin' that there Federal oath than you would of drinking a glass a water!"

She invited me in and went back to preparing her supper, while I fed and watered Soldier and left him to rest in their shed. Then she and her sixteen-year-old son prepared tea, knowing how hungry I must be. As we were having tea the husband Milam walked through the door. My first impression of the man was hardly favorable, especially after he sneered at his wife's introductory remarks about my being "a refugee from Yankee-land." He had very black sunken eyes that rolled about when he got excited.

"Damn Yankees run off my slaves, and if I ever catch 'em, I'll lash 'em 'til the blood run down to their heels. Damned if my slaves gunna go and help the damned Yankees," he barked, completely oblivious of how distasteful his timing was.

"Shall we speak about other matters, Milam?" suggested his wife. "We have a guest here—one of us."

Later he boasted to me how he had made a slave "confess" to stealing a small household article. Strapping the poor boy to the branches of a tree, he took his lash to him, tearing the flesh from the bones after rubbing the boy's back with coarse salt before delivering the blows with fiendish malice.

In vain the poor wretch screamed for mercy, protesting his innocence. Although this vile man knew it was in his interest to protect and save his slave, he recounted the story with gloating eyes. I suddenly realized that I despised Milam, despite his offering to help me find my brother.

"I reckon I can help you find him. It's very few over there," he said, pointing to the river," that don't know Milam or his partner, 'Old Baker.' I've run too many things across—hardware, muslins, sugar, tea, and coffee, aye, even muskets and ammunition—for them not to know me."

Cautiously and innocently, as if simply curious, I asked him my question. "Are you not afraid of getting caught?"

"Caught? Hell no! Ye see, up at Nashville, the damned Yanks think I'm a Union man because I've took the oath. Ye see, Old Baker, my partner, takes the goods through and disposes of 'em, so he can drive you in my buggy as far as General Bragg's headquarters." Now he stopped and threw me a twisted smile. "Provided you pay for it."

I responded calmly. "I am willing to pay liberally if it means finding my brother and helping him escape the persecution of the Federal officers in Nashville. I understand him to be with General Bragg."

With a heavy heart I sold this vile man my new best friend Soldier and the riding equipment. The following morning, I paid his man Baker for the use of his buggy and services as driver. As we headed towards the land of Dixie, I saw Milam leaving for Nashville, in quest of some runaway Negros, who had escaped from a neighboring farm. The last words I heard were his usual oath, that he would "lash 'em til the blood ran down their heels."

We traveled over the most terrible roads. If the little horse pulling the buggy had not been a good one, we would never have reached our destination. My endless journey lasted ten days, trekking through the long dreary woods over ruts and swollen streams. Incessant storms had produced mud as deep as the hubs of the wheels, and we often needed to alight from the buggy so Mr. Baker could extricate the horse and buggy from what threatened to be their tomb. I struggled to keep my wits about me.

At long last we arrived in Columbia. I was taken to a fine hotel kept by a man named Franklin. The cost was fearfully high, and I quickly spent the one hundred dollars in Confederate notes that were given to me for my horse and equipment. My fare included food, but I was completely disappointed in what they served me. Sidelings of bacon, fat and filthy, with rye coffee, were what composed our meals. Tired as I was, I rebelled against the food, and decided to procure a nice little chicken.

I found a slave lad outside and asked him if he wanted a dollar. His eyes glistened at the offer.

"But in exchange you must find me a real nice chicken—a little one, of course."

His face held the blank expression of dismay at even the mention of such impossibility.

"Boy, is that impossible?" Now I was becoming annoyed.

"I 'spect you'd tink so, Missis. Why dey hasn't seen a chikin' in dis house for a coon's age," he responded.

"If you bring me a chicken, I shall give you the dollar," I smiled back.

"'Speck I'll have to do without de dollar, den, Missis; but I see what I kin find."

After several hours, the much-longed-for delicacy arrived. He smiled as he handed me a tiny chicken, no larger than my hand, cooked in butter.

"You owes me four dollars, Missis. One for going to git it, two for de chickin itself and a dollar for cookin' it. Dey charged me for the butter too: fifty cents." He hung his head, shamefaced.

I responded with a broad smile. "Thank you for your work. Here's the fifty cents for the butter as well." He left, thrilled with his windfall. I was equally thrilled with the first good meal I had eaten in many days.

TWENTY-ONE

Antonia
LATE MARCH 1863

I was awakened by sunlight streaming through the barred window. My head and body were itching from the bedbugs and lice that infested my flimsy straw mattress. Wondering if the lumpy feather pillow was home to any creepy-crawlies, I shuddered at its grimy shine. My room, facing the prison yard and smelling of decay, measured a scant ten by twelve feet. It had been chosen intentionally to prevent me from seeing outside or being seen.

The morning air—cold, rank and pestiferous—seemed to gnaw at my bones. Dust and cobwebs hung everywhere. Larger rooms of the crumbling U.S. Capital Building had been partitioned off into cells, and this was where I would be living. I could hear the creaking of the doors and stairways as the prisoners moved through the rambling passages on their way to the courtyard. A guard told me I could go out to exercise after dinner, and I wondered if I would see my father there.

At three o'clock a servant brought my meal.

"What is this?" I asked with a frown, unable to recognize the dark mushy liquid.

She smiled and spoke in a low voice. "Irish stew." She handed me an apple, a piece of wheat bread and a stone jug of water. I placed them on the small table, next to my tin cup.

The thought of mingling with strangers in the courtyard made me uncomfortable, but I yearned to speak with my father. We were told we were not allowed to converse with fellow prisoners, but I needed the comfort his quiet voice would provide. As a guard escorted me to the courtyard, the late afternoon sun broke through a rift in the overcast sky with a wash of golden brilliance, but little warmth. After a few moments I saw Papa, standing under a pine tree near the corner. Leaving the guard behind, I ran to my father and fell into his arms.

"Oh Papa, how are you?" I whispered, wiping away a tear that slid to the corner of my mouth.

"I am well, my sweet Antonia. Please don't be upset with our situation. I pray that soon we will be free." He smiled down at me, but I saw the concern reflected in his eyes.

"Yes, Papa, so do I." My eyes met his. "Are you being treated well?"

He assured me that he was. I told him what had happened to me since I last saw him. Several guards noticed us talking and ignored it. Perhaps they knew we were related.

"Where are you living, Papa? Are we in the same building?" I was in the Carroll House, the building adjoining the Old Capitol Prison. I heard it was for the prisoners that Northern officials suspected of being Southern sympathizers.

Papa took my hand and squeezed it forcefully. "I'm here as well, in the central wing on the second floor. There are a few of us in a large room they call Number Sixteen. We have a dirty cylinder stove, a triple tier of bunks, two pine tables, and some stools. I believe you are on the third floor, correct?"

"I am, Papa. Now that I know you are below me, I shall listen for your footsteps." The thought warmed me.

He reached into his pocket. "Take this Federal money to buy what you need. I only wish I had more to give you." Papa pulled me close against him while I stuck the bills into my laced-up bodice. He whispered encouragement, rubbing my trembling hands in his.

"At least I have a cell to myself, and I am thankful for that," I said, smiling weakly.

Papa tucked my head under his chin and began to hum one of my favorite tunes.

Taking in a deep breath, I reached up to kiss him. "I promise you we will see each other tomorrow during exercise."

We were prisoners, and knew not if or when we would see each other again. Returning to my tiny room, I picked up my pen and began to write a letter to my mother.

Several days into my confinement, they announced I had a visitor. Hoping it was my mother, I hurried to the small parlor near the main door.

The guard cautioned me to speak in a distinct volume so he could hear the conversation. He also told me he might grant me thirty minutes for this interview, although fifteen minutes was the normal time allotted.

I heard his footsteps first, and then froze. Joseph Willard strode into the room.

"This is an outrage, my dear Antonia," he cried out, wrapping his arms around me. I relaxed against him, allowing his bulk to settle my angst. "Do not fear, Antonia. I will use my influence to get you released." He paused, studying me closely. "Are you well?"

I almost laughed in relief. "As well as can be expected. Oh Joseph, I see Mother was able to reach you quickly."

He sat beside me on the small bench and handed me a parcel. "Here, Antonia, I've brought you some good food. This will help you keep up your strength."

I was at a loss for words and weak with emotion. I asked him what he knew about my arrest.

"First of all, you should know that I have requested to be

reassigned from McDowell's staff to General Heintzelman's staff. He is the officer-in-charge of troops and prisoners in Washington."

"Thank you," I said quickly, laughing out loud. "You will surely be aware of what we prisoners are experiencing. You do know my father is an inmate as well, don't you?"

"Of course, and I have information to share with him when I return. But let me explain what I have learned about your arrest."

Joseph relayed that Stoughton's capture by Mosby nearly drove Secretary of War Edwin Stanton mad. He ordered Lafayette Baker to determine the cause of it and arrest everyone involved. It was decided that Mosby's knowledge of the movements of the forces pointed to the existence of traitors and spies and their communication with Confederate officers.

"Unfortunately for you, my dear lady, Baker read an article in *The Washington Star* about the speculation of an intimate relationship between you and Stoughton."

I blushed and blinked at him, my face burning hotly. "That is not true," I protested, swallowing hard.

He smiled. "I know that. But Baker focused on local Secessionists, and investigated your family. He assigned one of his most trusted female scouts, Frankie Abel, because he believed she could easily curry favor with you and your mother."

"And that is exactly what she did," I groaned. "And we fell for it. Frankie betrayed us, even as we reached out to help her." I hugged myself, shivering as though an icy wind had just blown through the room.

He reached for my hand. "That was then, Antonia. That is why you are here. Now we must work for your release." His gaze was gentle, and my eyes clamped onto his, seeking courage.

"But why would you help me? I am the enemy. You've already done more than I could have imagined."

He lowered his head, as if searching for the right words. "Because I care for you. I am a man of few words, but I deeply care for you and will help you in any way I can."

As he stood up to leave, he leaned down and placed a gentle kiss on my forehead. Then he stroked my hair back from my face, taking in the delicate lines of my cheek, my jaw and my throat. My breath shuddered softly as his lips followed the same path.

I could sense my cheeks reddening and felt a tear sliding down the bridge of my nose.

"I will try to visit you every day, Antonia," he whispered, tenderly wiping away the tear with his fingertip.

TWENTY-TWO

Antonia

APRIL 1863

I was intrigued to learn that Frankie Abel had been arrested in Washington City the same day I was. Although she told us she was going to Centreville, she went to Washington instead.

Wearing men's clothing the evening of her arrest, she gave her name as Frank Tuttle. The soldiers gave her permission to sleep in her boarding house and report to the authorities the next morning. At that point she arrived dressed as a woman (most likely in my outfit) and told them she was Frankie Abel, of Baltimore—a detective employed by Colonel Fisher. Lafayette Baker called her in to witness against some others they had detained.

People have asked me how I communicated with fellow inmates during my incarceration. We actually used quite an ingenious method.

The first time I heard a scraping noise in the wall, I watched incredulously as a dull metal knife slid halfway out a crack between bricks. Unsure of how to respond, I slid my dinner knife next to it, hoping to be enlightened. A rolled-up message then appeared like a tiny mouse between the two dull blades. We had very little information to share, yet we delighted in breaking the "no communication" rule.

After the prisoner in the next cell gave me her name and

unit, she mentioned having been betrayed by a Union spy—
and a woman at that!

Putting my knife away, the idea started me thinking. It had
never occurred to me that any women other than Miss Abel
might be doing similar work for the other side. *What had they
done before the war?* I wondered. *How effective were they as
spies? How well would we get along if the opportunity arose for
us to meet?*

This reverie was interrupted by the unexpected arrival of
another visitor—disguised in civilian clothing, and having
registered in the visitors' log with an alias.

When we were face-to-face in the parlor, I could hardly
contain my joy. It was my good friend John Esten Cooke, grinning from ear to ear.

"Oh, sweet Antonia," he murmured, low enough so no one
else could hear. "I am trying desperately to use my influence
to get you out of prison. I have contacted General Jeb Stuart,
who said he would write to Major Mosby, requesting evidence
of your innocence."

He searched my face. I returned his smile and reached out
for his hands. "Thank you, dear John Esten. As you can see, I
am fine, although thinner than ever before."

"But just as beautiful," he murmured, staring hard at me.
"And I've brought you some food to fatten you up. I am certain
it will taste far better than prison fare."

I smiled at him. "Will you kindly put in a good word for
my father and my neighbors who have also been arrested?" I
asked, remembering our shared plight.

"I already have," he assured me. "And I know that Major
Mosby has sent a statement to Fitzhugh Lee's headquarters
stating that you had nothing to do with the capture of General
Stoughton. It is my hope that we will get you an unconditional
release."

"Oh, John, have you seen my mother?" I asked him, changing the subject.

Again he whispered. "I dare not venture into your village, or I will end up here as well."

"So you have no news of her," I sighed. "I miss her so much."

We talked about people we knew, and I asked him about my brother Charlie. We talked about the family servants Octavia, Adam and Mathilde. We recalled the joy we had felt on January 1st past, when the bell of freedom rang for our Fairfax County's slaves.

"My only concern is that some of our enslaved population will join the Union forces, where they can serve as soldiers," said John Esten.

Finally, he asked me how I occupied my time.

"We play games, as they cannot completely separate us. The men like card games, but my favorite is Muggins, a domino game. Mr. Wood has allowed my mother to send me paper, pens, and yarn, and I am embroidering a lace cap and collar set that makes me concentrate so hard that I often forget where I am," I smiled faintly.

A few days later I was informed that I would have a cellmate. Abigail Williams, another scout, arrived like a wraith. Not strong or healthy, she ignored my questions and refused to eat. I was worried about her and made up my mind that she would be my new project.

I told her stories, taught her to work with lace, and made her recite poetry. I also gave her one of the shawls Mother sent to me, and that kept her from shivering when the small fire burned down to ashes every night. After several days she decided to eat.

"Abigail, we must remember to write to our families, as they are so concerned about us," I urged, working quietly on the lace collar.

"Do you think they actually receive our letters?" she asked.

"Yes, I do," I replied persuasively. I wondered what she had gone through to become so dispirited.

And then I received the letter from my Mother that she had written two days previously:

Fairfax, April 13, 1863
My darling Child,

I have not received a single line from you since the sad morning of your departure from home, nor have I seen anyone who could tell me how you were or how you were looking. I have longed for one line saying you were well. I have seen several who could tell me how your Father is. Keep up your spirit—by so doing your health may be better preserved. You were so sick the morning you left I feared seriously you were not able to stand the trip but trust in God, my dear child. He is able to accomplish all things and will not let us fall if we put our trust in Him. He has said: Call upon Me in the day of trouble and I will deliver you.

We are all well. All your brothers, Pattie, and the darkeys. Mary has been sick but is now well. She has been very anxious to go to see her mother but has not been able to get a pass. Since I hear your Father's favorite (of past summer) is the superintendent of the C. Prison, I am much better satisfied. If Mr. Wood will allow it, I will write you a note soon again and ask that you do the same. Just one line to let me know how you and your Father are will be a good comfort to me. To your Father, tell him not to feel uneasy about home—we are getting on very well.

> *Your devoted MaMa,*
> *Julia Ford*

Everybody that knows you sends love to you. Tell Father to try to keep up his spirits and not to trouble about Frank's eyes.

Lizzie, Murrys, send much love. All the neighbors are well except Mrs. Gunnell.

That letter, written one month after my arrest, made me cry with desolation and relief. I was saddened that Mother had not received any of my letters, but immediately reached for my stationery and pen to compose her reply.

My dear MaMa,

Mr. Wood has given me permission to write for my trunk, of which I gladly avail myself—being as you may imagine in much need of clothes. I am very comfortably fixed and very well; so is Papa. I see him occasionally. We don't want you to feel uneasy or distressed about us; we really are doing well, and but for the separation would be satisfied. Please Mother, make a clean sweep in gathering up my things, for (I don't want to distress you, but you must know it) I shall see Richmond long before Fairfax Courthouse. If it were possible for you to leave home how glad I should be to see you; but I suppose it cannot be affected. Papa says you had much better take the oath, if you can conscientiously.

All the gentlemen from Courthouse are well—tell Mrs. Powell, Benceley says his health hasn't been as good since Jan., as it is now. Tell Mary I leave you in her care. Tell Pattie not to cry her eyes out. Tell Frank that Papa talks of him every time I see him. Tell Clanie to fill my place for you. If you can't come to see me, pray do write me. In that case: put your letter in an unsealed envelope directed to me, and then in a sealed one to Wm. P. Wood ... Carroll Prison. Mother, can't you come down once while I'm here? We don't know when we'll meet again, and I'm so anxious to see you. If you can possibly get off bring Frank. I'm at a great loss for work; please put some in my trunk.

Give my love to the family, Mary included, and all who inquire. Please send to me the following essentials: plumes; bows; china mug; tea; spool cotton #18, 24, 30, 36, 40, 70; Les Miserables; music of "Bonnie Blue Flag" and "Dixie"; buckskin gloves; and stationery. Place them all in small bags then put neatly in larger ones, for gentlemen to take a peep in.

Keep any of the articles I've written for, if you want them for your own use.

Most affectionately, your child
Antonia Ford

Joseph Willard continued to visit several times a week, and I looked forward to our regulated times together. He avoided discussing his feelings for me, but I could read them in his eyes and behind his smile. My attraction to him was so strong that I knew I was also falling for him. That truly frightened me. I believed he was a good man, knew he was a Christian, and found him appealing and fascinating. Yet he was a Unionist and I a Confederate. And I could not bring myself to pledge the oath to the Union.

"Antonia, I bring you good news today," he grinned boyishly, approaching me and laying his hand affectionately on my shoulder.

"What is it, Joseph?"

"Mosby has denied your involvement in his capture of Stoughton, which will be beneficial when we plead your case. I am personally working on obtaining your release. A prisoner exchange would be your best option."

I smiled widely. "The fact that Mosby denied my involvement in his apprehension will assure my future usefulness as a spy as well, will it not?"

He looked away, his eyes darting to the floor, and it occurred to me that he was not pleased with the idea.

"Will you answer me truthfully if I ask you a question?" I wondered aloud.

He nodded, so I continued. "I entered prison a healthy girl, vibrant with life and energy. Do you now see me as a shadow of that girl?"

His eyes remained steadily on mine. "Your large eyes are the same, although your arms and body are thinner. But with good food and care, you will return to the blooming woman I met." His smile was honest, but his eyes were sad. "Here are the newspapers you requested, and also some chocolates I believe you will enjoy."

Smoothly changing the subject, he brought up the important question we had discussed during his last visit. "My dear, have you considered taking the Oath of Allegiance to the Union?"

Studying him intently through narrowed eyes, I said finally, "Yes, Joseph, and I simply cannot do it."

He nodded in silence, sorrow shadowing his hazel eyes. Joseph understood my love of the Confederacy, and his grasp of my loyalty warmed my heart.

Two months to the day after my incarceration, Mr. Wood, the prison superintendent, came personally to my cell.

"Miss Ford, you are to be sent for exchange to Fortress Monroe, and then to City Point, Virginia. Pack everything as quickly as possible."

He told me that on the following morning I and twelve other female prisoners were to be transported by train to Baltimore and then down the Chesapeake Bay to Virginia.

Joseph visited me later that evening. He stood up when I entered the parlor, then waited until the guard left the room. Sitting down next to me, he put his arms around me and held me close. Then he took a deep, steadying breath and said,

"There is something I need to tell you." He paused for a long moment.

"I am married."

My stunned shock was palpable.

TWENTY-THREE

Pauline

MID-JUNE 1863

The railroad track from Columbia to Shelbyville had been torn up by our troops, which compelled me to wait for repairs to be completed. This gave me some time to uncover bits of information about the Rebel movements by talking with refugees from the "Yankee tyranny."

Before returning to the Milams, Mr. Baker introduced me to Confederate Major Boone. Standing in front of his lodgings, the Major asked how he might be of assistance.

"My dear brother, a colonel in the Confederate service, has disappeared. I am trying to find him," I answered straightforwardly. The Major promised me that Confederate officers would immediately be notified about my search, and then introduced me to a quartermaster from Vicksburg named Captain P.A. Blackman. Both gentlemen escorted me around Columbia's Confederate camps.

I also told anyone who would listen about the wretched Federal officers who had driven me from Nashville. Although I was questioned and cross-examined by the idle and the curious, I repeated the familiar story so my true motives were never discovered.

A man named Kennedy had the most interesting story I heard in Columbia. He was eager to tell me about his escape from Nashville's jail.

"I managed to secure a file from one Rebel sympathizer visiting the jail. Using that, I slowly severed the heavy chain and ball holding my feet, taking care to do so near the iron staple that was driven into the band about my leg. I tied two pieces of iron chain together with string and strolled around the cell. No one suspected anything, not even the German guard: a round-faced, good-natured and kindly man."

Sitting back comfortably in his chair, he crossed his hands over his stomach and continued. "I entered into conversation with him over the days, and one day asked him to allow me to take a mouthful of fresh air outside the door. He agreed, only that the ball attached to the chain around my leg should remain in his grasp while I stood outside. We laughed about the impossibility of my escape with the guard holding the ball, and out I went. The moment I got outside, I took my hidden knife and severed the string which still held the chain attached to the ball."

"When did they discover you gone?" I asked in amazement.

"The poor guard was sleeping with the ball next to his feet when the inspection officer came by to call the roll. They woke him up when no one answered to my name. When asked where I was, the guard told the officer I was 'right here—just as snug as a bug in a rug.' Looking down at the ball, his eyes followed the chain to the spot where I had been standing, and he finally realized he had been tricked."

"But how did you get past the guards through the main entrance?" I asked.

He laughed. "I was brought a suit of citizen's clothes by Rebel friends, and donned them without delay. So I simply strolled past the guard post without question."

Experiences and stories like this one kept me intrigued and gave me a good feeling about my scouting days in Columbia. I spent part of every day with Major Boone and Captain Blackman, who naively kept me apprised of the war news.

They may not have been entirely honest regarding the motive for helping me so much, because they both appeared to be interested in me as a woman. I took note of that for further use.

When I was ready to depart to Shelbyville, they made my travel arrangements, ordering Mr. Baker to stay in Columbia and wait for my return.

The twenty-hour ride in an Army supply wagon was pleasant enough, through gentle hills and farmland in the mild summer sunlight. Soon after fording the Duck River, we arrived safely in Shelbyville.

I felt certain I had caused no suspicions by my actions or questions. After reserving a room at the Evans House Hotel on the town's square, I was disappointed to learn that General Bragg had left the area for parts unknown. Reporting on his movements had been the primary part of my assignment, so I needed to find other ways to make myself useful.

Two nights after my arrival, a small group of gentlemen were eating supper at the hotel's long table. An attractive young captain with long light-brown hair began telling his friends how hard he was working day and night to finish a drawing for Bragg's new fortifications, where his 47,000 soldiers could rest and reconnoiter. The soldier was an engineer, and I found myself intrigued as I listened to him.

After supper I introduced myself and my reasons for being there. I also showed him my "letter of safeguard," which seemed to pique his interest. After two glasses of port, he voiced his concern for my plight and offered to write his own letter of introduction to General Bragg.

When I retired that evening, I drew up my own plans, which would require disobeying my instructions by securing enemy papers. Whatever the risk, I was determined to obtain the engineer's drawings and carry them to Nashville. I would find a way to cross through the Federal lines.

The following morning I tapped lightly on his door. "Please forgive me for imposing when you are working on your drawings."

He smiled warmly. "Not a bother, Miss Pauline. I have finished my plans and was just about to step out." His eyes met mine. "Perhaps you can join me for a stroll about the area."

"I would have loved to," I answered in a disappointed tone, "but I suddenly realized I must leave earlier than I had intended. If it is not too great an imposition, could you please write me the letter for General Bragg that you mentioned?"

I saw his face drop as he surveyed my figure. "It is I who am regretful that you are leaving us so soon. For a short time only, I trust?"

Picking up his pen, paper and inkwell, he flashed a rueful grin over his shoulder. "I shall have to go downstairs and use the hotel's desk to prepare the letter."

The moment he stepped out I tiptoed to his bedside table, covered with drawings. Unable to resist the temptation, I picked up every paper that looked completed, and thrust them with trembling hands into the bodice of my dress. My hands were shaking as I secured them. Then I heard him climbing the stairs and jumped back to my previous spot in his doorway.

"You will not, then, forget us?" he grinned, handing me the letter.

"No, sir, I will not forget you," I smiled. *Nor do I think you will forget me, especially if I manage to deliver these papers intact.*

I made haste to leave Shelbyville, but was forced to stop at Wartrace, a small town just seven miles from Shelbyville. Numerous skirmishes between the Rebel and the Union cavalries were being fought in and around the village. A new idea blossomed as I traveled. If I could reach one of the roving bands of Union cavalry, I could give them valuable information. But I needed men's clothing to accomplish this.

In the dining room of my boarding house, a young man about my size was deep in conversation with another guest. I overheard him say that he slept in a room in the upper story. That night, I trod silently upstairs and stood by his door until I heard him snoring. The door was not locked, so I entered softly. I waited until my eyes grew accustomed to the dark, and then reached into the wardrobe and took a suit of men's clothing.

Dashing back to my room, I put on the stolen suit and crept out to the stables, where I quickly selected and saddled the best horse. In no time I was out of town and rushing through the moonlit woods. Tree branches on both sides of the road curved inward, forming a canopy. I crossed swampy areas and creeks—tributaries of major rivers.

I traveled approximately three miles before spotting a large watch fire with three armed men sitting around it. I dismounted and tied my horse to a tree, then crept closer to the fire to listen to their conversation. What I heard was bloodthirsty, wicked drivel against the Union.

"Oh Lord," I whispered to myself. "These men are Rebel guerillas." Their mongrel song was repugnant to me, and I flinched as I listened.

"The Yankees run, ha! ha! The niggers stay, ho! ho! It must be now the Rebs are going to have a jubalow!"

I had heard enough and noiselessly slipped away. Approaching the spot where my horse was tied, my foot landed on a tree branch, cracking out a warning.

"What's that?" shouted one of the Rebels, jumping up and seizing his pistol.

The captain ordered the men to grab their muskets and scour the woods.

By this time, overcome with dread, I jumped into the saddle

and galloped away. The guerrillas followed, and the chase was on. Genuine fear coursed through my veins. Panic burned in my chest.

A cliff loomed before me and I looked behind to see them gaining on me. Their horses were faster than mine. My heart was racing—stark terror charging through me. I saw the large rocky piece of land jutting out ahead of me and had only a moment to make a decision. Squeezing my eyes shut I spurred my horse, and the noble steed jumped off the rock into the unknown.

I felt myself flailing, knowing that rock bottom was somewhere beneath me, closing in fast.

My graceful steed landed on firm pasture land. Later, I found out that this promontory was about ten feet perpendicular. Directly below lay a gently-sloping grassy hill about a hundred feet above a small stream. I looked back, realized they had not followed, and felt tears of relief flooding my eyes.

Pushing into the adjoining woods, I was convinced I had escaped. Progressively, their voices and the hooves of their horses became more indistinct. I exhaled a long sigh of relief. I always found strength and calm in a forest. This was my first experience alone at night surrounded by imminent danger, yet the tree branches hovering above like clouds refreshed and revived me. I walked my horse slowly, every sense alert.

My horse abruptly stopped short. I sat up straight, terror pounding in my temples. An armed cavalryman sat on his horse ten yards down the path.

Stunned and panicked, I yelled out, "Stand aside or I will send a pistol ball through your head!"

"Stand down, comrade," he answered back in a feeble, breathy voice. "I do not wish to engage with you. I am critically wounded and it is all I can do to stay on my horse. My own warm blood is soaking my shirt and jacket."

"You are wounded? What brings you here, away from your comrades?"

His answer was faint. "We skirmished with you Rebs near here five or six hours ago. I was wounded and stayed behind."

"Then you are a Federal officer?"

"I am," he replied weakly.

"Heavens, then you can aid me and our country."

"Our country? Are you not a Rebel?"

I smiled for the first time that evening. "No sir, I am a Yankee: a Yankee spy and scout, and a woman."

His mouth dropped open. "A woman?"

"I am. My name is Pauline Cushman." I leaned closer to his face. "Will you help me?"

He agreed to help me, and I told him I had a plan to save both our lives.

"Do not be frightened by what I am going to do," I warned before firing my pistol into the air.

"Now then, I'll pretend to be a Rebel who just shot you. You must, therefore, swear that I did. You are severely injured, you surrender to them when they find you and save your life. You will save mine as well. I am transporting valuable military information to our generals that will be lost if I am captured."

The dear soldier replied, "I will do anything to save you. There is not a soldier in the Army of the Cumberland who would do as much as you are doing." I was humbled by his sincerity and gratitude.

We quickly put my plan into action. Rebel horsemen, drawn by the gunfire, galloped up to find the Union soldier lying at the foot of the tree, bleeding profusely. I was bending over him, pistol in hand.

Looking up at the soldier with honest concern, I spoke hurriedly. "Oh sir, I am a farmer's son near Wartrace, and I surrender to you. I have shot one of your fellows here, and only wish I had shot more of ye."

The confused Rebel was at a sudden loss for words. Just then, several more Rebel soldiers cantered up.

I continued. "I am only sorry I didn't kill more of you damned Yankees, who come down here and run off all our Negros."

The Rebels now concluded that everyone except the wounded soldier were Rebels.

Unfortunately, I could see that one of them wasn't convinced. Dismounting, he shook the dazed and wounded soldier. "I say, soldier, who was it that shot you?"

Rising onto one elbow, my new friend pointed directly at me.

"There!" yelled another Rebel. "He says the boy shot him. What more proof do you want?"

I shuddered and gulped a lungful of breath. So far it had gone my way. The Rebels lifted the wounded soldier onto his horse to take him to Wartrace for medical aid. But then the game took a new twist: they ordered me to follow them.

Riding behind them, I thought of how I might cause confusion and escape. As we filed through a narrow forest gorge, I lagged behind and rapidly fired five erratic shots. The Rebels, fearing a Federal cavalry ambush, galloped off as fast as their horses could run. I also rode swiftly and hard, determined to reach the camp before them. I was successful, and managed to return the horse and the man's clothing undetected.

The next day the Rebel gang could be seen strutting around Wartrace, bragging about their wonderful fight with many "Yanks." They boasted about their setting upon the damned Yanks and putting them to flight. I laughed gleefully at their boasts, knowing they never suspected that the fascinating Miss Cushman and the rude country boy were one and the same.

TWENTY-FOUR

Antonia

MAY 1863

A cold chill swept over my collapsing heart. When I was finally able to speak, I stammered, "What did you say?"

"I am married."

Tears filled my eyes. My heart ached as if it were ripped from my chest. We had been very close for almost a year, and he had declared his undying love for me on two occasions. Joseph was a Christian with a deep faith who knew I had strong moral values. Now, he drops this heated cannonball.

Lurching to my feet I charged toward him, a hand raised to slap his face. Joseph nimbly caught my wrist and pulled me to him. In a wavering voice, he said, "Please, Antonia, allow me to explain."

Looking down at my face, I knew he sensed my emotional upheaval through the tears swimming in my eyes.

"Come here, my love. Sit down and let me share my story before you judge me." His voice broke, but he kept a hold on his feelings.

I shook my head and the blood draining from my face left me giddy.

"You are pale, darling. I insist that you sit with me," he pressed, leading me gently to the chair. He knelt in front of me, one knee on the hardwood floor.

He drew a long breath. "I moved from my home in

Vermont to Troy, New York when I was twenty-four years old. I worked briefly at the steamboat company and then at the Astoria House in New York City. I attended parties, gambled, drank and dated many young women. Then I met Caroline Moore, who intrigued me even though she didn't enjoy reading and we had very little in common." Pausing, his eyes took in my features.

"Please continue," I implored, in a voice as low and intense as his.

"Her parents allowed me to visit her without a chaperone, which seemed highly inappropriate. I became fond of her as a sweet friend, and when she permitted, I took liberties with her. A young man's temptation is strong, and she didn't object. We sat close and kissed for long periods of time, until one night…," he tore his eyes away from mine, clearly embarrassed. "That night I had my way with her. She willingly consented."

I turned my head away, not wanting to hear this. He continued. "I am not proud of this, Antonia. I never told her I loved her, because I did not, but when she told me she was pregnant, I tried to do the honorable thing."

My throat closed and my cheeks were damp, yet I forced myself to hear him out. My fingers gripped the arms of the chair with such force that my knuckles gleamed in the faint glow of the dying parlor fire.

"I am so sorry to burden you with this gloomy story, my love." He swallowed hard, most likely at the sight of my stricken face. "But I have no choice with you but to tell the truth."

I nodded for him to continue. "We had a quick, loveless wedding ceremony. Shortly after, Caroline miscarried the baby and fell into a deep depression. A doctor prescribed pills to help with her emotions, but they did not work. She must have known that I did not love her, and soon she refused me conjugal rights." His eyes welled up. My heart ached for him.

"She began sleeping half the day, then stopped washing and grooming herself. I considered institutionalizing her. But my brother Henry, my confidant during this traumatic period, helped me bring her back to a kind of normalcy. She still refused to socialize with friends, and demanded her own bedroom. Five years passed."

"Oh, Joseph," I whispered, reaching for his cool hand. "How terrible that must have been for both of you."

"I was offered an opportunity to work as a cashier for Aspinwall and Company in San Francisco. The idea of striking gold was enticing, and I invited Caroline to join me. She refused, moving in with relatives instead.

"After two years in California, I returned to Washington City in 1853, where Henry and I purchased our hotel. Caroline and I lived together for a while in the hotel. She enjoyed having everything done for her."

I could see how weary and fatigued he was, but I needed to hear more.

"Joseph, please forgive me but I must know the rest."

"Yes, Antonia. You shall. Henry married Sarah Kellogg in 1855, and we decided to purchase a joint home one block from the hotel. But Caroline remained at the hotel, declining my wishes that she move into the home with us. I visited her there, and she asked nothing of me, probably because she lacked for nothing. She continues to maintain an elegant, carefree lifestyle in our hotel."

"And now?" I sighed, leaning toward him, every part of me on alert.

"Caroline certainly did not object when I was commissioned in the Union army. I have discussed divorce with her, but it is still unacceptable. Except for the social impact I do not believe she would object."

A shudder rippled through me. I tightened my lips and we

sat silent for a long time, until the guard announced that visiting hours had ended.

"Joseph, I am stunned and devastated by your duplicity. Yet I still care, and know you feel the same for me. I will prayerfully reflect on what you have told me." My mouth felt dry as I struggled to stay calm. "At this moment I am not even certain I want to see you again. If we do not meet again, farewell and thank you for your honesty."

I rushed from the room to my cell, where I cried inconsolably.

Poor Abigail came over and silently wrapped her arms around me. When she found her voice, she asked hesitantly, "Antonia, whatever is wrong?"

"Oh Abigail, my heart is broken, and I do not want to talk about it now. I did not know emotional pain could hurt so much."

She nodded, placed a cold wet rag over my forehead and eyes, and took me to my bed.

I slept through the night, and prepared to leave before the sun rose. I could not get Major Willard out of my thoughts. Kissing Abigail goodbye, I sat in the parlor awaiting the carriage to take me to the Washington depot. From there, I would make my journey on the Baltimore and Ohio train to Baltimore, thirty-eight miles away. I prayed I would sleep on the train and block out bitter memories of the previous night.

TWENTY-FIVE

Antonia

MID-MAY 1863

I n spite of my dispirited heart, I was enthusiastic about my arrival at the Gilmore House the moment I saw a real bed with laundered sheets. My first thought was to jump in and snuggle. Then I discovered a washbowl and soap, and I joyfully treated myself to a sponge bath. What a glorious feeling to be clean after so long!

An equally wonderful aroma of cooking food soon drifted up from the kitchen and restored my appetite. We enjoyed the delicious supper and pleasant conversation, and each of us spoke of our gratitude to be free. After supper, our hosts divided us into groups to play card games. It was late when we turned in for the night; despite my troubled heart, I slept soundly.

After a hearty breakfast, all thirteen former prisoners were driven to the steamer. A copy of *The Washington Star* was passed around the carriage on the way. To my surprise, my name appeared in an article entitled *"Females Sent South."*

The last lot of Rebel prisoners sent South from this city were accompanied by thirteen females, who had been in confinement in the Old Capitol. Among them were Mrs. Mitchell and her two daughters, arrested by General Rosecrans for persistently aiding and abetting the escape of Rebel prisoners, most intensely vituperative traitors as they proved to be while here. Also, a woman who had served for some months as a Rebel sergeant of cavalry, a regular bruiser. Also, the noted Miss Ford, of Fairfax County, Virginia, arrested for participation in Mosby's abduction of General Stoughton, and company. It is due to Miss Ford and we should state that her behavior while a prisoner here was so entirely modest and correct as to make friends for her all whose duties were about the Old Capitol, and to impress them with the conviction that General Stuart's commission appointing her as one of his aides-de-camp, which was found with her when arrested, was but a joke on the part of all concerned in it.

I pointed out the article to Mrs. Mitchell, mentioned along with her daughters. We were traveling together and began to share confidences. She laughed wildly about the article, and I joined her. It seemed we were popular again.

Walking toward the steamer, some Baltimore Secessionists waylaid us, offering gifts of food tied in multi-colored handkerchiefs. They embraced us, blessed us and agreed to mail any letters we might have written since being incarcerated. At noon we boarded the steamer *Juanita*. Being feted in the Officer's mess, the Captain arranged a lovely luncheon accompanied by iced champagne.

Our next two travel days were very uncomfortable. There were no beds and we were forced to sleep sitting up. The second afternoon I caught sight of a lighthouse facing Chesapeake Bay and was told we had arrived at Old Point Comfort. A transport approached our steamer, and Colonel Lafayette C. Baker stepped ashore.

"Well, Miss Ford, it looks like our paths have crossed again," he laughed shallowly.

I could only force myself to nod in his direction. He said he would be our escort from this point onward. He led us to a wooden building flying the Union flag—the Captain of the Port's Office. The male prisoners were taken immediately to waiting carriages, but the women were ushered next door into a fancy building to dine in the saloon.

Relaxing in mid-afternoon under a cool tree, I leaned back and tilted my face toward the sky to bask in the warm sunshine. Then a shadow moved across my resting body—the dark outline of a man's form. Sitting up swiftly, I rearranged my sprawled legs and untidy hair in time to recognize Major Willard's smiling face.

Bowing, he extended his hand and announced, "Antonia, how happy I am to see that you arrived safely. I came here as quickly as I could to take you home. Your mother is quite relieved to know my plan."

"You have come to rescue me?" I asked in disbelief.

Before he could answer, Colonel Baker approached. Speaking directly to Major Willard, he said, "I see you have an interest in this woman. Unfortunately, I also do, but only as an officer of the Union Army. She may only be released at the appropriate time and place."

Joseph turned to me. "Antonia, please agree to take the Oath of Allegiance so I will be able to take you north. Your father has sent you money for travel."

"My father? Has he been freed?" I could hardly believe my ears. Hope surged.

"Yes, Mr. Wood released him soon after you left due to insufficient evidence." Noting my relief, he added, "May I escort you home when the exchange is complete?"

I was infuriated that Major Willard had not consulted me in any of his planning, especially when I told him I had not decided whether I would agree to see him again.

"Major Willard, we are going north by rail," I said stubbornly, tossing my head. "It would be unsafe for us women to travel through Confederate villages with you in your blue uniform."

My words appeared to hurt him, but I did not care. My eyes were flashing by the time he finally answered. "As you wish, Antonia. I will take my meal in the dining saloon and come back to see you before you leave."

After his departure, Mrs. Mitchell lifted my hand and smiled kindly. "Antonia, you were too rough on that poor man, who is much enamored of you." Her daughters nodded in agreement.

"He has no right to come here and dictate the terms of my return home," I muttered, mostly to myself. Her reprimand took me by surprise and touched me deeply.

Joseph returned just as our coach was pulling up. Leading me to a private place, he quietly asked me, "Is there any hope of my courting you, or are you too angry about my marital situation to even consider it?"

"How do you expect me to think about these things now?" I retorted, anger surfacing again. "When I am home and at peace, I may take some moments to contemplate your question."

"Very well Antonia. I will see you at Fortress Monroe, since I also have business there. Until then," he nodded.

"Goodbye, sir," I told him, entering the coach with the other women.

In no time we pulled up to a picturesque and handsome medieval-looking fort, surrounded by a moat. The stone walls at the edge of the moat had windows large enough to shoot weapons. Spanning the moat was a narrow bridge with guardrails.

The guarded entrance, peeking from between majestic oak trees, was just wide enough to allow a carriage to pass. We rode to the Prison House and followed Colonel Baker to a room marked "Prisoner Exchange." The provost marshal, Captain Cassels, was sitting behind a large desk. He rose and asked us to sign the Oath of Allegiance.

"I cannot do that, sir," I proclaimed righteously as some of the other women put their signatures on the papers.

Colonel Baker spoke up. "You are making it very difficult for yourself, Miss Ford."

Staring intently into his eyes, I replied, "Sometimes the right way is not the easy way, Colonel."

Captain Cassels cut in. "Miss Ford, I will immediately release the women who sign, and provide them with passes to travel home. The others must remain here until I can document the exchanges."

Colonel Baker spoke up. "Each of you must promise to stay out of Federal territory and may not interfere in military affairs. Is that understood?"

"When do you feel our exchange will occur?" I asked Captain Cassels.

"Hopefully tomorrow. We have arranged military quarters for the night."

Mrs. Mitchell and her daughters had also refused to sign the oath. We followed the men to our rooms, hoping to be released the following morning.

The four of us who had not signed the Oath of Allegiance were again asked to sign it the next morning, and again we refused. A scowling Colonel Baker handed us travel passes, instructed us to gather our belongings, and sent us to the wharf to board the steamer *Belvedere*.

Mrs. Mitchell nudged me and pointed in the distance. "I think that is your beloved Major Willard approaching," she grinned. "Please resolve to be kinder to him today."

"He is not my beloved, but yes, indeed it is he," I snapped. My heart beat faster at the sight of him. How handsome he looked, yet he appeared to be exhausted.

"Antonia dear," he smiled, taking my hand and drawing me aside. "I pray for your safe travels, and I will learn of your destination from your parents. I will write you with news of your family and friends."

Dropping his voice, he whispered, "Just know that I love you." Bright color flooded his face as he sent me a sweet smile. "There, I've finally said it. I love you, Antonia." Moving closer, he gathered me in his arms.

I felt certain my gasp was heard by the women standing close by, but the tears glistening in my eyes were seen only by Joseph, who wiped them away as they fell.

With a shaky voice, I said, "I would like to hear from you, Joseph. I certainly need a friend."

Reaching up, I clung to him as though my life depended on it. I pressed myself into his arms and gave him my heart. For a long moment, we met each other's eyes and acknowledged the heavy tension in the air. I knew I now faced a far more dangerous situation than I had imagined.

Startled by this public display of affection, I backed away. There were surprised murmurs from the soldiers who had just observed a Southern lady consorting with a Federal officer.

We steamed forward all day, passing the time comfortably by reading, playing cards and enjoying two very tasty meals in the company of the captain and his charming wife. Reaching the mouth of the James River, we saw Confederate officers signaling us toward City Point. My eyes misted when I saw the Confederate flag proudly waving over the blue horizon. The Mitchells, a few other passengers and I remained on board that night as the soldiers and civilians disembarked. We would take a flag-of-truce tugboat the next day to the Shockhoe Slip in Richmond.

"Why a tugboat and not a steamer?" I asked Captain Hutch.

"Well, young lady, the area around Drewry's Bluff is

extremely dangerous for larger ships. We might run aground," he grinned, visibly pleased to see my interest.

I stood on deck, enjoying nature's beauty, as my eyes filled with the colors and textures of trees and springtime blooms. Warm winds blew across my face. Closing my eyes, I told God how grateful I was to no longer be incarcerated.

Drewry's Bluff rose precipitously ninety feet above the James River and I now understood Captain Hatch's concerns.

Pointing to the fort on the bluff from mid-ship, Captain Hutch cleared his throat and made an announcement. "I am proud to remind you that one year ago, Commander Ebenezer Farrand and his troops prevented the Union flotilla from advancing to Richmond. Captain Sydney Smith Lee, brother of General Robert E. Lee, has since taken over command of the site and has supervised its expansion into a permanent fort."

We docked at Richmond's Shockhoe Slip, then continued by carriage to the Exchange Hotel, conveniently located behind the train depot. After a good night's rest we met the others at the depot and boarded our Virginia Central train, then O&A at Gordonsville. My destination was Culpeper Courthouse. The Mitchells were heading to Warrenton, so we exchanged information and promised to stay in touch.

I was excited to see familiar church steeples in the distance, rising above tiny farms with picket fences. I had arrived. I hugged Mrs. Mitchell and her daughters goodbye and walked away from the train, frail and weary, hungry and thirsty. But I felt ready to begin planning my future.

Pauline Cushman. *Courtesy of the Library of Congress.*

Chased by Rebel guerrillas, Pauline gambled and spurred her horse and jumped from a rocky promontory. *Image: The fearful midnight flight, F.L. Sarmiento*, Life of Pauline Cushman.

Pauline Cushman in her theatre days. *Courtesy of Herbert Rickards.*

154 / DANCING DELILAHS

As an actress, Pauline Cushman often performed in scanty attire. *Courtesy of Herbert Rickards.*

P.T. Barnum's 1864 broadside advertisement with two depictions of Pauline Cushman. "In the Parlour" shows a figure in a dress while "In the Field" shows a figure in a military uniform. *Courtesy of the California Historical Society.*

Pauline Cushman's autograph. *Courtesy of F.L. Sarmiento's,* Life of Pauline Cushman.

Pauline was honored for her services as scout and spy. From 1864 to 1870 she lectured and performed throughout the East wearing this uniform. Showman P.T. Barnum billed her as "the greatest heroine of the age." *Courtesy of the University of Nevada–Reno Library.*

Pauline Cushman wearing a field officer's uniform with a sword and sash similar to those in her 1864 images in military uniform. Her short hair and bangs are combed in male fashion, with a side part, and she wears a false mustache and "imperial." Dress uniform epaulettes and a Grand army of Republic medal have been added. This 1872 Sutterley photograph was the basis for a drawing that appeared in the *San Francisco Examiner* at the time of her death. *Courtesy of the University of Nevada–Reno Library.*

"Major" Pauline Cushman, The Federal Spy Who Barely Escaped Hanging. *Courtesy of F.L. Sarmiento's*, Life of Pauline Cushman.

Pauline Cushman in a studio pose taken between 1870 and 1872 in St. Louis, Missouri, by J.H. Fitzgibbon. A copy of this image in carte de visite format, we well as several others taken by Sutterley in Virginia City, Nevada, was given by Pauline to Alf Doten in 1872. *Courtesy of Special Collections, University of Nevada–Reno Library.*

Courtesy of the Library of Congress.

Pauline Cushman in a studio pose taken in November 1872. This image, as well as several others taken by Sutterley in Virginia City, Nevada, was given to Alf Doten. *Courtesy of the University of Nevada–Reno Library.*

Pauline Cushman leaning on the arm of a posing chair, bare shouldered and wearing a coral necklace with a large cross, which was a fashionable accessory, in an 1872 Sutterley photograph. *Courtesy of the Nevada Historical Society.*

Casa Grande Lodging House

Casa Grande, Arizona.

JERE FRYER,   PROPRIETOR

FIRST CLASS ACCOMMODATIONS
AT MODERATE PRICES.

Corral, Livery & Feed Stable

In Connection with the House.

Stages Leave this House

DAILY FOR FLORENCE, PINAL, SIL
VER KING, GLOBE and surrounding
Camps.   2-3tf

Advertisement for Fryer Hotel in Casa Grande. It appeared in the *Arizona Weekly Enterprise* in June 1884 when Pauline and Jere Fryer lived in Casa Grande. *Courtesy of Casa Grande Valley Historical Society.*

Pauline Cushman "as she appeared when she married Jere Fryer" was the caption accompanying this drawing printed in the *San Francisco Chronicle* the day after her death. The image shows her as she would have appeared in 1879 or 1880. The drawing was based on a photograph, possibly lost when her belongings were taken to the coroner's office upon her death. *Courtesy of Casa Grande Valley Historical Society.*

Jere Fryer as he appeared during his marriage to Pauline Cushman. Fryer was a county supervisor and sheriff of Pinal County in the Arizona Territory during the 1880s. *Courtesy of Casa Grande Valley Historical Society.*

Pauline Cushman Fryer's tombstone reads: "Pauline C. Fryer, Union Spy." Located in Officers' Circle at the National Cemetery in the Presidio in San Francisco, CA.

When the Civil War broke out in 1861, Antonia Ford was the very attractive, well-educated, 23-year-old daughter of wealthy merchant and ardent secessionist, Edward Rudolph Ford. Fairfax was overrun by Union forces. In June, John Q. Marr became the first Confederate officer killed in the war in the Battle of Fairfax Courthouse in a cavalry skirmish that took place not far from the Fords' house on Main Street. *Courtesy of the City of Fairfax.*

Confederate Spy
Antonia Ford,
on honeymoon,
c. 1864, Philadelphia,
PA. *Courtesy of the
Library of Congress.*

Buckingham Female Collegiate Institute, Buckingham Co., VA. *Courtesy of the Virginia Landmarks Registry.*

Ford Building, 3977 Chain Bridge Road, Fairfax. This was the home of Antonia Ford, imprisoned as a spy following Ranger Mosby's night capture of the local Union commander, Brig. Gen. Edwin H. Stoughton, March 9, 1863. A search of the house had revealed an honorary aide-de-camp commission to Antonia from Gen. Jeb Stuart.

Laura Ratcliffe. *Courtesy of Great Falls Historical Society.*

To All Whom it May Concern

Know ye:

That reposing Special Confidence in the patriotism, fidelity and ability of Miss Antonia Ford, I, James F.B. Stuart, by virtue of the power vested in me, as Brigadier General in the Provisional Army of the Confederate States of America, do hereby appoint and commission her my Honorary <u>aide-de-camp</u>, to rank as such from this date.

She will be obeyed, respected and admired by all lovers of a noble nature.

Given under my hand and seal at the headquarters, Cavalry Brigade, at Camp Beverly, this seventh day of October, A.D., 1861, and the first year of our independence.

James E.B. Stuart
Brigadier General, C.S.A.

In 1863, *Harper's Weekly* learned that two years earlier, Jeb Stuart had presented Antonia Ford with a mock commission as his honorary aide-de-camp. They ran this cartoon with the following caption: "The rebel cavalry leader, Stuart, has appointed to a position on his staff, with the rank of Major, a young lady residing at Fairfax Court House, who has been of great service to him in giving information." *Courtesy of* Harper's Weekly *1863.*

Mosby's Rangers. Top row (left to right): Lee Herverson, Ben Palmer, John Puryear, Tom Booker, Norman Randolph, Frank Raham. Second row: Robert Blanks Parrott, John Troop, John W. Munson, John S. Mosby, Newell, Neely, Quarles. Third row: Walter Gosden, Harry T. Sinnott, Butler, Gentry. *Courtesy of the Library of Congress.*

Jeb Stuart. *Courtesy of the Library of Congress.*

John Singleton Mosby, The Gray Ghost. *Courtesy of the Library of Congress.*

Joseph C. Willard, 1862. *Courtesy of the Library of Congress.*

Joseph C. Willard, circa 1864. *Courtesy of the Library of Congress.*

The Willard Hotel, Washington, D.C., 1860. *Courtesy of the Library of Congress.*

The Old Capitol Prison, 1st and A Streets NE, Washington, D.C.
Courtesy of the Library of Congress.

La Pierre House, Philadelphia (Free Library of Philadelphia, circa
1876. *Courtesy of the Library of Philadelphia.*

The Willards' second son died in infancy in 1867 and Antonia died soon after giving birth to their third son, Archie, on February 9, 1871. Archie died on the 9th, Antonia died 6 days later. The Willards are buried at Oak Hill Cemetery in Washington in a plot marked by a large monument. *Courtesy of the Willard family.*

TWENTY-SIX

Antonia

END OF MAY 1863

One year ago, the Federals occupied and controlled Culpeper Courthouse. Now it was under Southern command after almost one hundred battles. Pedestrians in the town's main street included a few uniformed soldiers wearing gray, who returned my smile and salute.

My father had recommended the Old Virginia Hotel on Main Street, because he knew the Payne family and their kindness.

Mrs. Payne answered the door, dressed in widow's garments. Her husband had passed just two months earlier, so now she and her four daughters ran the hotel.

"Welcome, Antonia," she said brightly. "Your father notified me of your arrival. I am sorry to report that my hotel has seen much better days, but we will make you as comfortable as we can."

She explained that the rooms were being used as a hospital, and the Federals had stripped it of all furnishings except beds and mattresses.

She added, "They did leave the family's living quarters and rooms intact, so of course we have a place for you to stay, my dear. You may share a room with my daughters."

I enjoyed tea and biscuits with the four girls: Millie, Josephine, Charlene and Amanda. Their home, like ours, had been used by the Yankees as a command center who expected to be greeted politely and entertained. The daughters all played the piano well and were often requested to entertain with their music.

Millie, the true beauty of the family, giggled and stated, "They did not dare hang a national flag from our hotel. We forbade it."

Her mother Mary responded sharply. "Our kindness and attention to them is why our hotel is still in one piece. You saw the homes of other Southern supporters torn down and demolished, did you not?"

"But don't forget your barroom, Mother. That was a big draw," Josephine reminded her.

Mary laughed lightly. "How true, but keep in mind that Colonel Taylor closed the hotel last year because he decided our bar keeper lacked patriotic restraint in dealing with the soldiers."

After tea, they showed me to a bedroom. I fell asleep the moment my head hit the pillow.

In a letter to my parents, I told them where I was and how well I was being treated. I also expressed how difficult it was for me to wait in Culpeper, even knowing it was still dangerous to return to Fairfax Courthouse, only fifty miles away.

I missed them so much and longed to see my siblings. However, it was a blessing to be able to stay with Mrs. Payne and her daughters. Millie and her sisters lifted my spirits on a daily basis, helping me re-adjust to "civilian life."

Millie often received letters from her soldier beau Peter, who was away fighting in the war. She shared some of them with me.

"Oh, my. These are very intimate," I commented. "How can you give your heart so openly to any man?"

"Oh, Antonia. Do you not see how this war has taken so many lives? In this situation, propriety and restraint should take a back seat to life and death. Perhaps my expressions of love will be the last thing he will read before death. So I have resolved to always send him comforting and loving words."

I smiled at her. "Millie, you remind me of a very dear school friend, Rose Garnett. She jumped into life fully, and shared her love of life with all who met her."

Millie raised an eyebrow. "And what happened to her?"

"The last I heard, before I was imprisoned, was that she was teaching school in her small town. Of course, that may now be interrupted and she is most likely nursing the wounded soldiers."

Later, I thought about her words and wondered if I would ever feel like she did. I shared that uncertainty with her mother, who spoke to me of the strong love she and her husband had shared over the years.

"In the end, he could not walk or even speak. I believe the war was the final shock to his deteriorated condition. But the love we shared will sustain me forever."

Millie asked me about Jeb Stuart. "Is it true that you are his aide-de-camp? He was here in March, but he never mentioned it."

I frowned. "That was purely a parlor game that went badly, I fear. That silly document put me into jail! Pray forget about it."

Then the next day Jeb appeared on our doorstep.

"Antonia," he exclaimed, "I heard you were sent south and am delighted to see you are so close to home!" A wide smile spread across his face.

"What are you doing here?" I asked.

"General Lee's instructions were to guard the upper Rappahannock and monitor local Federal movements. But your timing is perfect, for in two days I will hold a grand review of my cavalry and horse artillery, with some four thousand men on parade."

"Oh, how splendid! I am in great need of some gaiety these days! I shall be there to congratulate them!"

The Paynes and I joined everyone from the village and surrounding areas at the magnificent event. Cavalrymen proudly showed off their polished metal adornments, saddles and well-groomed horses. Later that evening we were invited to a gala dinner and entertainment at the Bradfords' home. As we were dressing, I felt extremely embarrassed that I had nothing appropriate to wear.

Noting my discomfort and remarking we were about the same size, young Amanda presented me with a beautiful light green silk gown. With its scooped neck and embroidered flowers on the bodice and sleeves, the gown was exquisite. But I was much too thin to do it justice.

"In just a moment our seamstress will adjust the sides," Mrs. Payne assured me. "And just look at how well you look in light green. Why, it reveals your slender throat and the proper amount of creamy shoulders."

Once the gown was fitted to me, she smiled with pleasure. "Let us pin up your hair and secure it with a beautiful comb, so you will be the belle of the evening." Her enthusiasm was so contagious I laughed merrily along with her.

At their fine home that evening, we were warmly welcomed and escorted inside by Sam and Sally Bradford. I looked around the beautiful parlor. Its walls were covered in pale pink watered silk, while a deeper rose-colored ribbed silk upholstered the big overstuffed sofa, several chairs, and a small love seat set against the back wall. The tied-back draperies at the two tall windows matched the sofa and chairs, but were made of light, floating taffeta. Sitting on the small love seat was Mrs. Myrta Grey, the nineteen-year-old pregnant wife of one of Stuart's men, Major Daniel Grey, who was presently boarding with them.

I had just begun a conversation with her when two dear friends surprised me with warm embraces. I had anticipated Jeb Stuart's arrival and received him happily, but was completely taken aback when I was swept up into the arms of John Esten Cooke.

"Oh my goodness," I cried out. "I did not expect to see you here!"

"Well, Antonia, the moment I heard you were in town, I made up my mind to see you. Now, you must give me the time to catch up," he grinned. In a hushed tone he added, "It helps that Jeb's wife happens to be my cousin."

I was thrilled to see him again and be seated next to him at the dinner table. I noticed that Jeb teased Myrta Grey, saying that because her husband Major Grey was so important to him, he could not be spared from his duties to join us tonight. She put on a brave face, but I could see the sadness in her eyes.

A knock on the door interrupted him, and in walked Major Dan Grey himself. Jeb had, of course, arranged this rendezvous in his devilish covert manner. Their emotional meeting affected us all. The dinner was now a complete success.

We were entertained by Jeb's banjo-playing companion, and as I listened to him picking and stroking the strings, I thought about Joseph Willard. How I would have loved to have him at my side, holding my hand under the table. I cleared my head and joined the others in singing "Old Joe Hooker, Won't You Come Out of the Wilderness?" That was the song that Jeb Stuart and his troops had sung after the fall of General Stonewall Jackson at the Battle of Chancellorsville. What a fitting end to such a glorious evening.

The following morning, I was pleased to find another letter

from Joseph. True to his word, he was writing at least once every week, along with sending me books to read.

I loved reading his letters, but could not bring myself to write back. He wrote that I should be able to go home soon. Regrettably, even he did not have the power to assure me a safe return.

TWENTY-SEVEN

Antonia

JUNE 1863

Millie and I often rode horseback along the riverside and could hear the Yankee and Rebel soldiers conversing across it, from one bank to the other. We tried to steer clear of them because of stray bullets. Although there were many soldiers around since Commander Lee had relocated most of his men to Culpeper, we saw very little fighting.

Jeb Stuart and the other officers tried to keep up the morale in the town with frequent reviews of the cavalry and even impromptu outdoor balls near his camp. One evening he invited us to one of these at Brandy, seven miles away. On that particular evening, our dance floor was the grass and the lighting came from the bonfires. There was spirited music, dancing and alcoholic drinks. Jeb took me aside and told me there was someone I should meet.

"Oh Jeb, not another lieutenant, certainly. I do not wish to converse any more this evening," I quipped.

"Close your eyes, Antonia," he told me, a smile flickering across his face.

"Hello, sister!" My eyes flew open and I found myself in the arms of my brother Charlie. I screamed out his name, overcome with emotion. Tears of joy filled every part of my being.

"You are so thin," I cried, wrapping my arms around him.

He laughed. "Look at yourself," he said, pointing to my tiny arms.

We walked away from the others to speak freely about our lives since we'd last been together. Although he'd fought in many battles, he had never been wounded. We talked about my arrest, and I even asked for advice about Joseph Willard.

"He's married, Charlie. He admitted it and has been trying to talk her into divorce."

Tilting his head to one side, he looked into my eyes. "Do you love him, Antonia?" he asked gently.

"I do not know, Charlie," I said. "He intrigues me and says he loves me. I have not even given him permission to court me until I'm certain he has asked his wife for a divorce."

"Dear sister, have you given your life to Jesus?" His question totally unnerved me.

There was a brief but significant pause.

"I am still searching, but have not yet given Him my life. I do believe in Jesus, Charlie. We were raised in the faith, but from what I've seen in daily living, I often question His grace."

"Be strong, dear Antonia. Try to find peace with the Lord and give Him your troubles. He is what has kept me going through this horrible war."

Charlie kissed my cheek to offer me comfort, and that simple token filled up a lonely corner of my heart. He held me for a long, long time.

I gave him my current address, but told him I hoped to be home before long. I felt wrapped in more happiness than I'd known for years.

On June 7, Robert E. Lee established his camp near the courthouse. The following day Jeb Stuart staged another review, but not for the public. He wanted General Lee to see how well his soldiers could perform. Nearly nine thousand mounted soldiers passed Lee's reviewing stand. Twenty-two batteries of horse artillery walked and then cantered their steeds for their General's inspection. I was proud knowing that Charlie was one of them.

On June 9, we heard the sounds of gunfire, cannons and galloping horses once again. We were told that fighting was taking place at Beverly's Ford, Kelly's Ford and Brandy Station. Soon orderlies were carrying soldiers into the hotel, including a dying Federal soldier. I wrote a letter to his mother as he took his last breath.

In the end, Jeb Stuart lost seventy-five soldiers, with three hundred wounded. General McClellan's Federal losses were more than four hundred and fifty soldiers killed and wounded. Once again we worked as nurses with limited resources. Too many men died in our hotel over the next few days, yet we worked hard to save the savable. The less seriously injured were sent to Richmond. Our town held funeral services and buried the corpses.

Myrta Grey learned that her major was safe. Jeb assured me that Charlie had also pulled through without injury. I attended services at the Episcopal Church on Saturday, June 13, along with General Lee.

As I prayed for my loved ones and the soldiers we had cared for and lost, I remembered Charlie's conversation. I knew I had sinned against the very plans God had for my life. I had put God off and walked away from Him to follow my own will. The truth seemed clearer now. I decided to try to live for Him, and simply ask Jesus to forgive me and enter my life again.

On June 15, my friend John Esten Cooke came to visit and brought news that Stuart's cavalry would be heading north toward the Blue Ridge Mountains. He encouraged Myrta and me to relocate to Richmond, where we would be safer. She agreed to go, but I wanted to stay.

"I am so close to home now. I cannot backtrack. If I go anywhere, it will be to Warrenton."

The next letter I received from Joseph bore devastating news. His brother Edwin had been shot and killed at the Battle of Brandy Station. I had the terrible notion, which I tried to banish from my mind, that my brother might have been the one to kill him. Again and again I prayed for Joseph as I thanked God it had not been Charlie.

I received a letter from General Stuart's staff chaplain, Dabney Ball, a long-time family friend. He advised me not to go to Fairfax:

> *Do not become impatient or depressed; be the heroine you are. My Dear Antonia, please do me the favor to write, for me, to my wife—embody anything in this you think proper. I cannot possibly mail a letter from here. I haven't seen Charlie since I left Culpeper. He is well, and I expect to see him soon. Love to Mrs. Ashby's family, and Mrs. Payne's. Your devoted friend, Dabney Ball.*

My father, now in Warrenton at Joseph B. Hunton's home, also wrote to me:

> *June 28, 1863*
> *My dear Antonia,*
> *I left Warrenton yesterday evening very hurriedly. I had not intended leaving before morning, but met a friend who told me there were no Yanks at Fairfax Courthouse so I took off. I wrote you a short note saying I wish you to stay at the home of Mr. William H. Gaines until you hear from me. If it is safe for you to come home, I will come after you. Stay in Warrenton for the present. I spoke to Mr. Gaines about getting me some Confederate Stock, so please give him a check*

for $1,500 when you can. I will visit you there when I can.
Mr. Tavenner, the hotelkeeper, saw Charlie on Wednesday
between Paris and Winchester, where the fighting is happen-
ing. He said Charlie is with Stuart near Fairfax and is well.
If we can get him home now how very pleasant that would
be. We are 22 miles from home and walking through the rain,
carrying our luggage. I hope and pray you may keep well
and be comfortable. Try to keep up your spirits. We expect
to reach home tomorrow, with luck and if we do not meet
Yankees. Goodbye my Dear Child. May every blessing attend
you.

Your affectionate father, E.R. Ford

Mr. Gaines, a former mayor, retired merchant and wealthy
landowner, was now the Justice in Warrenton. I was hesitant
to relocate, but knew that was what my father wanted me to
do. I was also weary of the sounds of battle, and working so
hard and long in the hospital. But I was safe and comfortable
where I was, and had truly enjoyed the hospitality and friendship of the Payne family.

The following morning, I hugged each one goodbye, and
boarded the Orange & Alexandra train to Warrenton.

TWENTY-EIGHT

Pauline

END OF JUNE 1863

When I reached Columbia, I found Mr. Baker, per Major Boone's orders, awaiting my arrival. I spent only two days in Columbia, reporting my intelligence to Major Boone and Captain Blackman. I also accompanied Captain Blackman on horseback to tour the surrounding camps.

I was not able to get a message through to General Truesdail, and was unaware at that time that General Garfield had already prepared a detailed report for General Rosecrans on 12 June. General Rosecrans, after reading that report, ordered an advance of all available forces.

Captain Blackman was becoming increasingly clear about his romantic interest in me. It was unnerving, but I used it to my advantage.

"How lovely you look mounted on this steed, Miss Cushman," he grinned, as we sat atop a small hill, surveying the camp.

"Thank you, Captain. How kind of you to acquire him for me." I grew pensive. "I wonder how my horse Soldier is doing."

"Soldier?" he asked, turning toward me with a puzzled frown.

"The horse I had to sell to Milam when I came here. I hope to get him back one day."

"You shall need him when you accompany me in the

position of my aide, which I hope you will accept after your return from Nashville. I have already written to an acquaintance about locating your trunk. It should be awaiting you at Milam's."

I smiled nervously. How much did I want them to know about my past, and especially my trunk being held for me at Truesdail's headquarters?

"By the way," he continued, "I should like to have a military uniform made for you to wear when you serve me as my lieutenant. My mother would be pleased to have you stay with her, and she can make it for you."

His pride and personal admiration were obvious. I smiled broadly, as if happy with the idea. We went to his house to take measurements and she began sewing. I tried it on the following day, but it was too large.

"I can get this adjusted in Nashville while I am there," I told them. "Thank you so much for making this for me." I smiled gratefully at this gentle woman, who clasped my hand in hers.

I did not know then that the die was cast. My messages had not yet reached General Truesdail, but none of the information I would send in the following two weeks would have changed General Rosecrans' battle plan.

Mr. Baker and I returned to Milam's home, arriving late at night. His wife suggested I stay there until Milam's arrival the following day. Considering my distaste for the man, I surprised myself by giving him permission to travel to Nashville for my trunk. I knew he would not find it where Captain Blackman had sent him, since it was still with General Truesdail.

Milam walked into the house, sneering and suspicious. "Yer baggage ain't where you and Blackman said," he muttered. "Seems Truesdail has it. Why would that be?"

I pretended to be indignant and declared I would go get it myself.

"I need to buy back my horse and saddle in order to make the journey," I told him calmly, handing him ninety Confederate dollars before he could object.

"Yer horse is with Baker in De Mosses. I'll send word to bring 'im back."

Through his slanted eyes I saw his distrust. He certainly did not want me returning to Nashville and revealing the details of his secret smuggling operations. And I did not want him to turn me over to the nearest Confederate unit.

I waited until the next morning to depart and Milam once again disappeared. He returned some time later with his friend Shute from the Confederate scout station. Moments passed before another scout entered Milam's house by the rear door. Milam feigned surprise.

"Your pass, ma'am," the scout demanded smugly, holding out his hand. "You need a pass from Tullahoma to travel beyond our lines."

"By whose authority?" I inquired, struggling to release my elbow from his grasp. "I did not know a pass was needed."

"My name is Fall, and I am a Confederate scout. I am afraid you will have to come with me to our station at Anderson's Mills. General Bragg ordered the arrest of anyone going out of the lines without a pass. Come with me," he commanded.

Glaring at Milam, I snapped, "You have violated your duty as a host and betrayed me. Mark you: as sure as my name is Pauline Cushman, I will get even with you yet!"

Like most bullies, Milam was uncertain about how serious my threat might be. He scowled and scratched his head.

Turning back to Fall, I finally wrestled my arm free. "I cannot do that, sir. My horse is not here, and I will not leave without him." In the confusion, the scout failed to search me, so my gun remained hidden under my jacket.

They forced me to ride Shute's horse to De Mosses, where I

was reunited with my horse Soldier. He snorted happily when he saw me, and I was so happy to have him back.

Fall rode in front of me as we traveled to Anderson's Mill. Several times I considered pulling out my pistol and shooting him to make my escape. Once I even pointed it at the back of his head. Fall chose that moment to compliment me on my horsemanship, and I put the pistol away. I could not shoot him in cold blood.

In my haste to leave Milam's, I left behind my few belongings, including my new gray uniform and the sketches of the Confederate fortifications, hidden under the soles of my boots. Knowing those few scraps of paper were all the evidence General Bragg would need to hang a Union spy, I submissively entered Anderson's Mill and handed my pistol to Lieutenant Johnson.

He detained me as a "prisoner of war" and ordered me taken to Spring Hill, where the famous cavalry commander Major General Nathan Bedford Forrest was headquartered.

A few hours into our journey we stopped for lunch at the home of a well-known Secesh physician. After the meal, I was introduced to Brigadier General John Hunt Morgan, a noble, gentle yet manly figure. His smile exuded confidence. Mounted on a magnificent charger, with his splendid uniform of gray, braided-on shoulders and cuffs with broad gold cord, he presented as handsome a picture as I had seen. This general insisted on personally escorting me to Spring Hill.

"I take it upon myself to beg that you will allow me, henceforth, to be your guide in this excursion."

I smiled at his courtly manners. "Sir, rather than say you would be my guide, use the proper word *jailer,* for I am your prisoner."

"May I call you Pauline?" he asked through that charming smile.

I nodded my approval so he added, "And you must call me Johnny."

Smiling in his turn, he added reassuringly, "Pauline, I do not think you will find me a very severe guardian, for to tell you the truth, I am very susceptible, and if there are any prisoners here, it will be *I,* and your bright beautiful eyes the *jailer.*"

Johnny and I exchanged childhood stories and several of my thespian adventures. I found him to be gallant and as charming a companion as one could wish. I enjoyed our ride together so much, I forgot to try and discover any military "plums."

There were certainly women spies working for the South. It was difficult during that ride to separate my work for the national cause from my attraction to an officer on the other side. I wondered if my Southern counterparts faced a similar challenge, and if they were handling it with greater ease than I.

In Hillsboro, he officially turned me over to a group of scouts and ordered them to convey me safely to Forrest's headquarters.

"We shall soon meet again," he said, pressing my hand warmly. "Man proposes and God disposes."

On the road that evening, a terrible thunderstorm quickly made the roads impassable. The scouts stopped at a shack in the forest and asked for shelter. Regrettably, it was our bad fortune to have stopped in the home of a wounded Rebel soldier named Baum, who had lost both legs in a recent skirmish. I could hear him weeping and groaning all night, accompanied by the sobs of his unfortunate wife. They told me to sleep by the fireplace, next to an elderly black servant. After a brief conversation, I made up my mind to ask him for help.

"Please sir, I implore you to assist me with my plight," I whispered to this kind gentleman. I shared my plan as simply as I could.

"All you need to do for me is to run up the road a piece and back again, shouting loudly, 'The Yankees are coming!'"

I knew the people here feared an attack by General Rosecrans, and I wanted to take advantage of those fears. "I will give you a ten-dollar greenback if you do this for me."

He nodded and slipped outside. Around midnight the area's entire black population could be heard running up to the house, screaming out those terrifying words, "De Yankees is a-comin'! Blessed sakes, de Yanks is a-comin'! Run! Run!" Several even rushed through the house, awakening the guards and prisoners.

My plan worked! The guards fled, trying to save themselves. I grabbed a pistol belonging to the wounded soldier and hurried out to find Soldier. Leaping onto his back, I headed straight for the Union lines at Franklin. The pounding rain poured down in broad sheets while the ferocious winds made it impossible to see where I was going, so I was forced to stop at another house and seek shelter. I rested there for only a few hours.

Again Soldier and I braved the elements riding toward the Union lines. Apparently, there were six Rebel sentinels between there and Franklin. I also overheard the password, "a friend," and used it successfully through five patrols. One of the guards asked me for the "countersign."

I blinked in confusion. "I'm sorry, sir. I do not understand you."

He laughed. "Some of the Rebels have invented a countersign to assure that no Yanks get through. Do you not know it?"

Bile rose to my throat as I hung my head demurely and shrugged my shoulders. "No, sir. I am unaware of this countersign."

"Fear not, woman. I shall allow you through this time. For the future, the words are 'Jeff Davis and the Southern Confederacy.' Carry on!" I smiled dazzlingly and gave him my heartfelt thanks.

I passed smoothly through five stations. My luck ran out at the sixth.

"Where is your written pass?" asked the guard. "I cannot let you pass without it."

I tried every means of bribery possible with this older guard, but to no avail. He held me there at the sixth sentinel until four Rebel scouts arrived to arrest me. They demanded I mount my horse and follow them. I allowed them to detain me, and soon I again found myself in the presence of Johnny Hunt Morgan. This time he watched me sorrowfully while politely discharging the guards.

"I will personally conduct you to General Forrest's headquarters," he said, his face registering angst and heartache.

I nodded knowingly.

TWENTY-NINE

Antonia

JULY 1863

On July 1, 1863, I arrived at the Warrenton Branch train station. On the way to the home where I would be staying, I noticed many empty stockyards, shops and dwellings. This town resembled other villages I had visited, but fewer people were milling about, and not one woman. Most of the shops were deserted. No one spoke to me as I found my way to the home of the former mayor of Warrenton Branch—William H. Gaines.

"Hello Antonia! We were expecting you. Welcome to our home." After the warm greeting he ushered me into his lovely parlor and handed my bag to a young man.

"Mr. Gaines, I am so pleased to meet you. My father holds you in such high regard."

"There is no finer man than he. How was your train ride from Culpeper?" His smile showed a sincere interest.

"It was uneventful, Mr. Gaines," I answered honestly. "Your town looks picturesque, but I saw very few people."

"It remains picturesque because we have had no fighting here yet. However, the town is occupied by Yankees, which accounts for little interaction among our own folks."

"And how many people live here?" I asked, curiosity rising as he gestured for me to sit down on the plump parlor sofa. He gazed out the window for a long moment, as if peering into a fond memory.

"We once numbered about twelve hundred, including five doctors, fifteen lawyers, five schools and a large library. We had fifteen stores, three bakeries, three tailors, two boot makers, a druggist, a jeweler and two carriage makers. But last winter, most who could afford to moved away. We who remain are all stubborn independents, guarding our homes and properties."

"Are any of our men nearby?" I continued, hoping for news about my brother.

"Some small scouting parties travel between here and Culpeper; mostly Mosby's men, I believe."

Just then Mary Gaines and her children entered the room. Obviously younger than her husband, she still had the petite figure of a child although surrounded by her four small children. Beaming, she presented them to me.

"It is a pleasure to offer you shelter in our humble home, Antonia. We are so very fond of your father. Please say hello to Lizzie, eleven; Grenville, nine; William, seven; and Lena, five."

The precious children bowed and curtsied. Little William reminded me of my younger brother Frank, and I realized how much I missed him.

When two other boarders—Susan Foster and her father Thomas—joined us, we enjoyed coffee and a lively conversation. Mary Gaines apologized several times for the lack of sugar, explaining that even real coffee had become extremely scarce.

"So we often substitute a hot drink made of burnt rye, corn cake and bacon. But for today's special guest, I am serving the last of my real coffee," she said with a smile. Fresh berries and a crumbly sweet cake completed our treat.

Later, I helped Susan work on a quilt and asked her more about the town. The question seemed to make her weary and somber.

"Most of us are proud Secessionists. We find it difficult being civil to the Yankees occupying our town."

I smiled. "I have used insincere sweetness to my advantage, and communicating with them makes me privy to military information."

Mary broke in. "Antonia, was it dreadful being imprisoned? Were you treated badly?"

"No, I chose to see it as an adventure. They fed us three meals a day, but I became this thin due to the flavorless food. Yet my father was close by, and that helped me keep my faith."

Mary thoughtfully changed the subject. "I only wish we had fresh vegetables from the grocer, but we do not. We harvest some fruit and berries, and laying hens along with a few chickens give us protein. Oh, and several pigs. We use our livestock for the outdoor work."

"Please let me know what I can do to help you," I offered gratefully.

"Perhaps you can help the children with their studies. Your father told us you attended a women's college in Gravel Hill, Virginia. There used to be a girls' boarding school here on Lee Street. Of course it is closed now, but we acquired some of the materials they used, especially the books."

I grinned. "Just what I needed! I would love to work with them. We can begin tomorrow," I added, stifling a sudden yawn. They showed me to the bedroom I would be sharing with Susan, and I soon succumbed to a long afternoon nap.

My stay in Warrenton was restful, and I slowly began to gain weight. I tutored the children and accompanied them to the Presbyterian Church when it was open, praying for the safety of the soldiers, especially my brother Charlie and dear Joseph.

The year before, this same church was used as a hospital for the Federal troops, and its basement served as their stable.

Having a great deal of free time gave me a chance to reflect on what was happening between Joseph and myself. I eventually came to the conclusion that I cared deeply for him. In one letter to my parents, I told them they could give Major Willard my new address.

They wrote me that my brother Charlie made it safely through the Battle of Rector's Cross Roads, also known as Hanover, on June 30.

Susan and I shared women talk and spent time sewing quilts and clothing for the soldiers. We discussed *The Woman in White* by Wilkie Collins, written in 1860. Then we both read it a second time and discussed it with Mary and William Gaines. Of course I identified with the character Marian, who learns how to use her wiles to exist in the male-dominated society. Each afternoon I napped, roused myself for the evening meal, played cards with the group, and then read a little before falling asleep. My life, for the first time in years, was peaceful.

On July 15, at approximately three o'clock in the afternoon, Joseph Willard rode back into my life.

Susan and I were sewing on the shaded front porch when we heard a horse approaching. Lifting up our eyes, we saw a dashing officer dressed in blue approaching the house.

How handsome he looks, I thought to myself, then suddenly paled and felt faint.

Susan noticed my distressed expression. "Antonia, I am certain he will not harm us. Look, he is smiling."

Joseph walked up the steps and stood above us. "Good afternoon, ladies."

I recovered quickly. "Major Willard, allow me to introduce you to Miss Susan Foster. Susan, Major Willard is an acquaintance of mine."

Susan extended her hand and greeted him politely. Noting the way we looked at each other, she excused herself and retreated into the house.

"Perhaps you would care for a beverage, Major Willard," I asked him in a formal tone.

He laughed and lifted my hand tenderly to his lips. "Yes, Antonia, I would appreciate some water, please."

I went inside to get water and some biscuits. I found Mary and Susan whispering in the kitchen.

"Mary, is my friend welcome to visit me here?" I asked uncertainly.

"Yes, Antonia, but I cannot house any more Federals here."

"Oh no, he is not here to stay. He is on General Heintzelman's staff in Washington City." I smiled my relief. "Thank you for your hospitality."

I hurried back to Joseph.

"You look well," he fibbed gallantly, his eyes riveted on mine.

I smiled faintly. "Joseph, pray do not flatter me. I have not yet regained my strength, and am certainly not dressed to impress." I adored him for his thoughtfulness.

"You are a fine sight for these tired eyes. I can see a glow in your cheeks and your smile is beautiful, as always." Setting down his glass, he lifted my hands and held them between his. His smile, filled with charm and warmth, startled my heart.

"Antonia, how much longer will you be here?"

I stared into the face I had come to love and said, "I know not. Perhaps you can tell me if it would be safe to travel home."

"What I can say is that the Federals still occupy your town and are vigilant in sending suspected Southern scouts to prison."

I bowed my head and murmured, "Then I have no choice but to remain here." Lifting my eyes, I inquired about his life.

"I am primarily an administrator now. My field days are

over. The overseer is running our hotel mostly. Henry and his wife Sarah are faring well in New York with their young son."

"And your wife?"

He looked away. "She is the same—no better, no worse." I couldn't miss his quiet resigned tone.

"Joseph," the words somehow came out, "I have come to realize that I want to be with you if you should decide to get a divorce. I can no longer pretend you are not important to me."

The smile flitting across his face brought his eyes to sparkling life. "Oh my darling, I have prayed to hear those words from you."

Standing quickly, he put his arm around me and walked me a short distance from the house.

"Look at you, Antonia. Even without trying, your beauty is soft, angelic and genuine. Your innate warmth and kindness won me over so long ago, and will never leave me."

Holding me in his arms, he kissed my cheek, my neck, my hair. Finally, he caught my face between his hands and pulled me to him for a quick, hard kiss.

Overcome with emotion, I felt the tears slipping down my face. Still he held me.

Finally, he spoke. "I will get a divorce, my love. It will not be easy, since Congress only authorized them in Washington three years ago."

I pulled away slowly and locked my eyes with his. "How do you get a divorce?"

"I must establish grounds, and that is difficult. The only grounds that I know of are adultery, bigamy, lunacy, or impotence."

Finding my voice, I asked, "Would you be divorcing on the ground of lunacy?"

He nodded. "That is the only logical choice. I have already hired a lawyer and have initiated the process."

For a moment I simply gazed up, totally under his spell. He had done all of this for me without knowing if I would be in agreement. I felt a strong surge of respect for Joseph Willard, knowing he would take care of me and whatever came with me—the whole package.

"Joseph, let's walk," I suggested. "I never stroll around town as it is not recommended for women to walk alone." We talked about life as we strolled through town.

"The tide of the war has turned against the South after the terrible Battle at Gettysburg and the surrender of Vicksburg this month. I truly hope the war is nearly over." His words were spoken in sorrow.

The fragrant aroma of baked goods curling from a chimney drew us across the public square to the open door of the tiny bakery. A fresh batch of scones welcomed us from the table inside. The major escorted me through the open door.

"Sweet rolls, please," he said, pulling bills from his pocket.

"I've just two left," the baker smiled. "You are in luck."

I savored this sweet roll, made from real sugar. I wondered where he had found the ingredients. The price was dear, but we later agreed it was worth every cent.

As we passed the dry goods store, Joseph paused. "Wait here," he told me.

Returning, he made me close my eyes and open my hands. I felt paper and something a little heavier.

"A pen!" I exclaimed, opening them wide. Thank you, Joseph. It is beautiful." I leaned over and kissed his cheek.

He laughed delightfully. "Now you will have no excuse not to write to me."

"I only wish our lives could return to normal. Things will be like before, won't they?" I asked him, apprehensive. "Wouldn't it be lovely if I could just do what Southern girls are supposed to do and not worry?"

He gave me a long look. "And what are Southern girls supposed to do?"

I relaxed with a warm smile. "Well, we should be well-versed in etiquette, well-read, and dressed stylishly. It is even better if we master a musical instrument. We should have culinary skills and understand medical remedies. Home management skills are essential for undertaking the role of 'lady of the house.'"

"Do tell me, lovely Antonia. Do you wish to be a 'lady of the house' one day?"

For a moment, I simply stared at him. Then my eyes sparkled. "I am twenty-five years old and look forward to a happy life with a husband and a few children."

Joseph took me into his arms and began kneading my neck and back, much to the amusement of several spectators.

THIRTY

Antonia

AUGUST 1863

We celebrated my birthday in late July with a quilting bee at the home of my new friends—Annie, Fanny and Peggy Lucas. They invited two sisters named Janet and Elizabeth Weaver to join us.

The afternoon passed pleasantly, with a frank exchange of viewpoints on love, freed slaves and the war. Having honest talks with the gracious ladies filled my heart with hope as strangers discovered how much we had in common. We shared a belief in the rights of fellow humans, a strong faith in God and an abiding loyalty to our country.

Each of us had spent time nursing wounded combatants, grieving over lost loved ones, caring for beloved family members and looking toward the future with faith. I was certain the bonds we formed that day would last a lifetime.

August was steaming hot in Warrenton. Mother wrote me that the provost marshal had arrested Uncle Brower and sent him to Old Capitol Prison.

Papa suggested I stay in Warrenton through August, due to the Federal presence in Fairfax Courthouse. And John Mosby wrote us to describe a daring raid he had executed on August 4.

At Fairfax Courthouse a few nights ago I captured twenty-nine loaded sutlers' wagons, about one hundred prisoners and one hundred forty horses. I had brought all off safely near Aldie, where I fell in with a large force of the enemy's cavalry, who

recaptured them. The enemy had several hundred, and I had
only twenty-seven soldiers. We killed and captured several.
My loss: one wounded and captured.

Prices were rising everywhere. A pair of lady's shoes now cost
thirty dollars. Although I needed some badly, when a small
turkey now cost eight dollars, a horse two hundred dollars,
and four barrels of flour were sold at fifty dollars, I stopped
thinking about new shoes.

Our conversations seemed to be mostly about prices, the food
we missed, or our cravings for what we had not eaten for months.
Occasionally we discussed the war and politics, but those topics
were becoming too complex for a parlor conversation.

One day Mr. Foster told us that Major General Irvin
McDowell's engineering corps would re-surface the Springs
Bridge. Several people laughed, remembering its history as a
riverside building, a cheese factory and originally, a brewery.

Just then a servant rushed in to announce the imminent
arrival of two Union officers. We quickly hid anything of
value and secreted lighter items under our hoopskirts. Servants grabbed all our food and chickens and rushed outdoors
to conceal them.

After speaking with the officers on the porch, Mr. Gaines
gathered us together.

"Major Hitchcock came to personally apologize for that incident last week at a neighbor's home. His troops helped themselves to the family's food supply and were about to behave
indecently with the women of the household. Fortunately, he
caught them red-handed. Now he's on his way to apologize to
the family and offer his protection to them and other civilians.
He suggested we fly a United States flag and put it at an angle
between the house and a wing. As long as it is there, we will
not be bothered."

I groaned inwardly. The food situation was now critical, and Warrenton was becoming a ghost town. It was time to go home.

When the day of departure finally dawned, my dear Joseph came to Warrenton to escort me home by train. At Manassas Junction, we hired a carriage to drive us to my house. I enjoyed sitting beside him, engaging in light conversation about everything except his wife. I wanted nothing to dampen my joy at returning to my family, and my parents were still unaware of his marital status.

Turning the corner at Payne Street, I saw my home for the first time in six months. The vision became magical when my parents rushed out the door to meet us. I was at last in their embrace. Wiping away our tears, we were talking over each other in excitement.

"How I have missed you," we each cried out from the heart. "It is wonderful to see you again!"

Papa turned away from me to exclaim, "Major Willard, how can I ever thank you for bringing my child home safely?"

I could feel Papa's body shaking with sobs during our embrace. My brothers and sister had now joined the emotional maelstrom; everyone seemed overwhelmed with joy and gratitude.

"Frank, you are so grown up," I cried, studying my energetic five-year-old brother. He was now tall enough to join Pattie and Clanie in flinging their arms around me.

Mother, still brushing away tears, suggested we step inside.

"What news have you of Charlie?" I asked entering the parlor and warmly embracing a weeping Mathilde and a shaking Octavia.

"We've heard he's nearby and safe," my father answered contently.

Looking around the room filled me with love and a sense of happiness for the second time in months. I was home with my family, and standing at my side was the man I loved.

Our lengthy reunion featured constant hugs and kisses, explanations and stories of eventful past months. Finally, we could laugh from relief and put the cold darkness behind us. We were home!

Joseph leaned over to whisper, "I must depart now, Antonia. You are home and safe, and I must return to my post." He smiled as my hand reached for his.

Mathilde must have overheard him, for she directed her words to him. "Sir, this is a day of celebration, and I would be honored to serve you some tea and refreshments before you depart." Her words were warm and welcoming.

After a brief cup of tea he quietly slipped out, leaving me a stolen kiss. "Stay strong, my love," he advised. *Was that remark about telling my family that he was married?*

I grinned. "Yes, Major! And I think I shall call you that, as I like the sound of it."

My Major nodded his approval. "Coming from your lips, it sounds divine."

The following morning after breakfast, it took all my strength to address the issue. After a deep breath I blurted it out: "Major Willard is a married man."

Mother looked around the room as if in panic and covered her face with her hands so she wouldn't have to look at me.

Papa sent me a grave look. "Should I be concerned? What is going on with you two?"

"I have fallen in love with him," I answered sincerely, feeling completely liberated by voicing my emotional commitment.

"Then it grieves me to tell you I am disappointed and a little ashamed of you," he answered.

I heard a cry from my mother. Then Papa's statement unleashed another rush of tears.

"Please, Papa and Ma, I could not bear your anger or disappointment in me."

Papa rose and walked over, then silently put an arm around my shoulders.

At last he said softly, "Antonia, you are of age and have a mind of your own. I cannot forbid you from seeing him. I can only point out the emotional obstacles you will face."

Taking a deep breath, he continued. "Remember that he is a Union officer, and your allegiance is to the South. Divorces are extremely difficult to obtain, even following divorce reform legislation in Washington City."

Holding me at arm's length, he looked into my eyes. "But I will support whatever decision you make. Your mother and I believe in you, and we love you deeply."

"Oh Papa, dear Mama, the obstacles can be surmounted. Joseph is a good man who is already trying to divorce his wife. He has said he will resign his commission; once that happens, I have given him my word to sign the oath."

After a long silence, Mother spoke words I never expected to hear from her. "Whether we sign the oath now or later is of no consequence. And the issue of his being a Union officer will soon go away. The South will lose this war."

They continued talking softly together and I went to find Pattie. We decided to walk through town, which had been impossible to do in Warrenton.

"It's not changed much here," she said. "Union soldiers stay near the courthouse and jail, and pretty much leave us alone."

When we passed Papa's shop with a "closed" sign on it, I remarked wistfully, "At least we still have food and fuel."

"Yes," she agreed, "but we are only allowed to keep our shops stocked because the Federals need them too."

Back at home, Mathilde offered me some sweeties she had set aside for my return. "I will have to fatten you up, child," she laughed. "You are shrinking and are even smaller than your sister Pattie."

Adam and Octavia also sought me out. "We be workin' together on a saddle for ye, Miss Antonia. I dun sum toolin' and Octavia put a likeness of your face on de side."

Adam stood before me, grinning from ear to ear. I hugged them both and kissed their proud faces. It was indeed good to be home.

That Sunday, at church services in the courthouse, I sat in the midst of Union soldiers and townsfolk. There were obviously very few men except for soldiers and the elderly. Happy to see many children and women I knew, I stopped after the service to greet our neighbors.

Less than a week later, we received a visit from Captain Dennis of the Centreville district and Colonel Lowell, Fairfax Courthouse's military commander.

Father answered the knock and stood outside with them for several moments. We heard raised voices, then watched him escort them into the parlor.

"Antonia, these men have come to arrest you on charges of disloyalty." A deep sigh shook him as sorrow filled his eyes.

"Miss Ford, pack your belongings now. We will leave shortly," commanded Colonel Lowell.

"My daughter will not go alone. I shall accompany her," insisted Papa.

"Where is your Federal flag? Have you taken the Oath of Allegiance?" he demanded.

Mother and Pattie had been sitting quietly during this exchange, the color slowly draining from Mother's face.

"We have not taken the oath, and the Federal flag has not as yet been placed on the house. If you cannot give me reason to arrest my daughter, I will not release her to you." Papa stood firmly to show his determination.

"Sir, I am arresting you too, for resisting my orders."

Clanie appeared at the doorway, his eyes blazing.

"Do you have an arrest warrant?" he inquired defiantly.

"That is not necessary. Would you care to join us?" mocked Captain Dennis.

"Stay out of this, Clanie," warned Papa in a low voice.

We packed two small bags and left with the men for Alexandria, riding in an ambulance. Arriving at the provost general's headquarters, we were escorted into his office.

"Colonel Wells," Captain Dennis said in a self-important manner. "I present these disloyal citizens for your disposition."

"I will review their situation. Please take them to the waiting room."

In a room in the house next door, my father and I were handed some food and water and told to prepare our beds on the floor. I hugged Papa as we said good night.

"Fear not, Antonia. This matter will be cleared up tomorrow," Papa said, embracing me tightly.

The following morning we met again in Colonel Wells' room, along with three other men accused of disloyalty.

"I am sending all of you to Lieutenant Colonel J.H. Taylor, Chief of Staff in Washington, for his disposition."

Color suffused my father's face. "Sir, do you not have the fortitude to release us on your own accord? We are innocent citizens who have never caused trouble to anyone. Take pity on my daughter who has been through so much already, and is innocent. Just look at her frailty!"

To my surprise, I heard the murmur of assent from the other men in the room.

The colonel replied tersely. "I take my orders from the Chief of Staff Taylor and he wishes to see you—all of you."

On that note, we were dismissed.

THIRTY-ONE

Antonia

Colonel Taylor still possessed the same unpleasant attitude as when I had seen him last in the prison.

"Will you take the oath?" he asked gruffly.

"No, I cannot in good conscience do so," I replied intractably.

"Very well. Then you will remain here a sufficient amount of time to reflect on your foolishness."

The next morning I accepted an invitation to take exercise, where I looked for my father and others I knew were there. My father stood alone, waiting for me.

"Antonia, I have been thinking. I believe we must take the oath, even if we do not believe in it. My compatriots have decided it's best for all of us."

I studied his face, and his eyes told me we could pronounce this untruth in exchange for our freedom. Papa was being pragmatic and I needed to follow his example.

We parted. I returned to my cell, the same one I had occupied some months before. My roommate Abigail had been released, and I could get no information as to where she might be now.

I slept, and was awakened from my short nap and told I had a visitor.

Major Willard came toward me as I entered the room. Ignoring the guard's shocked expression, he embraced me tenderly. I studied the hazel depths and unguarded emotion in his eyes, and felt a rush of tenderness.

"Darling, I have prevailed on Major General Samuel Heintzelman to release you if you take the Oath of Allegiance. Please tell me you will," he implored, deep concern clouding his voice.

I had already decided I would; however, I saw this as an opportunity to negotiate.

"Joseph, I will do so as long as you promise to resign your commission in the Union Army."

Taken aback, he stared at me for a long moment. Then he smiled.

"I have been thinking of doing that very thing. I will begin the process immediately. I have brought a document to show you." He handed me a piece of paper.

Headquarters, Dept. of Washington
September 16, 1863

Major Willard, ADC, will administer, in accordance with instructions from the Secretary of War, the Oath of Allegiance to Miss Antonia Ford who will afterwards at proper time be transferred to her home at Fairfax Courthouse, receiving a written authority to remain at that place with her family.

By Command of Major General Heintzelman
(Signed: J.H. Taylor, Chief of Staff, AAG)

I laughed after reading it. "So, you already suspected I would take the oath?"

He nodded affectionately. "Yes, ma'am. It is for our future, and I dare believe you want it as much as I do."

We sat down at the table and he dictated what I should write. I did as he asked.

On being released from my arrest, I, Antonia Ford of Fairfax Co., Va, do solemnly affirm that I will support, protect and defend the Constitution and Government of the United

*States against all enemies—whether domestic or foreign; that
I will bear true faith, allegiance and loyalty to the same, any
ordinance, resolution or law of any State convention or leg-
islative to the contrary notwithstanding, that I will not give
aid, comfort or information to its enemies, and further, that
I do this with a full determination pledge and purpose without any mental reservation or evasion whatsoever. So help
me God.*

> *Antonia Ford*

*Sworn and subscribed to before me this 16th day of Septem-
ber 1863*

> *J.C. Willard*
> *Headquarters Department of Washington*

Joseph signed as my witness, handed me a copy of the day's
Gazette, and left a light kiss on my cheek before departing with
the document.

I spent two uneventful days in prison and saw my father
only once during that time. He had also taken and signed
the Oath of Allegiance. Now we would languish through the
waiting period and hopefully be released together.

General Heintzelman kept his word. Major Willard came
to take me home on September 18, 1863. He proudly handed
me the letter signed by the general.

*The bearer Antonia Ford, having taken the Oath of Alle-
giance to the United States, is hereby permitted by direct
authority from the Secretary of War to return to her home
in Fairfax Courthouse—there to remain subject to orders
from these Headquarters. Excepting under instructions from
Headquarters, Washington, she will in no case be molested or
interfered with by any military authority. The Provost Marshal of "Rug's Division" will see that this order is carried out.*

It was signed by Major General Heintzelman. I threw my arms around Joseph and clung to him, trembling. He carried my light suitcase to the waiting carriage and once again, we traveled home together.

Father also reached home that afternoon. A Union flag now flew in one of our front windows. We had done all we could to keep peace and harmony in our home. Now I would finally rest, and wait for Major to keep his word in our covenant.

Late one evening, just as we were preparing for bed, we heard a loud knock on the door.

"It's John Mosby," he shouted. "Let me in. Hurry!"

Papa grabbed his arm and pulled him into the foyer. "You are putting us at peril, John. We have taken the oath. What is going on?"

"Sorry. I am in great need of medical supplies and ammunition," he blurted.

"Are you injured?" asked Papa.

"Not I, but I have injured men. I've captured over one hundred horses and mules, several wagons with valuable goods and about one hundred prisoners. Among them are three captains and one lieutenant."

Mother returned with what she could find. "Do take care, John," she said, with a gentle smile.

Mosby grinned. "I am protecting Fairfax by waylaying their troops' communications and preventing them from operating. Tomorrow night we shall attack a cavalry camp at Falls Church."

He left as quickly as he arrived. I took the letter I had begun writing to Joseph, hoping to finish it by candlelight in my bedroom. Mother came to bid me goodnight and saw the letter spread out on my bed.

She lifted her brow, and I grinned. "You know it is to my beloved. He has told me each letter from me is a 'feast.'"

Sitting down beside me, she tucked a stray hair behind my earlobe. "You do love him dearly, do you not, Antonia?"

I nodded, and asked, "May I sign my letters 'yours faithfully', or is that too forward?"

Mother frowned. "You may, but he cannot."

"Mother," I protested. "He is as good as divorced. They have had no marital relations for years."

She shook her head slowly. "I pray you are right to believe in him so."

We continued to exchange amorous letters for several weeks. Then one day in mid-November, with a warm fire burning in the fireplace to hold off the chill, he appeared at our front door.

"What a pleasure and a surprise!" I exclaimed, hugging him close. "I expected you on Saturday."

He laughed. "Today is my birthday, and I had to share it with the woman I love," he said. "I am an old soldier now, perhaps too old for you."

Reaching up to cup his face in my hands, I asked, "Just how old are you, old man?" I liked the way the bristle along his jaw tickled my palms.

"Forty-three years of age. Old enough to be your father." He studied me seriously.

"Joseph, we must celebrate. I shall let Mathilde know and perhaps we shall open a bottle of brandy."

Mathilde frowned at my request. "We have no flour. What shall I cook?" I encouraged her to be creative and left the kitchen carrying the teapot and biscuits.

"Joseph, leave a bit of water with the tea leaves and we can read them together," I suggested coquettishly.

"Dear one, your mother and I have warned you that reading

tea leaves is the work of Satan. We find it un-Christian, as would your minister."

I laughed dismissively and instructed him how to proceed. "Take the cup in your left hand and swirl it around clockwise three times. I will do that too. Then, cover the top of your cup with your right hand and swirl the leaves up and around the sides and rim."

He obeyed with a puzzled expression on his face. "Now what?"

"Now, you read mine and I'll read yours," I smiled. "Oh look, there is a bird on the bottom of your cup. That is a sign of good news! Changes!" I was delighted with the reading.

Joseph's eyes sparkled. "Why look, I see a ring on the rim of your cup!"

Clapping my hands together, I squealed with pleasure. "That's a wedding ring, Joseph! And because it is on the rim, it means a life-changing event. How lucky I am!" Then I stopped, and blushed. "Oh, maybe it's not for me. Do you know any other couples contemplating marriage?"

Instead of responding, Joseph took my hands in his and pulled me toward him, kissing me urgently and passionately. We broke it off quickly as footsteps came near. Mathilde had baked him a birthday cake, just as I knew she would.

"Beautiful," I gushed. "What do you call it, Mathilde?"

"It is a molasses crabapple stick cake, and I've just invented it," she grinned. "Happy Birthday, Major Willard."

The rest of the family joined us for a wonderful celebration, including a grand supper. We sang and danced well into the night. I felt incredibly happy and very blessed.

THIRTY-TWO

Pauline

FINAL DAYS OF JUNE 1863

Geneeral Forrest was physically imposing and intimi-dating at two hundred-twenty pounds and six feet two inches tall. As erect as an Indian, his dark blue eyes radiated harshness and bitterness.

"Well, Miss Cushman," said the famous cavalry leader, "I am glad, indeed, to see you. I've been looking for you a long time. You are pretty sharp at turning a card, but I think we've got you on this last shuffle. Let's get to the point."

I felt certain scorn was flashing in my dark eyes, but I answered him politely.

"On what shuffle do you have me, sir?" I inquired, my breath catching in my throat.

His facial features hardened. "You have certain documents about you, and should their evidence show you to be, as I suspect, a spy, nothing under Heaven can save you from a hanging!"

I gasped, unprepared for such cruel candor. He was mea-suring me with a savage gleam.

Answering slowly and in a soft voice, I responded. "Well, sir, suppose you proceed now and uproot the whole thing." I smiled tentatively. "I am ready." My pulse thundered in my ears.

In the sharp skirmish of cross-questioning that followed, I fell back on my wit and theatrical training to sow doubt in the general's mind. At one point, I even slandered Colonel

Truesdail, in response to his comment about washing his hands in Yankee's blood.

"The only one in whose blood I would like to dip my hand," I said with absolute conviction, "is Colonel Truesdail, of Nashville."

"Ha, is that so?" he cried out. Anger radiated off him in waves. "I'd give the world to capture that man, and I've given strict orders that, if ever taken, he shall be hung on the first tree, and his body brought to me that I may embalm it for a curiosity. Damn him!" His gaze connected with mine.

After what seemed an eternity, he finalized our meeting. "I have no more time to investigate your case. I am going to send you to General Bragg's headquarters at Shelbyville."

But then he surprised me. His face softening ever so slightly, he added, "In the hugely unlikely event that you should prove your loyalty to the South, you may depend on me for protection. Yet I am sorry to say that I find that nearly impossible, so prepare for the worst, for hanging is not pleasant." He reached across the table and cupped his hand over mine.

With these momentous words ringing in my ears, I was led back to my quarters and placed under heavy guard. For the first time in years, I reached out for reliance on Him who guides all things. Strangely, I also felt very devoted to my country, the Union. I wondered if I could muster up the strength to die for it without the slightest regret.

Little did I know that the worst was yet to come.

I could not sleep that night. My quarters were in a tent ill-suited to a woman—a canvas covering, a knapsack for a pillow, and two government blankets stolen from our soldiers was my bed. The noisy carousing of the Rebels camped around me continued until midnight. I sat up and scrutinized the quarters, searching for a possibility for escape. After a long while, hearing no movement, I gently lifted a corner of the tent. All was quiet, and the posted guard seemed to be sleeping. Forcefully wedging my body through the small opening, I glanced up to find a menacing sword pointed at my breast.

"Miss Cushman, you are very sharp, but I have foiled you this time. Now please retire to your blanket and remain there, or I shall have to issue orders that will not only be repugnant to my feelings but ungallant to your sex." Despite the darkness, the large man's erect form and deep voice standing before me could only be General Forrest.

To increase security, General Forrest ordered a squad of men to position themselves near my tent. Lying there awake and shaking with frustration, I listened to General Forrest's inhuman orders to his men. I could only press my hands over my ears to block out the words. The room spun around me and my stomach lurched. I could hear some of the men whispering uneasily that the general risked the prospect of being shot by his own soldiers.

Can such things be, and Heaven not fall to crush their fiendish perpetrators? I whimpered in my head. Remembering my mother's Godly teachings, I added, *Father, forgive them. They know not what they do.*

Finally, I slept. Several hours later I hailed the morning with a bit of awe as I watched the gray dawn steal softly up the eastern sky, and heard the Rebel drums and bugles sound the reveille. Last evening the outlines of the distant hills had been indistinct, but now, with their gauzy veil of mist lifting, they appeared dyed in a thousand tints of melting purple and vivid green.

After a humble breakfast, I prepared for my fateful journey. Thanks to General Forrest's unpredictable kindness, I was conveyed in a guarded ambulance. He must have noticed how deep fatigue, sustained perturbation and loss of sleep had wreaked chaos on my body. Indeed, I felt as decimated as if rising from a sick bed.

As the ambulance passed the front steps of General Forrest's house, some of the soldiers pressed around it, as if I were a traveling show.

"Oh, look at the Yankee spy!" one exclaimed. "Ain't she pretty?"

"Damn her!" another shouted. "She might be as beautiful as Venus, but I'll be damned if I wouldn't hang her on the highest tree."

I turned my head from the curtained window and covered my ears until I was past the threats and on the quiet road, attempting to collect my thoughts for the upcoming interview with the well-known Rebel, General Bragg.

Just then a horse drew up to the ambulance, and its rider leaned toward my window. "I came out to say good-bye and Godspeed. I pray we shall meet again, where we will share something better than corn bread baked in ashes." I smiled and lifted my hand to wave to Johnny Morgan. A warm breeze billowed the lace curtains.

The journey to Shelbyville took two and a half days. Upon arrival, I was taken directly to General Bragg's headquarters at the camp's center. Watching my tentative arrival was a bony, angular, sharp-pointed man, with small dark-gray eyes, iron-gray hair and whiskers.

He bowed in acknowledgment of my salute, and the guard handed him my papers. Glancing coldly at them he began his interrogation, a celebrated skill for him.

"Of what country are you a native, Miss Cushman?" he asked, waving me to a chair.

"I am an American, sir, but of French and Spanish parentage."

"Where were you born?" he again asked.

"In New Orleans, General."

"Hmm!" he coughed doubtingly. "How is it that your pronunciation has the Yankee twang?"

"It comes, most certainly, from the fact that I am professionally an actress," I promptly answered. "And as I am in the habit of playing Yankee characters frequently, it may be that I have caught the 'twang' and now show it in my ordinary conversations as well as on the stage."

"I see," grunted the general. "But what brought you to the South?"

"I was not *brought*, sir; I was *sent*," I answered defiantly, daring him to question me.

"By whom, may I ask, Miss Cushman?" In his frustration, his voice rose an octave.

"By Federal Colonel Truesdail."

"Aha! *Sent? Why?*" he inquired, with a sly look of incredulity.

"Because I gave warm utterance to my Southern feelings, and refused to take their Oath of Allegiance." At this point I began to sniffle, clearly on the verge of shedding tears. I tried to smile, and when my eyes crinkled, a tear spilled from the corner of the left eye and tracked down my cheek.

The general studied my face for a long moment, and then continued. "What was the main charge that the Federals had against you?"

"I had publicly drunk to the success of the South and our Confederacy on stage at the Louisville Theater, at the request of two paroled Confederate officers. If they were here now, they would confirm this." I went on to relate the entire story, slowly and carefully, watching him beneath lowered lashes as I gave my rendition of that performance.

"Well, what happened next?"

"I was at once discharged from the theater, and went to Nashville, where I got a fresh engagement, only to be sent away by Colonel Truesdail, the Chief of the Federal Army Police. He heard of my Southern sentiments and the drinking of the toast, and ordered me to leave the Federal jurisdiction. Why, he wouldn't even allow me to take my trunk or my theatrical wardrobe with me." I felt a spark of fire in my eyes.

I watched the effect my words had on him. After a brief pause, he resumed his questioning in a more kindly tone. "Miss Cushman, this statement of yours may be correct, but still I should like to have you give some *positive proof* of your loyalty to our cause; for, as it stands, I must say it appears at best very doubtful."

I gazed at him firmly and pointedly. "General, I have been seized and brought hither to meet charges laid against me, I presume, but assuredly not to investigate and decide my own case."

I rose smoothly and stood before him as the wronged and gentle lady, wounded dignity gathered around me like a cloak. I recognized my weakness and dependence as my most charming traits. Yet beneath my hand of velvet I knew I was twice his match. My time with the bold Indian youths and lasses had given me unusual strength and quickness, but now was not the time to exhibit my advantage.

"General, you cannot be expected to believe my statement; therefore, I say to you: produce your charges and the evidence. You will see that my loyalty to the South will shine with as bright and steady a luster as does your own." I gave him one of my sweetest smiles.

He listened to my final words and, after a long pause, smiled and dismissed me for the afternoon. I felt so exhausted; I returned to my quarters and fell into a deep sleep.

THIRTY-THREE

Pauline

First days of July 1863

The cross-examination continued the following morning. General Braxton Bragg was notorious for two things: being a bully and hating spies. I considered this as he shut the door behind him, scrutinizing my untidy state with a quick look.

I felt grateful that he mentioned it first. "Good morning, Miss Cushman. I trust you slept well. I will arrange for you to bathe yourself once our conversation is finished."

"Thank you General. Perhaps that will help me regain my composure."

"Hmm, I am curious. Please tell me why you have no baggage."

"Colonel Truesdail gave me no time to prepare it, nor did I have the means to transport it."

General Bragg nodded. "How do you expect to get it?"

I shook my head. "General, I do not know. I hope to find my brother, Colonel Asa A. Cushman of the Confederate service, and obtain his assistance."

Apparently he had not heard about this yet. He drew in a quick surprised breath. "So you have a brother in our service, have you?" He took a moment to consider this. "What will you do if you fail to find him?"

"If I can get my wardrobe, I shall apply for an engagement at Richmond or Atlanta."

At this point he began drilling me on questions to which he knew the answers, hoping to trip me up. "Is Colonel Truesdail a married man?"

I acted disinterested. "I believe so. I learned he had a son boarding at the City Hotel, where I stopped."

"Where does Colonel Truesdail reside in Nashville?"

I glanced at him with surprise. "Sir, I have never visited his home. When I was arrested, I was taken to his office, in a house on High Street, near the capital."

"Miss Cushman, please describe the man." He raised his eyebrows.

He saw me attempting to clear my parched throat and sent a guard to bring water. I drank it in several gulps. "He is about medium height and slight in nature. He has gray hair and heavy black whiskers. His complexion is rather dark, and his eyes are black. I only saw him once, but I remember him well."

"What appears to be the popular sentiment at Nashville?"

"It varies every day, just as the tide of battle rises and falls. When the Confederate arms have persevered, everyone is strong Secesh. When they falter, Union men are plenty. But they are driving almost all the Southern sympathizers across the 'lines.'"

"Who is in command in Nashville?" he asked. I knew that he knew.

"General Mitchell has been for some time past, but was superseded a few days ago by Brigadier General Morgan."

"Tell me about the military forces there." Now he sat back comfortably, expecting a complete answer. I decided to tell him only part of what I knew. I hoped that with unsatisfactory answers he would not require me to tell him about the movements and intentions of the Federal troops.

"I noticed a large number of encampments in and about the city. The capital is heavily fortified. There are..."

At this point he interrupted me with an impatient wave of his hand. "Are they arming the Negros?"

"I do not know. I noticed them working on the fortifications."

He studied me from across the table. "Where is General Rosecrans' army located?"

I was honest. "I do not know. I heard his headquarters are at Murfreesboro."

He shot me a mocking smile. "I wish to meet him. We have been waiting for some time. When he comes, I shall give him a warm reception." His face broke into a puckish grin.

I nodded, not certain of his meaning.

"As for you, Miss Cushman, I have to inform you that there are serious charges against you. I will hand you over to Provost Marshal General Colonel McKinstry, who is a humane and just man and will treat you kindly. Your fate will depend upon the result of his investigation."

"Colonel McKinstry is precisely the man I desire to see. For through him the proof of my innocence will make these charges disappear. And when my blamelessness is proven, what then, General Bragg?"

"You will be acquitted with honor," he replied easily.

I nodded in agreement. "How though, if I am found guilty?"

His eyes narrowed. "You know the *fate of spies*. You will be hanged."

His words fell like the icy hand of death upon my heart, but I braced myself. "General, I don't think I would look well dangling at the end of a rope. If I must die, I hope you will allow me to choose the manner of my death."

My words caught him off guard, but he recovered quickly. "I cannot promise that, because you might prefer to die a natural death," he replied self-righteously.

Now I wanted him to see what I was made of. I drew in a deep breath.

"No sir. If I must die, I would prefer to be shot, as I don't believe it would hurt too much." *If I must die, at least it will be said that I died for a noble cause. I will speak my last words—"the Union"—and know that I died for my country.*

He nodded at my words, and I wondered if he had also read my mind.

"Where did you get the pistol you had in your possession when you were captured?"

"I took it from a house where we stopped at Hillsboro. It belonged to a wounded soldier."

"What did you intend to do with it?"

"Self-preservation, General. The scouts had left me, and Federals were reported to be nearby." Anxiety held me by the shoulders.

This remark seemed to have considerable weight with him. He bowed his head on his hand for a moment, as if in deep and deliberate thought. Eventually, he spoke.

"Miss Cushman, you must go to rest in your chamber. You appear to be ill. I will give you several days to recover before sending you to Colonel McKinstry. He is a just and kind man. If you are telling the truth, you have nothing to fear. Good day now."

I knew it wasn't going to be as easy as he was making it sound.

On the third morning of my enforced rest, a guard came to tell me I would be taken to the quarters of Provost Marshal General Colonel Alexander McKinstry. I was allowed to bathe, and the freshly laundered dress was returned to me.

I found Colonel McKinstry to be a gentleman whose ways

reminded me of Colonel Truesdail. Although his duty required him to be stern and implacable, he quickly adopted a softer, courteous manner. Physically he barely resembled Colonel Truesdail, with deep lines also furrowed in his face and similar hair and eye coloring. But their mannerisms were almost identical, and both carried out their provost duties to the letter.

After asking many questions, he eventually inquired how I became possessed of the Confederate uniform found in my satchel. Knowing that the truth would serve me best, I told him frankly that Captain P.A. Blackman, Confederate Quartermaster, had professed the warmest regard and affection for me. I explained that he proposed that I should accompany him as his lieutenant.

McKinstry replied, "It is astonishing how a pretty woman will make the best of our officers forget their duty!" He stood up abruptly and rang a small bell, instructing an orderly to send a certain captain to him. When the captain arrived, the provost marshal told him to issue an order for the arrest of Captain Blackman.

I rose to my feet. "Sir, you would not arrest my poor friend, would you?" I pleaded, eyes widening in dismay. I felt dreadful that he would suffer because of my disclosures, and I struggled to convince McKinstry that Captain Blackman was not to blame.

He was unyielding on the matter. "An officer who would serve his country must learn to resist a pretty face, as well as the charges and onslaughts of the enemy."

Then he took the wind out of my sails. "A Confederate officer's uniform would have been an excellent disguise for a spy, you will confess. One might be able to penetrate to the heart of every camp in the Confederate States, to every fortress and even to the councils of our generals."

He scrutinized me as I calmly responded. "It is true sir, but

I can assure you that the manner in which I received that uniform was entirely through the diligence of my friend, Captain Blackman."

"Good Lord. Did this Captain Blackman take so great an interest in you that he wished you always to remain near him?"

I blushed. "He loved me, or thought he did. If you need any proof of that, I have a number of his notes and letters addressed to me that will confirm this." I reached into the bodice of my gown and removed the one I had received just before my arrest. "In this, I do not doubt, you will find mention of the position as lieutenant which he designed to honor me with." I shrugged, pleased with my nonchalance.

After reading the letter, he muttered, completely bewildered, "It is indeed so." Looking at me with a puzzled expression, he asked, "Would you have gone with the captain in your new uniform?"

With an air of mock reserve, I replied, "Ah! That remains to be seen."

I noticed that the colonel could not repress a faint smile as he drew in a breath, juggling his words. "Your statements, thus far, Miss Cushman, seem to be perfectly correct. Sadly, I have proof which, I regret to say, will overwhelm you." My heart folded.

Very slowly, he opened his drawer and brought out papers, one at a time. With a jolt of alarm, I recognized them. I tried to conceal the trembling of my hands, for these were the very papers I had extracted from the table of the Rebel engineer-officer at Columbia.

He also proffered sketches and memoranda I had drawn of the various fortifications at Tullahoma, Shelbyville, Spring Hill and several other sites. All had been stashed and carried with me under the cork soles of my boots. While at the wounded soldier's home, my boots and these papers had been pilfered from my satchel.

How could I have disobeyed the specific instructions given to me by Colonel Truesdail: "Make no written statement and no drawings. Carry everything in your memory."

The provost-marshal asked gravely, "Do you recognize these documents?"

My heart screamed at me to deny it, but my mind would not allow it. Assuming a light manner, I admitted that I did.

"Miss Cushman, what was your purpose to formulate these sketches?"

Once again I called on my theatrical skills. "Oh, they were mere fancy sketches. Simply guesswork; something I could offer the Yankees when I found myself among them asking to recover my wardrobe."

In spite of his convictions regarding my guilt, I could see that my bold, careless assertion staggered the provost marshal.

His facial features hardened, and then he snorted, "Hum!" and placed me in the charge of his assistant, Captain S.E. Pedden. Before walking away, he gave me his last instruction. "That will do, Miss Cushman, you may retire." His obvious uneasiness undermined his words.

As I left the office, I overheard Colonel McKinstry's voice, "That woman is the very devil, and would almost convince one that black was white." That statement hurt me more than anything else I would hear throughout the remainder of my career.

THIRTY-FOUR

Antonia

NOVEMBER 1863

I was now writing letters to Major Willard every day, and was elated to see his loving script on envelopes arriving several times a week. My family also celebrated each bit of news from Charlie. In November, we read in his own words that he was well and had been promoted.

I spent the cool, rainy afternoons before the fire, creating clever, enticing notes to Joseph.

On November 12, I wrote:

If I were ever so much inclined, my dearest friend, I could not forget you; your kind attentions are unremitting—one favor is not dim in my remembrance, ere another claims attention. I shall be compelled to search the vocabulary for language to express my indebtedness. You sadden me by your continued melancholy. I know you are in some respects unpleasantly situated; but life is not all dark. Remember Longfellow's lines in "A Psalm of Life:"

Not enjoyment, and not sorrow,
Is our destined end or way;
But to act, that each tomorrow
Finds us farther than today.

If I don't write as often as you wish, pray remember I am very busy; as you know my baggage is in the country, and I'm replenishing my wardrobe somewhat.

Ma's kind regards and good wishes always understood if not expressed. I didn't receive a line from you yesterday. What was the matter? I felt uneasy—feared you were sick and dear knows what all.

Write long letters to Yours Truly, Antonia

My brothers always sent little messages, and when the Major visited, he brought them sweeties or little gifts. He never forgot Pattie either, and often brought along something for my parents.

Several days later he came to visit me. I was so relieved because I had so much to tell him in person.

"Oh Joseph, your last letter to me was the best written and most complete reply I've ever read," I gushed, taking his arm as we walked through the windy town. The sun created long shadows in the street, but the air lacked warmth. The fields lay hard as iron. Smoke rose from the chimneys, curling in whimsical configurations.

He laughed lightly. "You must be referring to my response on whether it is possible to fall in love at first sight."

"Yes! I never thought that possible," I affirmed, tilting my head to look up at him. "And to be honest, it did not happen to me. But knowing you felt that way sends thrills up my spine."

He squeezed my arm lovingly. "And yet you still fret that I do not tell you often enough how much I miss you. Please know, my darling, that I think about you constantly and wish to gaze on your beauty every day of my life."

Just then we crossed paths with one of the neighbors. The Major tipped his blue officer's hat at her courteously and we wished her a good day. She answered me curtly and ignored him, tossing a judgmental look over her shoulder. After she walked by, I explained.

"I have received unsolicited advice from friends and neighbors concerning you. They wonder at our relationship and have asked questions. Perhaps I should not have admitted that you are married and seeking a divorce, but my heart wishes to speak of us."

"Perhaps the less you speak about us, my love, the better," he said with a frown.

"Yes, you are correct. I am sorry about that error in discretion. It won't happen again."

We passed by a small cottage near the hill. A door opened and a cat emerged, followed by a woman with a basket of washing. The cat wound itself around her ankles. She stopped her work to stroke the cat. I smiled and waved at the woman.

I took hold of his hand. "Joseph, please take care of yourself. I want to be the reason for your happiness, and for your life." I wondered if I had said too much, but he drew me close in response.

"Darling, I know you are impatient with the amount of time this divorce is taking. I wish I had more time to pester my commanding officer, the judge, my lawyer and my wife, but I do not. I have other responsibilities to attend to, and then I only want to sit down and pen loving words to you."

I gave him a radiant smile. He did have a way with words. "I shall try to be patient, my love."

When he left, I knew he would return soon. In the meantime, I let his written words soothe my soul, as quilting did for Mother.

I became discouraged when I learned that four of my six letters had not reached him.

My dear Major,

I was very much astonished to learn from your note this evening that my letters of Thursday have not reached you. Where can they be? I gave them to the orderly myself—I fear there is something wrong. Perhaps you can investigate the

matter. That is the sixth letter I've written you, and only two
have gone safely—do you understand this?

Come at once if possible and we can discuss the affair at
length. I do not know that this will reach you. Thank you for
the papers.

Yours very truly, Antonia

Ma's kindest regards. Frank says to tell you these words, "I am
Union now—that is the strong side." Please come tomorrow.

Sometimes we wrote our own secret code. I enjoyed this
underground, clandestine communication, perhaps because
of my spy days, which I was forced to accept were truly over.
Nevertheless, I missed the thrill and excitement of those days.

I sent him a lock of hair, tea leaves and dried flowers. He
seemed to appreciate them and I found pleasure thinking up
unusual gifts to share.

On the last day of November, I opened his letter with great
anticipation. He had regularly mailed me words of love and
affection, even including poems. This one was different.

My dear Antonia,

You are always in my thoughts, no matter where I am or
what I am doing. Your sweet smile and gentle mannerisms
make me feel so warm and safe that I never want to leave
you. Our last visit was particularly enchanting. I yearn for
your kisses and to caress you. Your womanly scent when we
are close together drives me to distraction. Caroline used to
give me pleasure, and I enjoyed her scent, but not as much
as yours, Antonia. When I see her now, at the hotel, I feel no
love whatsoever. I then think of you, and my heart beats rap-
idly and my attention strays from whatever task I am doing.

My dearest, are you sure you want to be married to a
divorced man? We could go somewhere where no one knows

us, set up house, and live happily ever after, unmarried. I
could liquidate my savings and start up a hotel in parts far
away. Think about it. Until our next meeting,

Yours truly,
Joseph

Angry tears streamed down my face. A rage swept over me
that frightened me with its intensity, and I fought for control.
I ran upstairs and threw myself on the bed.

Pattie heard me sobbing, and came in to check on me.

"What happened, Antonia?" she asked, alarmed.

"I hate him! He's a miserable insensitive creature. He talks
about bodily functions, his wife and me in the same paragraph!
What a beast!"

Pattie took the letter in her trembling fingers and read it,
wide-eyed and open-mouthed. "He wants you to live in sin
with him?"

"Yes, it appears so, but mentioning his wife and my name in
the same paragraph is what angers me the most." I shook my
head, incoherent from weeping. My nose ran and I knew my
face was blotched.

I wrote my response to him that afternoon and included the
paragraph that offended me, clipped from his own letter.

Monday night: 8 o'clock, Fairfax Courthouse, Nov. 30

Your letter was received at the usual time this evening, Major,
and the shock at reading one sentence was greater than you
can conceive. I enclose that paragraph as I cannot allow it
to remain in my possession. I have never had such language
addressed to me, and never in all my life have heard of it
being used to a <u>decent girl</u>, much less a <u>lady</u>. And to think it
came from <u>you</u> to <u>me</u>, your beloved?

Answer me just this one question: did you mean to insult

me? Great God, what am I to think? Hasn't my suffering been sufficient? Is there a bitterer drop yet in my cup of anguish? Am I mistaken in <u>*you*</u>*! Is it, can it be possible you intend adding the deepest to the long list of degradations I suffered at the hands of Federalists?*

Major, Major, answer me in Heaven's name what you meant. Are you going to keep me in horrible suspense over your intentions? I close now, perplexed and wondering.

Yours truly,
Antonia

My poor Joseph. He truly did not understand what he had done to hurt and anger me so, and apologized profusely on his next visit. He also brought me a gift—a costly gold necklace with a topaz stone. While he was seated at my side, I explained clearly what *not* to write in future letters to me.

A silence fell between us as I waited for his reply. He sighed deeply and spoke.

"Antonia, I cannot get you out of my mind. I don't even try to analyze it, but I do know that everything changed color when I walked through your doorway and saw you—your perfect oval face, high cheekbones, large blue eyes, sensual mouth. It was the color of your hair that truly captivated me—a dark spun gold. I had never seen that before." He raised his eyes to meet mine.

"So when I imagine you, my thoughts turn to images of possession. I want you to be mine in every way." Some of the tension left him, and he ventured a sardonic smile.

"Joseph, I understand completely. My life is purposeless without you." I was wiping at my eyes when he folded me into his embrace.

In early December we housed Union officers who were ill but not ill enough to be sent to hospital. We often heard them coughing and hacking into the night, and I feared they may have been carrying the extremely contagious tuberculosis. I still managed to find time to write and send my feelings to Joseph with the orderly who came by almost daily. I was also making Christmas presents for my family and trying to find some holiday spirit.

THIRTY-FIVE

Antonia

CHRISTMAS 1863

Christmas was wonderful. I was in love, home with my family, and safe. Mother wanted the focus to be on the Christ-child's birth. She also looked forward to giving six-year-old Frank a "real" Christmas this year.

Several days before Christmas we found a small cedar tree in the woods and decorated it with homemade ornaments, as well as a few baubles and trinkets of years past. Pattie and Frank cut strips of paper and made chains to wrap around the branches. Mother and I made paper fans with embroidery-threaded tassels to hang from the boughs. Papa helped the boys string popped corn with holly berries, forming a beautiful garland to dress up the tree.

Octavia and Mathilde had been collecting dried rose petals, lavender, rosemary, and apple slices since the beginning of autumn. They sprinkled grated nutmeg and cinnamon in the mix, and closed it up in a tight container. Two days ago they opened it up and poured this sweet-smelling potpourri into lovely porcelain bowls. After we placed the bowls in the windowsills, our home was blessed with Christmas aromas.

I wove a wreath of pinecones and pine boughs for the front door, and we hung mistletoe from the ceiling in the entry hall. Holly bushes flourished in our little village, so we cut berries and hung them from chandeliers, columns, and woodwork.

Pattie and I also spread the berries and greens across tables and mantles. Holiday preparations lifted everyone's spirits, and captivated little Frank.

The night before Christmas we vigilantly placed hand-dipped candles on the branches.

"Ma, can we keep this all year?" Frank asked persuasively.

"No dear. The tree will die. But we shall have another one next year," she answered him.

"But why do we do this?" he wondered aloud.

"The tradition of the Christmas tree began about fifty years ago in England. Later, around 1841, the German Prince Albert, who was the husband of Queen Victoria, decided to decorate a large one at Windsor Castle to remind him of his childhood Christmas celebrations in Germany. So, here in America we have adopted the custom."

"Did we ever have a decorated tree before?" he asked.

"Yes, but not for several years. Not since the war began."

Papa placed his hands on Frank's shoulders. "Young man, we will begin that tradition in our home this year, and you will help us carry it on. Is that good?"

Frank grinned, and then suddenly frowned. "But I want Charlie to see it as well. Will he come home in time?" His face puckered up.

I nodded and smiled. "We can pray that he will come home to enjoy it with us."

We walked through the neighboring village streets and began an impromptu caroling. My favorite song, "God Rest Ye Merry Gentlemen," was sung again and again, along with other favorites. Afterwards we returned to our house to read the Bible, pray and drink hot beverages. Papa and Clanie built a roaring fire and tossed in pinecones for crackling sounds. As I looked around the parlor, I noticed there were no young men, except Clanie. I missed Charlie and my Major.

After a bountiful and delicious breakfast, we lit the candles on the tree, added more logs to the glowing fire and sat down to open our gifts. Naturally, Frank had the largest pile spread out before him. He worked through it slowly so it would last even longer. Each unwrapped gift was accompanied by an excited shout and shining eyes. Clanie had carved him a beautiful wooden horse. The theme for his gifts seemed to be "battle," as he also received a toy drum, a cloth soldier and also a top.

I had sewn a pair of silk slippers for Mother. It pleased me so much that she had no idea I was making them for her.

"Where did you get this gorgeous silk, Antonia? It looks familiar."

I giggled. "Of course it is, Ma. I used Pattie's silk dress from last year to produce several gifts. Are you surprised?"

"I am delighted, my clever girl, and I love them. Thank you so much!" Mother looked regal and peaceful. Her heartfelt smile warmed the room.

Papa loved the monogrammed tobacco pouch I embroidered for him. He was a hard person to gift, and when I saw how much this touched him, I was pleased.

"Thank you, dear. I needed a new pouch, and I am proud of your beautiful handiwork."

Pattie was now thirteen and had begun quilting, so the family gave her a sewing kit. She immediately started working on her first square patriotic quilt: red, white and blue. Then she surprised me with a lovely needle case she had embroidered, bearing my initials: AJF.

And our Clanie was now almost grown up, so he received a muffler that Mother and I knitted. My final words to him, after wrapping it around his neck, were: "Keep warm, my handsome brother, and do not even think about joining the army." He folded me in an awkward embrace as we laughed and crossed our fingers for good luck.

Papa's gift to Mother was the best surprise of the day. It was wrapped in a plain sack tied tightly with a piece of twine. As she opened it slowly, a puzzled look crossed her face. She gasped when she unearthed her treasure chest: coffee, tea, flour, sugar, honey, nutmeg, cinnamon sticks and ginger.

"Darling, wherever did you find all of this?" she asked, tears springing to her eyes.

Father simply grinned and said nothing. Again, I thought of Charlie and Joseph. If only…

We gifted Mathilde, Octavia and Adam new clothing and half the day free to do as they wished. As the three trusted slaves began putting away their gifts, Papa leaned back in his chair and said the most unusual thing.

"One day you will gain the freedom you deserve…freedom to live, raise your families and work where you choose. Whatever the outcome of this war, I hope that thought pleases you." Smiling broadly, he continued. "I know it pleases us, and we will do what we can for you when that day arrives."

There was a sudden silence. Mathilde finished straightening up the living room as Adam stood still, hands dropped heavily at his sides. Octavia finally looked up from under her eyebrows and asked, "Does dat mean you wants us to move away sum place?" She looked anything but pleased.

"My word, so many of us want you to be happy and free, even if it causes us personal hardship. Would you actually be happier leading the lives you have now?"

There was another silence, longer this time. This was obviously not a conversation they had prepared for. Finally Adam spoke, almost in a murmur.

"So many bad folks and situations 'round here recently, Master Ford. We jus' ain't certain life could be better for us den it is here wif you and de family."

Mathilde's sharp look toward him told us they had said

enough. Noticing this, Papa tried to restore the festive spirit with some reassurance.

"Just as long as you all know we want what is best for you. We will always do what we can to show you our sincere esteem and affection."

I expected Joseph for dinner at three o'clock, but told myself I would have to swallow my disappointment if he could not get away.

I was not disappointed. At 2:45 I heard his horse, and peeked out the window as he dismounted, handing the reins to Adam. I didn't wait for him to rap on the door but opened it wide, flying into his welcoming embrace.

"Merry Christmas, my lovely Antonia," he whispered into my ear.

"Come in, darling. Merry Christmas to you," I answered, wrapped in happiness.

Joseph carried a bag under his arm and stopped in the parlor to place his gifts under the tree.

Mother and I made certain the table was beautifully set for our Christmas meal. Mother brought out her lovely white damask tablecloth, upon which she placed her silver cutlery and glassware. Mathilde and Octavia had added colorful boughs, ribbons and candles, bringing out the "hidden" silver candlesticks for this merry occasion. We dined on turkey, potatoes, cheese, bread and cranberry sauce. I could not remember when we last enjoyed the flavor of turkey, and was delighted we had found two small turkeys to share. Papa poured a little homemade wine into each glass. Frank declined in anticipation of dessert, which he had helped create. Plum pudding was everyone's favorite.

Clanie asked Joseph if he knew President Lincoln.

Turning to him, Major Willard smiled and nodded. "I was invited to his Inaugural Ball on March 4, 1861." This was news to me. But then, I had never asked him if he knew the President.

"That is amazing," squealed Pattie. "How did you meet him?"

Joseph set his fork noiselessly on the edge of his plate. "I will tell you, and it is an interesting tale. President-elect Lincoln arrived at our hotel at the end of February, 1861, late at night and in disguise, because the 1860 election had been a bitter contest. In 1861, the sentiment against him was running high, and we wanted his presence at the Willard to remain a secret."

As we continued our dinner, I looked around and saw that he held everyone's rapt attention.

"In his haste, President Lincoln realized that he had failed to pack his bedroom slippers. At that late hour we could not purchase any for him, so my brother Henry and I decided to gift him a new pair of slippers belonging to our grandfather, former Vermont Congressman William C. Bradley. We knew our grandfather had large feet, like the president, and he had never worn the slippers."

"Did they fit?" asked Frank, taking in every word.

"Indeed they did," smiled Joseph. "In fact, we offered to let him keep them, but he left them at the bedside at the end of his visit. Thanks to our hospitality, he made certain that Henry and I were honored guests at his Inaugural Ball, held a week or so later."

There were so many things about my Joseph that I did not know. I was eager to discover them all. Papa turned to him and asked about the morale among his men.

"Sir, it is as well as can be expected. They know the North will win, but know not when." He looked down, uncomfortable with having to answer Papa's question thus.

Frank broke in. "Major, did I see you bringing in gifts? Is there one under the tree for me?"

Everyone laughed and the joviality returned.

"Frank, you know better than that! Where are your manners?" reprimanded Mother, her words soft but firm.

"Ma, you know he always brings me little gifts. Perhaps today it is a big one!" His face lit up expectantly.

I took his hand. "Shall we go and see?" I asked smiling, leading him to the tree.

Everyone followed us into the parlor where Joseph told him to look for the brightest gift. Frank found a shimmering green package which he quickly and silently un-wrapped. He pulled out a large box of hard sweeties—his favorite delicacy. "Oh thank you, Major!" he squealed, popping one into his mouth with sheer delight, without even thinking about sharing his bounty.

Joseph reached under the tree and handed me a beautifully wrapped box, containing a hymnal and prayer book bound in black monkey-skin, and monogrammed in silver with my full name. I was utterly astounded by his thoughtfulness.

"Oh Joseph, how exquisite this is! I adore it, and the thought that you put into it." I ran my fingers over it slowly and tenderly, finally passing it around for the others to admire.

"My gift to you needs an explanation," I began, pulling a tiny wrapped item from under the tree. "You see, it is a bit selfish as well. I wanted to make you something that you would hold close, so you will always think of me."

His eyebrows rose, and we all watched as he opened it, slowly removing a hemmed handkerchief.

"I sacrificed some of my hair strands to embroider your monogram on it. Do you see them?"

His eyes danced. "Oh Antonia, your hair is your glory and your sacrifice is my treasure!"

I felt so happy. My handsome Major always knew just what to say. I was speechless as he added, "I will always keep this close to my heart."

That Christmas was the best one in my life. I said a silent prayer that the next year we would share it together as man and wife.

THIRTY-SIX

Antonia

JANUARY 1864

L ate New Year's Eve I wrote a heartfelt letter to Joseph. I reflected on all of our divided opinions and dissimilar viewpoints, but added that I knew that in our hearts, there was no separation. Our love for each other was stronger than anything else.

You know I love you, but I can never consent to a private marriage. My parents and relatives would be mortified and distressed to death; acquaintances would disown me; it would be illegal; and above all, it would be wrong. I cannot claim to be a Christian (unfortunately) but do have a conscience and am governed by it. I dislike saying 'no' to one so dear, but there is no alternative in this case. I will grant any request which is right and proper, and would make you the happiest man in the world if I could without compromising myself...I (will not) place a barrier between myself and all friends. It would be wrong for you as well as for me. Neither of us could be happy, for the curse of God would be cast upon us.

You have asked for my "heart and hand." The heart is yours already. When your hand is free and you can claim mine before the world, then that also is yours. Notwithstanding my unalterable determination in this matter, I love you dearly, and will love you as long as I live. I wish you a very

happy New Year, so happy that all your preceding life may
seem darker than ever by contrast.

Our love defies logic,
Antonia

Joseph had spent the evening with my family, and we welcomed in the New Year together. But our conversation had not been what I had hoped for, and we left several issues unresolved.

"I have reasons for not accepting to do a private marriage," I told him.

"Antonia, darling, what are your reasons, other than my not having obtained my divorce as of yet?"

"Even with the strong love and longing I feel for you, we must not do what I feel is wrong in the eyes of God. You and I both wish to consummate our love...our longing for the forbidden is fierce. But I must wait until your hand is free and you can profess me as your woman before the world. Then you will have me entirely, and I will have you." A deep blush imbued my features. I had never spoken so intimately to him.

He groaned. "I have waited since the day I met you to caress your smooth skin, know you deeply and be your man in every way."

I touched his hand. "Please remember, dearest, that the obstacle is yours, not mine. My hand is free."

But he had more to say. "Fate has not been friendly to me. A soldier's life is unpredictable, especially in this broken war. I curse the cruel fortune that has disconnected us in the past, and I fear another separation."

I gave him a warm smile. "Joseph, fate brought us together. A power stronger than both of us, our destiny, *threw* us together. I do not believe it would take us apart now. Do you?"

After several moments, I saw him force a smile. I also saw sadness reflected in his eyes.

He held me closely and whispered, "No, never. We are meant for each other." Kissing my nose and my lips, he added, "I love you so much and will continue loving you as long as I live."

Tilting my face to search my eyes, he asked, "Do you believe me?"

Nodding, I told him that I felt the same. After he left, I found I could not sleep, and put my thoughts to paper. Now I wondered when I would see him again.

I saw the Major next on January 9. My family and I were visiting my Aunt Mary and Uncle Robert Simpson's home in Sangster's Station. The last time I had seen them was shortly before my first arrest.

Aunt Mary held me close, and straight away asked me if I were well.

"I've lost some weight, Auntie, but I am regaining my strength. Do not worry. It will take some time, as we are deprived of sugar and fatty foods for the time being."

Joseph arrived on a snowy evening to join us for supper. First he regaled us with updates on the war, after which he beat all of us at cards. Finally, we retired to the library and sat together before a roaring fire burning brightly in the grate.

"Do you know if your relatives have taken the oath?" he asked me later, completely throwing me off guard.

I frowned. "Oh, I feel almost certain they have," I mused, believing they had not, but not wishing to disturb the pleasant moment. I settled back into the warmth of his embrace.

The sound of horse hooves surprised us. My father and my uncle opened the door to a Confederate soldier, who handed Papa a parcel, then mounted his horse and quickly rode away.

"What business could he have with your father?" wondered

Major. "Your entire family has taken the Oath of Allegiance, and that prohibits aiding the enemy."

Indignant at his accusation, I shot back, "Joseph, you know we take the oath seriously. Unlike you, who promised to love and cherish your wife."

A long silence ensued as Joseph gradually removed his arm from around my shoulders.

Leisurely lifting his eyes to meet mine, he responded. "And do you, Antonia, conduct business with Confederate soldiers?"

"No!" I bristled, taking great umbrage at his question. "I have not met with any Confederate soldiers lately. But I do love one dearly—my brother."

"You must realize that this would look bad for me if other Federal officers knew what happened here. I do want to trust you, however."

"Then trust me, Joseph! Your constant remarks and attention to this are extremely insulting, and your suspicion is leaving a poisoned trail in your own heart."

He cleared his throat and refused to meet my eyes, maintaining his silence for several long moments.

"Antonia, why don't you clear this up with your father? Ask him what his interpretation is of the Oath of Allegiance, and let me know." He stood abruptly. "I must return to headquarters now. Good evening, Miss Ford." Without a backward glance, he left.

At that moment I felt certain I hated him.

After some time had passed and shortly before retiring for the night, I asked Papa about the man at the door.

"Oh, he's a neighbor, asking the doctor (my uncle) for some medical advice about his son," he answered untruthfully. "Did your Major leave without saying goodbye to us?"

"Yes, Papa. He left with a few angry words, and I sent him away with my own. It was our first lover's quarrel, I fear."

His eyes crinkled. "There are apt to be many more, my daughter, but remember: love will conquer all. He is a good man, of that I am certain."

The following day, Papa and Clanie went home, leaving the rest of us behind with my relatives. I wanted my father to carry a message to Joseph. I had decided to test his love.

January 10, 1864
Dear Major Willard,

If you doubt my loyalty to the Union, that is your choice. I will assume by your mistrust of my family and me, and your abrupt departure yesterday, that you wish for our engagement to be broken. By the way, you had better burn my letters, for God forbid if someone should read them and think you were collaborating with a known spy! On the other hand, if you wish to apologize to me for your suspicions, please do so.

Antonia Ford of Fairfax

I heard nothing from Joseph. So I tried another ploy.

January 11, 1864
Dear Major Willard,

I have missed hearing from you, my love, these last few days. My young heart is breaking over you, and I think that would move you if anything would. Major, I'm tormented constantly by a verse of my saddest song: day and night. Since your last letter came, it has rung through my brain...

"I've loved thee too deeply, the dream shall pass by.
The cistern is broken the fountain is dry.
And the angel that sent o'er the brink of the maze,
Now weeps in the star light of love's early grave."

I ask myself, is this ominous, does it predict my fate? Heaven forbid! Surely our love is strong enough to stand one shock.

After what we've written and said, "Shall a light word part us soon?" What say you?

My dear Major, how dear you are to me. You cannot imagine, and would hardly believe if I was to tell you. My <u>darling</u> (oh! Just see what I've said, but is it any worse to feel it than write it?) How can I give you up? I would not write this if I did not know <u>we are</u> both unhappy at this estrangement. I admit I am for <u>I love you.</u> And Major, this moment <u>you love me</u> and as you read these lines your heart <u>thrills</u> to every word. You can't gainsay it. I repeat it exultantly: <u>you love me,</u> and you love me devotedly too: that is my only comfort in these unhappy moments.

Do you think, poor fellow, that you were the only sufferer? <u>Another</u> would find the sunshine of life unmoved and darkness in its place beside yourself—that ought to cheer you; the old adage says, "Misery loves company."

I will send everything except the letters and pictures; if you wish those, come after them, and I will give them up directly. If after reading this, you still wish the engagement broken, I'll be <u>dead to you</u> henceforth; if you wish it to stand I am now and forever your own and yours only.

Antonia

It took Joseph two more days to respond. When the orderly handed me the letter, I ripped it open, looking forward to reading the words of his sweet apology.

Washington City, D.C.
January 12, 1864

Miss Ford,
Please burn my letters to you, and therewith let the "dead facts" be consumed.

J.C. Willard

I dropped my head into my hands. Thinking myself alone, I began to sob. Mother approached me quietly and took me into her arms.

"What is it, dear?" she asked discretely. "You are very pale. What has happened?"

"Oh, Ma, it is over with Joseph," I sobbed. "He's asked me to burn his letters."

"My sweet girl, it is simply a misunderstanding. I feel certain you will work it out," Mother soothed.

I buried my face into Mother's chest, weeping as if my heart were breaking. Aunt Mary stepped up to console me, giving Mother a break.

"What should I do?" I continued to wail, fear and anxiety gripping me tightly.

The older ladies looked over my head and grinned knowingly. "Nothing for the moment. Tomorrow, when you are calm, you can write him another note," suggested Aunt Mary.

I followed her advice. I wrote a simple loving plea, pouring out my heart. I was humbled and heartbroken when two days later I still had not heard a word.

I did not know that pain could cut so deeply that it spilled every bit of emotion from you. I simply let go, allowing the fraying ends of control to slip through my fingers.

That was when Mother decided to take matters into her own hands. She wrote to Joseph.

January 15, 1864 Friday morning
Oh Major, for mercy's sake come up tomorrow or Sunday if but for an hour. The wildness of my poor child's anguish is alarming since the reading of your last letter. It has really made her ill. She has neither eaten nor slept since you left. Her prudishness has been the cause of her present distraction. I beseech you come if possible. Mr. Ford knows nothing

of her last letter—he is very much disturbed. Pardon me for interfering.

Your friend, Julia F.F.

I am not deceiving you when I say she is ill. Please write you will come.

The following day the orderly stopped by and told Mother that the Major would visit as soon as he could get away, and would write in the meantime.

THIRTY-SEVEN

Pauline

END OF JULY 1863

I was escorted by Captain Pedden to the house of a Mr. Morgan near Duck River and placed under guard. My room had the appearance of a dungeon, with barred windows and doubly-fastened doors. Captain Pedden was a man of compassion and gave orders that I be cared for with kindness.

This was not to be, however. The Rebels who lived there never came near me. I took ill and waited, burning with fever, until Captain Pedden returned to check on me.

"Oh my dear Miss Cushman, you need a doctor," he exclaimed, greatly distressed. I nodded and tried to smile.

If my memory serves, a doctor came shortly thereafter. With fever medication I was finally able to sleep for longer periods of time. But my sleep was haunted by horrific nightmares.

Past and present became muddled in my mind. Sometimes, people came to me from as far back as my childhood. The feverish deliriums terrified me: huge faces (including those of my dear children) ballooned and then shrank away menacingly. Their features were distorted and sometimes hideous, threatening and deformed. I woke up screaming, soaked in perspiration and sobbing into my pillow.

But I told no one that I wanted things—my life—to be as it once had been.

Several days passed, and Captain Pedden visited every day.

He brought along a Confederate soldier, Private Athan R. Smith, and left him in the home to take care of me.

I must have been highly medicated since I slept through most of the days. I only vaguely recall brief visits from Generals Bragg, Forrest and Cheatam.

Private Smith called me Pauline and spoke lovingly to me when I was awake. He spoon-fed me gently, and arranged for a young woman to come in to bathe me and change my borrowed clothing.

"Private Smith, do you know what my illness is?" I asked weakly when I awoke to find him seated at my bedside, rubbing my hand.

"Yes, Pauline. You are weakened by the fever. With our attentions, you are improving each day. Captain Pedden has insured that you will have the care you need." He smiled and after pausing to study me, told me that although I looked strained, my intelligent expression never changed.

"Are you always here with me? Each time I open my eyes, I see your face."

With one hand under my chin, he gently tilted my face upward. "Look at your skin. It is nearly translucent."

Then he answered my question. "I spend most of the day and part of the night here, per Captain Pedden's orders. He is also here a great deal of the time," he said softly, placing his arm around my thin shoulders.

"Oh my. I must look a sight, and so very thin."

"Your beauty is evident even in your illness. Your caretaker has kept your long raven tresses clean and brushed, and your eyes are large and lovely despite the pallor of your features."

Fatigue threatened to drown me; I could scarcely breathe. My eyes fluttered closed as he dropped the lightest of kisses across my lids. I trembled when he kissed away the traces of bitter tears of frustration from my cheeks.

Lying awake for long periods of time, I mourned my life, hanging onto consciousness like an unraveling threat. I knew nothing about my family; there was no way to get information about my children.

What will become of them? I wept. *I am so frightened about the verdict. I know I will not be brave enough to calmly face my own execution, which tears me apart. Where are you, God? I need to hear from you! How can I find the courage to face this?*

A tear seeped from under my lashes and inched down my face. "Oh God," I whispered to myself, "I would rather die now."

The generals who had interrogated me continued to visit, trying to distract me with conversation. General Bragg made another comment about General Rosecrans.

"I hold him to be the greatest of the Federal generals. He certainly has, thus far, shown the largest amount of military genius. I esteem it my particular good fortune to be opposed to such an illustrious chief." He grinned at me. "And I expect to meet him any day now."

One day Private Smith surprised me with a clear sign of his devotion.

"Pauline, if you should be released from your situation, I can offer you a good home with me in my pleasant, sheltered farm in Tennessee." The dear man looked me in the eyes and leaned close to place a kiss on my forehead.

I have heard of patients falling in love with caregivers, but rarely the other way around!

Ten days after my arrival, Colonel McKinstry came by to tell me that a court-martial had been held to investigate my case, but as yet, there had been no decision. Captain Pedden accompanied him, and asked if he might pray for me. I closed my eyes and nodded.

He called on God to save me from execution. Then he

opened his arms and folded me inside them. I rested my head against his chest, listening to the rapid beat of his heart and breathing in his masculine scent. There was real comfort in his embrace.

Both of them returned the following morning, entering my room with solemn expressions.

Instantly alert, I jumped from the bed. "Tell me the worst. Remove this dreaded uncertainty. I cannot bear it any longer."

Kneeling beside me, Captain Pedden placed my trembling hand in his palm to steady it with his own.

"Prepare yourself then, Pauline, for the worst."

My body shuddered forcefully against the side of the bed. "Tell me then. Has the court found me guilty?"

Colonel McKinstry spoke quietly. "It has."

"And have they condemned me to…to…" The sentence hung in the suddenly thick air. My face lost all its color. I folded to my knees and crumpled, clutching myself in a frantic attempt to staunch the primal wound now ravaging my spirit.

"To death, my dear," nodded Captain Pedden, speaking softly. "You have been condemned to be hanged as a spy."

I cried the ugly kind of tears that follow numbness and an overwhelming pain in the heart.

"Great God of mercy! It is just as I feared."

They held me protectively as I fell apart. At long last, I wiped away the tears and asked the question that burned into my heart.

"Will I be the first female spy hanged during this war?"

They nodded, but then Captain Pedden offered me a small piece of solace.

"Pauline, the Rebels will not carry a sick woman to the gallows. They will wait for you to get well, so you have time."

That was his attempt to reassure me that there was still hope. Union forces might yet save me. Although they had frequently tried to take Shelbyville, they had been thwarted each time. I could only pray that they would try again and succeed.

"Are you aware that a substantial Union force is advancing toward Shelbyville, Pauline?" asked Colonel McKinstry. "That may be your salvation, and give me the opportunity to finally meet your General Rosecrans." Despite being spent and weary, the old colonel had come to offer me hope.

For a moment, a spark of optimism flared in my heart, quickly followed by reality and renewed pain.

I asked to be left alone.

Forcing my eyes to close did no good, for they quickly flew open. Shadows dancing across the walls taunted me. It was evening now, with the moon full and bright.

Yet I was doomed to darkness.

THIRTY-EIGHT

Antonia

FEBRUARY 1864

apa wrote to us at Sangsters during the rest of January, explaining that it was still too unsafe in Fairfax for us to return. He also wrote us about my brother Clanie's disobedience and punishment. Apparently Clanie had been forbidden to leave town, but decided to do so anyway. His excuse was a visit to a friend, whom it turned out had a sister Clanie had long admired. Clanie left the house in secrecy but returned in no time, alarmed and unsettled.

Here is a portion of Papa's letter.

I started going to the stables to look for my wayward son when I saw him sneaking into the house. One look at his face, and I knew something had happened. I asked him what the meaning of his disobedience was, and he replied, "You were right, Papa. I should not have been out. I witnessed twenty of our men attack the picket at Flint Hill. The picket fell down, injured, or worse."

I thanked God that Clanie had not been shot.

Clanie continued, "Our men were driven off after a single volley, which surprised me—being scared off so easily. That was my cue to turn around and come home."

Angry with Clanie, but also relieved, I punished him by sending him to the woodpile to work off his restless energy by chopping until he exhausted himself.

I received several letters from the Major, but they were not as warm as the ones he had written before our rift. After reading Papa's letter, I wrote urging Joseph to be extremely careful when he traveled in that area. Much as I considered John Mosby a friend, I worried that he might capture my Major.

Finally, on January 30, Dr. Simpson drove us home. Arriving in the evening, we saw that Mathilde had prepared a blazing fire in the parlor. She had also lit softly shaded candles, giving the room a welcoming glow. I found my favorite chair, sat with my back to the fire, picked up my pen and wrote to Joseph.

Fairfax Courthouse, January 30, 1864
My dearest Major,

I am at home again as you'll perceive by this, and right glad to get here; glad simply because you wished one to return, and that I can now receive and send letters to you regularly. It was so provoking at Sangsters. I wrote four times and do not know yet that one was received. Your orderly told Pa today he had a letter for me, and Pa said better not send it down as I was expected home; but he found a good opportunity and sent it. I feel disappointed about it, for I anticipated a treat in reading it. Never mind, it will be sweet when it comes; and I hope to have a long one to relish.

You wish to know my birthday—it is the 23rd of July, and my birth room is the one you occupied at Fontainville. No, I do not think you are "an old soldier for a young lady"; I think you are very suitable for the young lady; she wouldn't have you changed a particle, as regards age or anything else.

I found the bundle awaiting me; I am very, very much obliged; the matchbox is very pretty. Ma will write to you very soon. She said today coming home, "I wish the Major

would come by tonight." I fully echoed the wish, I assure you.
Do come next week, will you not, dearest?

Captain LaMotte knocked on our door this evening.
Father and Mother declined to entertain him. I emphatically
declined to make my appearance. Stars have no attraction for
me. I much prefer the leaf. Capt. LaMotte is housed with the
General nearby.

Good night, write every day.
Yours affectionately,
Antonia

Several days passed before Joseph was able to visit me. He greeted my family warmly and shared light news. As soon as we could, we retired to the parlor to speak privately.

"Oh, my darling," he whispered, "how I've missed you." He ran his fingers through my flowing hair, which I had purposely worn down, gracing my back and shoulders. The room was cozy and welcoming with the fire crackling.

Kissing me softly, he sent my senses spinning. Stroking my hair, he told me how much he loved it. "May I have a lock of your copper-golden hair to hold close to my heart?"

Laughing warmly, I took the embroidery scissors and cut off a strand. "This is a charmed lock—a talisman to keep you close. You will always feel my presence, and that will give you joy and peace."

He held me close. "I do so enjoy your way with words, my dancing Delilah. Only this time you have cut off your hair, not mine!" After another kiss, he added, "Your heart gives off an innocent love."

Creasing my forehead, I looked up at him. "Are you attempting to quote Lord Byron? You have the idea, but your words are flawed."

He lifted a tuft of my hair and tucked it behind my ear. "I wanted to see if you would correct me," he grinned. "And you did."

My parents entered the room at that moment to join us. I had no idea what they would say, but Mother quickly relieved my curiosity.

"Joseph, how are your divorce proceedings going?"

I noticed his eyes widen. Without missing a beat, he answered calmly, "Unfortunately, they are moving slowly. I do have Major Bradley intervening for me, but the courts move at a snail's pace."

"Is your family aware of what you are doing?" asked Papa politely, studying his reaction.

Joseph nodded, taking my hand in his. "Indeed they are. My wife has also filed for divorce, so it will come as no surprise to anyone in my family." Now I was surprised! This was the first I had heard that his wife had filed.

Mother had more to say. "What about your military commission, Major Willard?"

I knew the answer to this one through his letters. "I have resigned my commission and believe that will come through by the end of the month."

It was my turn. "Joseph, when will we be able to marry?"

He turned to me with a loving gaze. "My hope is sometime in March." I smiled my gratitude at his words, proud of how he had handled my parents' questions.

My father pointed out that no one in Fairfax Courthouse could issue a marriage license, to which Joseph replied, "We shall have to marry without one."

My reaction was immediate. "No, Joseph, we shall not. Please check in Washington City. I would feel much safer there, as each time you plan to come here, I fear you will be caught by Mosby."

Papa agreed. It was decided that Washington City was the prudent place for us to marry.

I noticed how tense the Major had become with this twist in the conversation. "I would offer my hotel for the ceremonial place," he stammered, his face growing flushed, "but it is full of Federals and also is in disrepair."

For a brief moment I wondered if he were so embarrassed to marry a Rebel that he did not want it known among his hotel friends and family. I forced myself to erase that preposterous thought from my mind.

"However, I know that hotelkeepers in town offer one another professional courtesy for the use of their hotels. My brother Caleb runs the Ebbitt House, and he would certainly offer it. But I would prefer the Metropolitan Hotel, formerly the Brown's Hotel, as it is quite elegant and suitable for our joyous ceremony."

I wanted to reach over and plant a kiss on his lovely lips. But my mother and father did not seem as impressed as I.

"Yes, I know the Metropolitan is nice. And there should not be as many Federals staying there as in the Willard, correct?" asked Mother.

"No, ma'am, there are not. So, may I presume that you and your family will transport yourselves to the Metropolitan Hotel for our wedding?" Joseph asked calmly.

"Certainly not!" My father's face was flushed and his voice raised. "I believe our family is in more danger from your men than you are from Mosby. Only with you in the conveyance would we be assured safe passage." Stunned silence filled the air.

Joseph suddenly stood up and announced he was due back at his headquarters. "Seeing you was certainly a pleasure, as always. I shall return next week to finish this dialogue."

He scarcely embraced me as he headed for the door. My parents and I simply stared at each other as he departed.

Finally I spoke up. "Ma, did you need to be so inquisitive about his affairs?"

She snorted. "Absolutely, my child. I am simply showing my concern for my daughter, whom I happen to love." I nodded at her expression of affection.

Later in my room, I decided to write to Joseph, making the most of the soft candlelight.

I suffered very much with a headache this evening after your departure, remembering your kind sympathy. Your gentle attention lived again in my memory, intensified by the thought that we are now parted—that sixteen cruel miles stretch their length between us. The fact is, Major, I miss you. I want to see you. I cannot get accustomed to your absence; when a bell rings I jump as if to meet you, but alas, "he cometh not!"

Ma was very much worried and disappointed at your reserved manners. She thought you were displeased at something—what was the matter? I felt your altered behavior very sensibly; I think and hope, however, I could have brought a smile to your lips by less animated talk. Am I mistaken?

Come whenever you can, and write as often as you feel like it. Do not forget me and stay away from pretty young girls, especially Blanche Helm.

Yours faithfully,
Antonia

They say a lady's postscript is invariably the most important part of her letter. I leave you to judge its correctness in this case, the pith of mine being—when will you see Major Bradley again?

Of course I knew I was expressing in my letters the sentiments I could not speak to Joseph personally. Writing was the emotional purification that allowed me to convey my deepest emotions.

Several more days passed as I enjoyed time with my family. I took the time to write a detailed letter to my friend Rose, bringing her up to date on our lives. I knew she would respond quickly. Perhaps we could plan a visit to each other's home in the near future.

I had not heard another word from Joseph, but I felt the soothing reassurance of our love. My thoughts were consumed with him, and I was astonished to discover such passion. Sometimes I was overwhelmed by the intensity of my ardor and obsession. How I longed to become one with Joseph. Fortunately, common sense prevailed, yet I continued to share my strong feelings through the written word.

Tuesday, February 2, 1864

I miss you, and wish you were with me right now. I am pleased to hear that your wife is being cooperative. A solution that has come to mind would be to bring about a match between her and Major Bradley (is he single?); if she should wish to marry again, of course. Perhaps she simply wants her freedom and in that case could liberate you. Suggest it to Major Bradley. Above all, do not let her hear my name. I think if in addition to my other troubles, an infuriated female were to start in pursuit, I should show the white feather and take refuge in inglorious flight.

Do not be surprised at my flow of spirits. You must remember I have no Major Bradley to depress me by long prosy law talks, but instead of that the pleasant countenance and agreeable conversation of Lieutenant Henry Gawthrop.

Sad to relate he expects to leave tomorrow; can't you use your influence for the 4th Delaware to remain longer?

Am I not a good girl to more than fulfill a promise? I said I would write half a dozen lines a day; this is only Tuesday, and see how many half dozen are on this sheet. I hope you appreciate the magnanimity of such conduct. I charge you eight full pages for it. Let me know which style you prefer—the <u>sentimental or comic</u>, neither is exhausted, and I can enlarge indefinitely on both. Just specify your choice.

Write immediately, if not sooner.

Yours faithfully,
Antonia

Joseph Willard's resignation was accepted on February 12, 1864. As soon as we heard, Mother reminded me to ask him about the marriage license. "It would be just like a man to forget that most important of documents," she said laughing.

I wrote him regarding his status of becoming a civilian: *Your successor, Mr. Willard, will be as dear to me as the major has been.*

Strangely enough, right after my letter had been sent, a neighbor came to visit. "Congratulations on your marriage to the newly decommissioned Joseph Willard." I laughed, corrected her hypothesis, and realized that rumors would now be flying willy-nilly around Fairfax Courthouse.

THIRTY-NINE

Pauline

Rumors were spreading that Union forces were near Shelbyville. By this time, my health and the anticipation of my hanging had weakened me to the point of keeping only to my bed. I feared I could not walk even if I chose to. I also felt symptoms of some terrible sickness creeping through my frame, harassing me with the uncertain fear that because I was away from my home, this would be my end.

I could hear the sounds of the approaching troops, and felt tears coursing down my cheeks at the commotion of the shouts and gunshots. Suddenly, all went quiet.

General Bragg entered my sickroom with paperwork in his hand.

"By heaven!" he exclaimed. It seems your 'old Rosy' is really at work, for this dispatch announces that the Federal troops have entered the 'pike.'" His tired eyes lit up at the news, and then he departed. I heard him give orders to furnish the troops with three days' rations and hold them in readiness to march at once.

Captain Pedden came to me with the news that Union troops were moving through the city. Because I was too weak to be moved, he would take me to the home of Doctor Blackman. His final words stung my heart.

"I am agitated at the thought of parting from you, but I must leave quickly with my men. As you must know, I care deeply for you, and God willing, we shall meet again. When this war is finished, I will be honored to claim you for my bride. Until then, I shall know no other thought, no other wish." He ran his fingers along the side of my face, his voice rough with emotion. He searched my eyes, and for a brief second, my own fear edged in on the moment.

I could not tell him that his hopes were useless. All I could do was thank him for the kindness he had shown me.

"You will not be hanged now, my dear Pauline. I am moving you to a safe home, and when you are able to travel, you will be taken to Nashville. In a day or two Shelbyville will be completely occupied by Federal troops, so I am leaving you in good hands." We both cried at his words. He reached into his pocket and handed me a small gift—a cake of soap. Then he leaned down to kiss my parched lips.

"I can never thank you for all you did for me, dear Captain. My heart is overflowing with gratitude. I wish you well." I leaned against him as he stroked my hair. I felt so small in his arms.

Captain Pedden wrapped me in a feather bed and carried me to the house of Doctor Blackman. I was blessed to learn that the doctor was a Union man at heart, and both he and his wife treated me kindly during my brief stay in their home.

I had been unable to sit up for several days, but once moved, I began to recover. My prayers had been answered, and my strength returned as the roar of artillery filled the sky. The next day I saw the stars and stripes float by my window, bathed in a golden light that rivaled its own splendor.

Aroused by the stirring events, I pushed up from the bed and wrapped myself in a blanket. Incredibly, I reached the porch in time to see Major Fullerton pass by, followed by General Granger and General Mitchell. I called out to Fullerton, and was stunned to see that my weak voice had reached his ears.

Major Fullerton dismounted and entered the house. After embraces and tears of relief, I asked him who commanded our troops.

"Generals Granger and Mitchell are the commanders," he answered proudly.

"Where are they, sir?"

"Close by, Miss Cushman."

"Thank God then!" My eyes swam with tears. "I am safe at last! I am safe!" I threw up my hands as I thanked God in my heart. *Oh God, you did not abandon me.*

Generals Granger and Mitchell stopped by to see me twice that day: at five-thirty in the afternoon, and as late as eleven o'clock in the evening.

"Miss Cushman, do you know that on the very night you were at the house of the wounded Rebel soldier, no fewer than ninety Union scouts were out scouring the country in search of you?" asked General Granger, holding my hand.

"Dear me!" I answered, in surprise. "How did you imagine I might be there?"

The General smiled. "Your arrest at Milam's, by the Rebel scouts, somehow got into the wind. I believe he was impudent enough to brag of it, so we set out to rescue you between there and Hillsboro. But though beating up all that area, by some mischance they failed to find you."

I thought about his words. "Oh dear, that accounts for the two Rebel scouts found killed near the forks of the road. They believed I was the murderess." My eyes closed, forcing the tears between the lids. I thanked them for their attempt to rescue me.

I rested my face in my hands for a moment, just to gather strength.

They assured me of my protection, but it required some time

for my enfeebled mind to comprehend the joyous, life-giving fact: I would not be hanged!

Now that my safety was assured, that false strength born of excitement left me just as suddenly. I sank back into the chair, totally overcome. Late afternoon, kind Mrs. Blackman laid me gently upon the couch, and I fell into a deep, untroubled sleep.

CHAPTER FORTY

Antonia

LATE FEBRUARY–EARLY MARCH 1864

J oseph and I planned to marry just as soon as a judge in
Washington City granted him the divorce. My siblings
and I, and indeed Ma and Papa, were absorbed in the
flurry of wedding plans.

Mother and I wasted no time, rushing here and there to prepare for this glorious day. A cedar hope chest was filled with
wonderful embroidered pieces including linens, bath towels,
and table toppings. Quilted and knitted items, crafted by my
family and friends, complemented gorgeous velvet and silk
dresses purchased over time. My dear mother had recently
sewn for me two lovely cotton nightdresses and evening robes
with lace adornments, using material acquired by Major.

Now that Major had resigned his commission, we had only
to wait for the finalization of the marriage. Romantic Pattie
was convinced that Joseph would adore me always and forever.

"He loves you so much, Antonia," she cooed. "Just look at
how he smiles constantly at you and always holds your hand."

Mother added her insight. "I can see and feel the abounding
love between the two of you. I know you shall be blessed with
him, my child."

My superstitions rekindled my anxiety. Until I held the
divorce decree in my own hands, I could not be certain I would
actually be Mrs. Joseph Willard. And then, to make matters
worse, Pattie came to me with a new rhyme.

*Monday for health, Tuesday for wealth, Wednesday the best
day of all
Thursday for losses, Friday for crosses, and Saturday no luck
at all.*

I asked her, "What about Sunday?" Neither of us had an answer. I shuddered, having imagined my wedding would be on a Sunday.

I asked Pattie to be my maid of honor and my school friend Rose Garnett to be my bridesmaid.

In mid-February Mother and I traveled to Alexandria to commission a seamstress to sew my bridal gown. It would be a one-piece silk frock in the color of burnt umber and green floral. The bodice's classic V-back featured a carefully rounded jewel neckline and dropped shoulders. The waistband was pleated, the skirt was trained and the dress was full-sleeved. It was utterly exquisite, and when I tried it on, I nearly passed out from happiness. We also purchased kid leather shoes—beige, trimmed with pale green ruffles, and short lace gloves.

I knew the pale tan color of my wedding gown would raise eyebrows. I did not want to wear white, since the umber color complemented my skin tone and gave my complexion a glow. Some brides chose purple dresses to represent the courage of our fallen soldiers, but the color did not flatter me, and my Major had not fallen.

Thrilled with anticipation, I still worried that Major would be stopped by a Confederate raiding party when he came to escort us to the hotel.

As the family discussed details of the wedding arrangements, we were interrupted by another knock on the door. None of us were expecting visitors, so we ignored the knocking and continued discussing the procession into Washington City. We agreed that my parents, Joseph, and I would ride in one carriage while Pattie, Clanie and Rose would follow us. Frank would remain behind with Mathilde, Octavia and Adam.

When the loud knocking continued, Papa rose up from his chair to answer the door. Returning stiff-legged to the parlor, he sank into his chair as if into a bottomless pit. His entire body trembled and his eyes sought a way out.

"You're as white as a sheet! Darling, what happened?" asked Mother.

His mouth opened, but raw emotion closed off his throat. Finally he spoke.

"It's Charlie," he rasped almost inaudibly. His head jerked once. "I was just notified that Charlie has been killed in a skirmish." His face fell into his hands as he wept in sorrow.

"Oh no! Dear Lord, no!" wailed my mother, stumbling to embrace Papa as if to hold him steady.

We were all numb, at a loss for words, lost in pain like a dirge.

Helpless and devastated, we climbed the stairs to our beds and fragmented futures.

The following morning we received two more shocks, the first in a note from Jeb Stuart. He wrote the dead soldier had been someone else—Charlie was actually alive and well! As we crowded around Papa's chair in emotional turmoil and cascades of relief, a horse noisily approached our front gate.

Mathilde opened the door and showed our visitor into the parlor.

"Oh, my Lord! What are you doing here in the middle of the week?" I asked Joseph, as he held out his arms to embrace me.

"I have news, my love. Where may we speak privately?"

"Dear Joseph, so much has happened in the last twenty-four hours. Let us go to the porch and sort it all out."

I related the unfortunate news and the frightful scare we had experienced. Then I asked him, "Did you see any pickets along the road?"

"No, my love. Not a soldier in sight." Dropping his hand on my shoulder, he squeezed gently. "I am here to tell you personally that my divorce is as good as resolved."

I threw my arms around him, overcome by so much news and emotion. My head was whirling and I felt shortness of breath.

Papa came through the front door.

"Joseph, welcome," he smiled, extending his hand. "I feel certain that Antonia has told you of our immense grief, and then widespread relief, at the news about Charlie. We are not the same as before but nevertheless, we do welcome your visit."

Joseph nodded, and smiled. "Now that I am a civilian, I hope you will consider me a friend to you, your family and your village."

Papa grinned. "Joseph, you became a friend the moment you helped my daughter."

I had something more to add. "And our neighbors all consider you a friend, even though we understand you must remain loyal to the government. I love you all the more for that, because you are true to your cause. None of that matters now, since soon we will be united as man and wife."

We then spoke about the wedding plans. We brought up his deceased brother Edwin, and how he would be with us in spirit. Our short time together ended with high hopes for a blissful union.

Less than a week after his visit, Joseph wrote me the details of his divorce proceedings.

On March 2, Caroline and I were required to go before a judge at the courthouse, sitting in equity. I described to the judge the sad circumstances of our marriage and life together.

My wife was calm and agreeable to the financial settlement that the lawyers had worked out. The judge, as respondent, stated that he believed it better that the marriage should be severed and joined Caroline in her petition. He felt that divorce would promote "the happiness of both."

My relief was so immense at the receipt of this news that I could do nothing but sit on my bed and weep. Eventually, I descended the stairs to share the letter with my family.

Another letter reached us at about the same time. Charlie wrote from Albemarle County, six miles north of Charlottesville, telling us about the Battle of Rio Hill on February 26. His unit had faced the famous Union General George Armstrong Custer. According to Charlie, Custer's only opposition came from our friend Jeb Stuart's Horse Company. My brother proudly related that he and the other infantrymen had chased Custer from Albemarle. Sadly, that was only after the Federals burned the covered railroad bridge and gristmill on Rivanna River.

That tumultuous week's final letter came from Joseph. Only one sentence, but perhaps the happiest one he had ever written. *I shall come for Antonia on the morning of the tenth.*

FORTY-ONE

Pauline

July to December 1863

T he next morning I awoke bright and early, determined to start at once for Murfreesboro and get as far behind the Union lines as possible. The doctor examined me, then told me and Generals Mitchell and Granger that I was in no condition to travel.

"Miss Cushman, you would die on the road trying to reach Murfreesboro. I cannot release you to travel."

"Oh no, sir. I will not perish. Not after all I've been through. I shall go on foot if you do not allow me to travel."

Finally, after a great deal of pleading and arguing, I agreed to stay for another day or so, in order to build up my strength and wait for the constant rain to subside. To keep me entertained, General Granger shared a letter he had written to Major General Rosecrans the day before.

SHELBYVILLE, TENN., June 27, 1863 — 8 p.m.

GENERAL: We occupied this place at 6 o'clock, captured three pieces of artillery and 300 prisoners, among them one colonel, one lieutenant-colonel and a score of other officers. The "Stars and Stripes" floated from many windows and housetops, and we met a hearty welcome. Bragg left here this morning at 6 o'clock, for Tullahoma. Carts were running all night, removing the stores, sick, and wounded. We saved the bridge over Duck River; intercepted the enemy at that place.

Mr. Caldwell, a Union man, reports Bragg had 27,000 at this place and Wartrace, about 18,000 of them being here. Very few stores are to be found. I move at 9 o'clock, in pursuit of their wagon train, on the south side of Duck River. It cannot possibly be more than 9 miles distant, and the roads are very heavy. I hope to be able to destroy it.

G. GRANGER, Major-General, Commanding

He told me that Garfield was at the Army Headquarters at Beech Grove with Rosecrans, being briefed on my situation. Rosecrans was anxious to speak with me, but was still detained with his forces. I was anxious to leave.

At eleven o'clock the following morning Granger brought my ambulance around, furnished with bed, pillows, blankets, and a mattress. He and General Mitchell carried me down on a stretcher, while Fullerton held an umbrella to protect me from the continuing rain. The officers mounted their horses and accompanied the ambulance out of town on the road toward Murfreesboro, forming what they dubbed my "escort of honor." Eleven miles out of Shelbyville, Granger was ordered to return. We stopped at a Mr. Fletcher's home at six o'clock and remained there until noon the following day. When we finally reached Murfreesboro, I was tired but happy, knowing I was going home.

On June 30, I was placed in a railroad car headed for Nashville, Tennessee. Both Granger and Fullerton saw me off. Captain Sedgwick of Granger's staff accompanied me on the train. A carriage received me at the Nashville Depot and took me to City Hotel.

As we drove through the city, I experienced a peculiar thrill. *Nashville had been the turning-point in my destiny!* It was here that I began my perilous expedition, after receiving the warm-hearted handshake of the brave servant boy with his hearty "Godspeed." Yes, God had sped me, and then returned me, as if by a pre-determined miracle.

I immediately sent word to Truesdail's office of my desire to see him, unaware that he was no longer there. Several hours later I learned that he had been transferred from Nashville to Murfreesboro on June 2. His business affairs had been called into question, and his control of the mails, newspapers and speculation in the cotton market came under intense scrutiny. No official wrongdoing was discovered, but it was conveyed to me that many of the residents were relieved to see him go.

That evening I was visited by two officers on Rosecrans' staff, Captain Fyffe and Captain Temple Clark. Captain Clark was the special inspector appointed by Rosecrans to investigate Truesdail. He told me that Truesdail was at Tullahoma, and when notified of my return, said: "Let every care be taken of her."

I was watched over by the kind men on Rosecrans' staff, but I fell into an incomprehensible overpowering sadness. Once again I collapsed into a debilitated state. Great tears stole unconsciously down my face several times a day. The doctors attributed this to the exposure to the elements while traveling, as well as the stress and hardships I had endured during my adventures as a scout and imprisoned spy. On July 14 they put me in a private home, where I would receive more attention than at the crowded hotel.

Miss Jenny Williams' house was on Union Street. Because I was not well enough to get around on my own, they moved me two days later to a boarding house run by Mrs. Kirdell, at the corner of Church and High streets. Mrs. Kirdell showed me every kindness in her power. My friends, General Granger, General Garfield and Major Fullerton, also spent hours with me sharing war news. They also asked me what I knew about shipments of supplies and guerilla band operations in the vicinity.

"I can remember a great deal about what I overheard, but will it still be useful?" I wondered.

"Oh yes, Pauline. More skirmishes will be fought, and anything you tell us will be shared with the generals," answered Major Fullerton, with absolute conviction. I felt pleased to be of service, even in my weakened state.

My recovery in Mrs. Kirdell's boarding house continued.

"How can I afford to stay here with such costly care?" I asked her.

"You need not worry your lovely head about this," she answered. "General Garfield has authorized the U.S. government to take care of it."

During the following weeks, Major General Garfield, who insisted I call him James, visited my boarding house almost daily. We became good friends. I shared many of my spying adventures with him; he listened attentively. After one particular story, he stood up and came over to my bedside.

"That reminds me, Pauline, that I have just ordered the arrest of that scoundrel Benjamin Milam. After all you went through because of his dishonesty and duplicity, it was the proper thing to do."

I clapped my hands as a laugh burst out of me. The sound of my own laughter surprised me. It felt good. "Oh thank you, dear James. I never thought he would face the consequences of his crimes. Justice has been served." I was growing quite fond of this gentleman.

One evening while Garfield was visiting, a closely veiled lady entered the drawing room. James stood to ask her name and business. She did not answer him, but came directly to my chair and spoke softly.

"We have never met, but your deeds of patriotism and daring have given you a certain claim upon the sympathies of strangers. Hearing that you were indisposed, I have taken the liberty of bringing you a nice pound cake, which I made myself." Setting it on the side table next to some fruit the General had brought me, the lady smiled gently at both of us. "I hope you enjoy it."

"I cannot thank you enough for your thoughtfulness and kind regard for a stranger," I responded.

"Misfortune makes us all akin, you know," answered the lady pleasantly, moving toward the door.

"That should be so," I said to her. "But unfortunately it is not always the case. We do not often meet with such good Samaritans as yourself."

The General held the door open for her as she departed. Once again he asked her to whom Miss Cushman was indebted for this kindness. She declined to answer and disappeared into the dusk. "How very odd!" he exclaimed, turning to me with a baffled expression.

Neither of us was hungry since we had just dined. After General Garfield left, a neighbor's child came by to visit "the beautiful sick lady," as she had christened me. I offered her some fruit and a piece of cake. The little girl preferred the fruit, but gave the cake to the dog.

Several hours later, the child returned sobbing, shrieking that her dog was acting crazy. I followed her next door and found the dog writhing in convulsions on the floor. He soon expired in great agony, his body swollen to twice its natural size.

The following morning Garfield came to visit and I told him the story. He was greatly alarmed and wanted to test our suspicions. He gave another piece of the cake to a troublesome cat that kept us awake with its caterwauling. In a few moments, the poor animal gave up every one of the "nine lives" which common superstition had granted it, and swelled to an inordinate size.

"Dear Lord," I moaned. "This cake has been poisoned!"

The General was incensed to find his suspicions realized. "That woman, accursed may she be, would fain have had the sin of murder upon her guilty soul. Oh, heavens, is it possible that people can be so vile?"

He organized a search to find the culprit who had put the arsenic in the cake, but they were unsuccessful. They concluded that it must have been a proud Secesh woman determined to rid the Confederacy of a dangerous enemy, at whatever price. I felt grateful for this most providential escape, and humbly returned thanks to my Almighty Father for constantly watching over me.

As I continued to gather my strength, I felt almost as strong as before my scout days. Then I received some unexpected praise from Generals Granger and Garfield, who honored my Union services with a testimonial of appreciation, and proclaimed me a "Major of Cavalry."

They issued me a special permit to procure the military furnishings that a major was entitled to wear. In the initial report, written in July of 1863 and signed by Brigadier General J.A. Garfield, of the Army of the Cumberland, Garfield stated:

> "Miss Cushman was employed by William Truesdail, chief of the army police, to make a trip within enemy lines. She was captured upon her return within eight miles of Nashville by Rebel cavalry. She was taken to Bragg's headquarters, suffering from severe exposure during her trip. She was taken sick and found today in this condition by General Granger's command. General Granger ordered her removed to Nashville."

Because of this honor, I became known to the soldiers as *Major Pauline Cushman*, and although a little embarrassed by this, I felt very proud of this distinction. Garfield told me that he had written to President Lincoln and given him "*an account of the black-eyed spy the boys had dubbed 'The Major'"* before presenting me with this great honor. President Lincoln responded: "Let her keep the title."

The loyal ladies of Nashville, deeply moved by such an honor conferred upon one of their own sex, prepared for me a shining blue riding habit, trimmed in military style, with dainty shoulder straps, and presented the dress to me with all the customary honors.

An article appeared in the *Nashville Daily Press* on December 1, 1863.

> The dress was *"made of the most costly material and is beautifully but modestly ornamented with national emblems. Miss Pauline Cushman is the daring heroine who has done so much service to the United States—a lady who occupies the warmest niche in the patriotic heart of almost every American soldier."*

My recovery was nearly complete, and I now took daily drives around the city to visit friends and return the kindness of devoted mothers, wives and sisters of the noble soldiers. One morning, after returning from one such drive, my maid stopped me.

"That man has been here again, Miss."

"What man?" I asked her in surprise.

"The one who calls here nearly every day but never finds you home."

"Annette, what do you mean?"

"I thought I had told you; the reason I perhaps neglected to is probably because the man acted so queer, I began to suspect he must be crazy."

She led me to a lounge chair. "One morning you had not gone on your drive, because you felt weak, and when he called I told you were in and would see him, because he looked like a soldier and I know you always see *them*. He followed me upstairs and then stopped, laying his hand on his heart and told me, 'I cannot do it today. I feel my courage leaving me.' So he took to his heels and ran straight out the door, leaving me standing there."

I laughed, and she continued. "I came to the conclusion that he was some Secessionist who had come to murder you, inasmuch as he said he hadn't the courage to do it that day."

"Did he appear to be a soldier?"

"Yes, Miss, and now that I think of it, he was an Irishman, and they are generally on the right side."

I giggled at her logic.

"Today he hesitated a moment, then left a little package. He told me he would call this evening for an answer."

I opened the package, wrapped with clean white paper, and sealed with a wafer. Breaking the seal, a small scrap of faded ribbon fell out.

"Oh, my goodness. It is the very same one! How did it come all the way here?"

In my prison at Shelbyville there was a young Irishman who had been completely devoted to me. I had given him some trivial favor, half in jest, a little knot of ribbon which had once bound my hair, after all he had done for me. I told him that when he became a good man and stopped fighting against the Union, he could send me this, and if I weren't married or dead, I might be induced to have him as my husband. It was mostly in jest, but seeing the ribbon again made me curious to hear his story.

That evening I scarcely recognized the noble, sturdy figure standing before me. Instead of the dirty gray clothes of the Rebel service, he now wore the true blue of the Union, and was as fine a looking soldier as one would wish to gaze upon.

"Jimmy," I asked in amazement. "How is it that I see you in the Federal uniform?"

"Faith it is, marm," he answered. "Sure, as you know, my heart was never in the cause down yonder. I told them I was an alien, but they did not mind at all and just clapped me into the army. So I said the first chance will see me off, and here I am."

"Well done, Jimmy!" I was highly amused at his words. "But what made you enlist in our service?"

"Well, faith again, marm. When I saw your fair self-suffering and dying for the Union, without so much as a murmur out of you, I told myself that any cause for which a *woman* can die in that way *must* truly be the right one. So I made up for my sin of once being a miserable Rebel soldier and listed up in the same cause as you."

I was deeply touched. "Bravely done! And as a reward, you may wear this ribbon next to your heart, knowing that its former owner's prayers and blessings will ever accompany you."

"Faith, marm, it came off my heart when I gave it to your servant. I will put it there again, and when next year you see me, it will be with all the dishonor of ever being a Rebel washed out of my own heart's blood."

That literally came to be. After the fearful Battle of Chickamauga, I received the little knot of ribbon again. It was dyed a deeper red this time and accompanied by a note from the colonel of the regiment in which brave Jimmy had served. The note said:

"Jimmy, one of my best men, though deserted from the Rebel ranks, fell today literally covered with glory. He seemed desirous to retrieve, by his present conduct, the crime of which he had been guilty against his country, by joining its enemies. Three times he was shot down, and the dear old flag humbled in the dust, when Jimmy sprang forward, and, seizing it, bore it proudly and grandly aloft. At last, wounded in three places, he sank upon the torn and trampled sod, which proved his death-bed, pressing the colors still to his heart. I

was the nearest to him at the moment, and stopped to raise the old banner again, and to cheer my men. I saw him take the enclosed piece of ribbon from over his heart, and he told me: 'Send this to Miss Cushman, the Union scout—the bravest woman I ever saw; the dearest friend I have. She will under-stand.'

That night I offered up my heartfelt prayer for Jimmy, thanking God that as an agent of his intervention, I had been able to convert at least one Rebel. I begged Him to bless the poor but noble fellow, who had died fighting at last for the Right.

FORTY-TWO

Antonia

MARCH 10, 1864

W e rose early on the morning of the wedding and ate a light breakfast. I put together my toiletries in a small valise, smiling at the thought that today I would become Joseph's wife. As I was writing in my journal, I heard my sister opening the front door to welcome my closest friend Rose.

Pattie and Rose assisted me in getting dressed. Pattie brushed my hair until it shone, and then arranged it atop my head with a pearled comb. Rose lined my eyes with a kohl pencil and applied rouge to my cheeks and lips. She warned me, "Antonia, once we have finished, you must not look into the mirror again until after the ceremony."

"Why not?" I asked her, guessing the answer.

"That would be terribly unlucky, and I know how superstitious you are."

I laughed. "I've had more than my share of frightful luck already. Now it is time for sheer happiness."

My eyes sparkled as I shared a fact I had just recently discovered. "Do you remember how I've always dreamed of marrying a man with the initials J.C.?" They nodded, intrigued. "Well, Joseph's middle name is Clapp! That is one more dream coming true!"

Just then Mother came through the doorway, smiling at our

merriment. She was the first person I told about Major's middle name.

Mother reached down to pin a small pouch to my wedding petticoat. "This contains a piece of bread, cloth, wood and a single one-dollar bill," she said. "You will always have enough food, clothing, shelter and money." I smiled at her, having forgotten this marriage custom.

We fastened my short-sleeved chemise and straightened out the various hoops of my crinoline. Finally Mother, fighting back tears, tenderly rested the lace veil she had worn at her own wedding on my head. It tumbled down to settle about twelve inches from the floor.

Now it was my turn to hug my mother and wipe away her tears. "Ma, you are not losing a daughter. You are gaining another son," I whispered in her ear. "Save your tears for the ceremony." My smile was wobbly but wide.

Mother had chosen my bouquet with a selection of flowers symbolizing a blossoming woman. Its lavender crocuses and snowdrops were tied together with a lavender bow. Mother realized that the snowdrops represented "hope."

We walked to the parlor where Papa and Joseph waited. I stopped, stunned by Major's distinguished appearance. Dressed in a starched shirt, gleaming gold cuffs and bib front with a shining black silk cravat, he stood before me, honorable and handsome. His fancy silver silk vest peeked out from under a single-breasted tailcoat, with a knee-length skirt in the back. His black trousers were gray-striped, and a pocket watch swung from his front vest pocket. I could not stop staring at his white gloves and highly polished walking stick, complete with a silver handle.

"Darling, have you never seen me dressed up before?" he asked, arching a brow and trying to conceal his amusement.

"Yes, sir, in dress uniform, but I have never seen you quite this dashing," I murmured.

"But it is you who are transformed," he answered softly. "Always beautiful, always elegant, but today...you are simply spectacular! You are the loveliest woman I have ever seen." His eyes danced as he presented me a small package, which I opened posthaste.

"Oh Joseph, how exquisite! I have never received such a fine gift," I gasped, awestruck and a little lightheaded, as he fastened the solid gold baroque watch to my wrist.

"Our names and our wedding date are engraved on it!" I murmured, drawing in a deep breath.

He smiled, reaching for my hand. "Yes, darling. And now we must be off, as my brother Henry and his wife are awaiting us at the hotel."

Two carriages pulled up to the house. Clanie, Pattie and Rose got into the first one, and Papa, Mother, Joseph and I followed behind. The first carriage left a few minutes before we did, to avoid attracting attention. We overheard pieces of the soldiers' conversations as we drove by them.

"Yep, I tell you that one of our majors is marrying a Rebel here at the courthouse today," remarked a young private.

"You don't know that for a fact," quipped his partner. "It might be anyone going off for a wedding anywhere." We grinned as we passed them; I refrained from waving.

Today was one of the first balmy days of the year—blue skies, sweet-smelling, and peaceful. Buds were swelling in the trees, and the moor was misted green with young bracken. My joy was unbridled and fulfilling, and I wanted to shout it out from the rooftops.

I watched Major fretfully finger the pass he was given by Major General Augur, giving us passage across the bridge to enter Washington City. We were brought to a standstill by a Rebel soldier, and I recognized the man as one of Mosby's soldiers.

"Halt! Who goes there?" he demanded.

"Ford of Fairfax," answered my father from the carriage window. "I am taking my daughter to Washington to see a doctor." I wondered if the soldier could see my wedding outfit, although I was covered by blankets in the back of the carriage.

Major wrapped another blanket around my shoulders and held me tightly, feeling my shivers of anxiety through the thick wool. Cupping my cheeks with both hands, his thumbs trailed along my cheekbones, a gesture I was beginning to love. He drew my face toward his for a quick, hard kiss.

Soon we were boarding the train to Washington City. Another carriage was secured, and we finally stepped down at the entrance of the Metropolitan Hotel. I exhaled a sigh of relief upon our arrival.

I loved this hotel and had always admired the wood paneling on the walls. Every entryway was surrounded by ornate, carved wooden cornices and pillars. Lavish thick draperies hung across the tall windows, and gilded-edged pictures garnished the walls. There was an oval mirror on an end table, but I carefully looked away in case my best friend's superstitious warning was true.

Our luggage was taken to our room while we convened in the private dining room where our wedding ceremony would be held. The rest of the party was already there, including the Reverend Phineas Gurley. Joseph's brother Caleb looked handsome and aristocratic, and I was happy to see that his brother Henry, wife Sarah and little Henry had traveled from New York to join us.

Sarah hugged me and whispered, "This reminds me of my own wedding, except that we were able to marry at the Willard. Now it would be impossible, with all the troops there. Still, I want you to know how happy I am that we are now sisters." Her warmth and sweet nature made me feel welcome.

I smiled at her. "Yet I do love this hotel. Major has told me a bit of its history. Did you know that President James Madison's second inaugural ball was held here in 1813?"

She nodded. "Yes, and both of James Monroe's inaugural balls were also in this lovely venue several years later. I believe it was 1817 and 1821. So your wedding is being held in a providential setting."

We took our places in front of the large room, surrounded by softly burning candles and flowers cascading over windowsills and floor areas. My bridesmaids stood on my left, with Pattie proudly clasping my spray of flowers. Henry, Clanie and Caleb stood on Joseph's right, and the other guests sat in front of us. For a brief moment, an intense sadness tucked itself into my heart as I realized that Charlie was not with us.

It was twelve o'clock, and the ceremony began. Moments later, Reverend Gurley pronounced us "husband and wife." I had insisted on a double ring ceremony, to serve as a visual reminder that our union was sacred to both of us. Our gold bands were engraved with our initials and the date. A ring was the accepted sign of infinity, and I felt that the two end lines of our lives were now circled together. We *have come full circle*, I thought blissfully.

My heart swelled with even more joy as Joseph lifted my veil and kissed me passionately after our introduction as "Major and Mrs. Willard." A photographer later gave us the photos of our blessed moment.

We had set up the wedding breakfast in the same room, and sat around one large table, draped with lovely silvery linen. Violinists played harmoniously throughout the meal. Joseph had seen to every detail.

My parents sat at each end of the table, while Joseph and I were together at the midpoint. We were served great quantities of eggs, cured ham, a variety of sweet-smelling breads, hash-browned potatoes and copious cups of steaming coffee.

Our two-tiered wedding cake was smothered in white icing, embedded with a constellation of charms attached to ribbons. Each bridesmaid was invited to pull one ribbon, receiving a wedding souvenir.

"Pattie, you got the pansy, which is the symbol of blooming love," I exclaimed. "And Rose, you have the church charm. It looks like you will be the next one to marry!"

I was not meant to pull a ribbon, but my curiosity got the better of me. As I tugged on it, it broke halfway out to reveal a heart in hand, symbolizing a life filled with love.

"Oh Joseph, our life together will be bursting with love," I cooed, "just as we knew it would be."

We cut the cake together, placing small portions into each other's mouths.

When no one was within hearing distance, he whispered in my ear: "My beloved spy. Who would have imagined that you would marry your captor?" I was startled, since that same reflection had been dancing in my head since the previous day.

The toasts began and my heart turned over when Henry raised his glass of excellent wine and spoke.

"This 'best man' concedes the entitlement to Joseph, truly the best man I know. Love and cherish your wife, my brother, always and forever." He turned to me. "Welcome into our family, Antonia. Health and happiness to both of you."

More memorable toasts and well wishes followed. After a while, Pattie, Rose and I slipped away so I could change into my going-away outfit.

"Oh girls, I am perfectly happy today. My dream has come true! I truly feel like a princess," I giggled as they pulled the dress over my head.

"Antonia, now that you are married, will you stop referring to Joseph as Major?" asked my little sister.

"Why? I like it. And sometimes Joseph sounds a bit 'old-fashioned' to me," I replied, laughter bubbling up from inside.

I gave each bridesmaid a flower from my spray. Then, dressed in my gray silk traveling dress and bonnet, I told them I was ready to travel. I would have chosen a happier color, but out of respect for Joseph's sensitivity about his recent divorce, I did not want to risk being inappropriate.

Shortly after two o'clock we said our goodbyes and caught the train to Philadelphia. Henry went on ahead to take care of our luggage.

"Goodbye, dear Ma and Papa," I told them as I kissed them goodbye. "We will see you soon. Stay well."

We boarded a carriage drawn by four white horses while our friends showered us with rice. As we drove away, the guests threw a pair of satin slippers at us, as was traditional. The left one landed in the carriage and I clapped my hands together gleefully.

"Superstitious lady, this is perfect indeed," smiled my husband, pulling me to him. "The left slipper means good luck forever." He kissed me deeply, in full view of our wedding guests. I could only wonder what glorious events he had planned for later.

FORTY-THREE

Antonia

MARCH 1864

O ur wedding train trip from Washington City to Philadelphia lasted six hours. Joseph promised me he
would take me to the grandest hotel in Philadelphia,
and he did. La Pierre House, designed by the renowned Scottish architect John McArthur, measured one hundred feet in
width, and sat on the widest street in town.

The doorman greeted us with a smile and the words,
"Welcome to the most splendid hotel in America—La Pierre
House."

My eyes widened as I tried to take in everything at once.
High atop the six-floor building was a sculpture of an enormous golden eagle.

The reception room featured a thick, light-colored carpet
under white sofas and chairs. Marble floors and walls gleamed
brightly in the late afternoon sun, enhancing the "bride-ready"
atmosphere in my imagination.

Joseph noticed my expression of awe and whispered, "Just
wait until you see the room. We have the bridal suite." He
stopped, as though this were all there was to be said. Gently
grasping my elbow, he said, "Come then, my darling."

Joseph swept me up and carried me over the suite's threshold as I squealed in pleasure. The bellhop grinned at our light-
hearted antics.

My eyes took in our spacious suite, feeling overwhelmed

and totally under Joseph's spell. The décor was similar to the reception area with white marble, light carpeting and gold and white decorations. Gas lamps lit the sitting room and led to the bedroom, where a fire was burning.

"Oh Joseph, just look at the bed," I gasped. It was the loveliest bed I had ever seen, with a gold and white canopy and eyelet lace drooping over the sides. It was covered with a velvety satin spread, sprinkled with tiny yellow roses.

"My dear Major, who designed this perfect hotel?" I asked awestruck.

"A friend of mine named John McArthur. He designed it in 1853, as well as two other beauties in Philadelphia: the Girard House and the Continental Hotel."

"How I would love to meet him to give him my sincere compliments," I added.

The indoor plumbing was the most modern I had ever seen, and I gratefully went in to freshen up. I was tired, not very hungry and more than a little nervous. My dear husband gave me time to conquer these emotions before inviting me downstairs to the restaurant.

I nodded. "Just for a light snack, I'm sure."

We dined in the splendid grand dining room, and I was only able to sip some tea and nibble on crackers. Joseph enjoyed a full supper, and regaled me with stories of past visits to Philadelphia.

"Tomorrow, when you are rested, I shall take you to the theater. Would you like to go see a Shakespearean performance, or perhaps visit the opera? I do believe *Il Bacio* is on the opera stage these days."

"Oh Joseph. I certainly would. Just let me recover some of my energy, and I'll be eager to explore this wonderful city with you. After all, we have two weeks, so I feel certain we'll do it justice."

As he signed for our dinner, I excused myself and returned to the room. Still anxious and unsure of what was expected of me, I needed some private moments. I bathed and perfumed myself, brushed and dressed my hair in a loose, girlish style, and selected a pale rose silk nightgown. I tied it loosely around my waist with a broad pink ribbon belt.

Pulling back the covers and settling in between luxuriously smooth cotton sheets, I smiled and inhaled deeply. I very much wanted to please Joseph tonight. We had waited so long.

He entered the bedroom quietly, his face softly lit by candles and the hearth. Smiling, his eyes filled with warmth, Joseph leaned into me and cradled my shoulders with his arm. His warm lips found my cheek and then my waiting mouth. The fire burned low. The warmth was comforting, and I felt he could read my mind when he stood up to throw another log onto the glowing embers. The log instantly flared and sparks flew up the chimney, lighting our love nest.

Joseph pressed a kiss against the top of my head, looking longingly into my eyes. He caressed my cheek as he whispered, "Your golden hair frames your lovely face; your eyes, so soft, so warm, glow with hidden fire."

The full moon, visible through the window, coated everything in the room with a layer of silver. My mouth trembled as I tried to speak. His voice was husky with need. Kissing my open mouth freely, he buried his face in my neck and sucked its warmth to the surface. My senses swam and my legs became weak as my heart pounded against his chest.

"You are a fascinating enigma, sweet Antonia; a paradox. You are totally open and hide nothing, yet you are the most mysterious woman I've ever met."

I reached for his hand and thrilled to his touch, all the way to my toes. Lacing my fingers through his, I gasped, "Are you trying to drive me mad?" in a voice choked with frustration and laughter.

My heart was beating so loudly I wondered if he could hear it. Clinging to him, I allowed my eyes to flutter close. When my lips found the skin of his throat, I kissed it. He began rubbing my scalp with the pads of his fingers, sending me unbridled pleasure. I peeked through my lashes at his slow, tender smile.

Joseph's kisses were slow, deliberate and devastating. His tongue slid into my mouth...so warm, so soft. A sudden chill danced up my spine. He lifted me slightly and buried his face in my hair as he fondled my body through the silk gown. Despite the urgency of the physical demands, his kisses floated dreamy and sweet over my senses.

As we became one at last, his eyes took on a smoky hue. I felt my own bonfires blazing, and let them smolder slowly and deliciously. Like warm rain, my gratification felt soft and quiet and soothing. I tried to smile; when my eyes crinkled, a tear spilled from the corner and down my cheek. Joseph lifted my head, kissing my face, and pointed out the moon, peeking through the trees.

This was the closeness I had forever yearned for—the fusion of male and female that shaped the ancient ritual of the night. Washed by emotions beyond my understanding, I snuggled into his arms while he cradled my exhausted body, as if I were the most precious creature in the world.

I fell asleep, saturated in grateful love.

FORTY-FOUR

Pauline

LAST DAYS OF DECEMBER 1863

I am about to publish a little book about my scouting adventures! I wrote it during my long convalescence at the boarding house in Nashville, and I titled it *An Inside View of the Army Police (The Thrilling Adventures of Pauline Cushman.)* The publishing date is December 15, 1863, but it will not be available for sale until January 1864. Included in this publication is my favorite photograph of me in the military dress uniform.

I was finally able to return to Louisville on December 2, and the Louisville Journal welcomed me back with the following article.

ARRIVAL OF MISS PAULINE CUSHMAN—This distinguished lady arrived in our city yesterday. She will be heartily welcomed by her numerous friends and admirers. The Nashville Press of yesterday gives a glowing description of a rich lady's riding dress presented by the loyal ladies of Nashville to Miss Cushman—the daring heroine who has done so much service for the United States—a lady who occupied the warmest niche in the patriotic heart of almost every American soldier. The dress is made of the most costly material and is beautiful but modestly ornamented with national emblems. The career of this lady since she left our city has been one of the wildest romances, and perhaps the most eventful of all heroines who have figured in this war. Her achievements during the past year will fill one of the brightest pages of history.

A few days later I left for Cincinnati, where I am now working diligently to get my book ready for publication. I am including news of other female scouts and spies who I learned about after returning. Belle Boyd, a fascinating woman whose story is quite similar to mine, is one of them. I am also writing about Lizzie Compton, who served in seven different regiments and fought in several battles.

My friend General Rosecrans returned to Cincinnati in mid-December. We shared several meals together and talked about our new circumstances. He was chosen to be the president of the *Great Western Sanitary Fair*, and during the opening ceremony, he told the story of "The Union Female Spy" as I stood at his side. He explained how I had accepted the dangerous mission and succeeded by virtue of my profession as an actress.

He went on to say, "She braved the danger, and went through my lines. She was gone longer than we expected. At last when we took Shelbyville, we found her in prison, condemned to be hung as a spy! She awaited her fate like a patriot and hero, suffering from sickness throughout it all. We rescued her in time and sent her to Nashville, where she spent months recovering from her illness."

Drawing in a deep breath, he took up again. "I gave her all the money I had the right to draw from the public funds. From our conversations, I now know she has been two weeks in this city, working to obtain means to take her to friends in New York and then reunite with her children. She needs help to pay her bills here and her fare to New York. I am going to give you all an opportunity to show your appreciation for her devotion, by contributing something to relieve her present necessities."

A collection was taken up and, less than an hour later, a purse of three hundred dollars was raised. How grateful I was to these wonderful people! I was able to pay my boarding and set the rest aside until the New Year, when I would at long last return to my children.

It had been almost a year since I'd held my own children. I learned that they now resided in two different states. My daughter Ida was in Sandusky, Ohio, living with my deceased husband's relatives. My mother-in-law Ellen passed away and left both children under the care of Mary and Jim Ferris. But then Mary became pregnant and could not care for them both so they sent little Charlie to another aunt in Vermont. I will visit them as soon as I can, grateful that after so much time and heartache, we will finally be a family again.

Just before the Christmas holiday, I gave a recitation of my experiences at Mozart Hall, where the best professional talent appears along with fine vocal and instrumental performances. *The Cincinnati Daily Gazette* wrote the following:

> MISS PAULINE CUSHMAN—*A large audience was present at the entertainment given by Miss Pauline Cushman at Mozart Hall last evening. The lady did not present the appearance of one who had undergone the perils from which she was fortunately rescued by General Granger, but rather that of one who never had a care, but had been surrounded by the good things of this life. She is of medium height, with large dark and expressive eyes and delicately molded features. Her part of the entertainment consisted in the singing of several songs, which she rendered in a pleasant manner.*

Then two days later, an audience of more than two thousand people assembled at Mozart Hall to hear me recount more of my daring adventures. It seemed the ladies of Cincinnati were curious about me. My share of this large gate (at twenty-five or fifty cents a ticket) added several hundred more dollars to my income. Naturally I shared the proceeds with The Sanitary Commission and other organizations, feeling so blessed to receive it.

General Rosecrans no longer commands an army, having been ordered to take charge of the Department of Missouri. James Garfield is now in Washington, D.C., serving as a congressman. It is now time for me to go east to find my children. Upon my return, my book will be published and I will continue my career as an actress, reciting my thrilling adventures for those who want to read them.

Pauline

P auline flourished and suffered through the Civil War, the coming of the railroad and the settling of our Western frontier. She briefly interrupted her career as a theater actress to ride horseback as a Union messenger through Kentucky, Tennessee, Alabama, Mississippi and northern Georgia. In late 1864, she returned to performing.

Between 1864 and 1870, Pauline lectured about her adventures as a spy, often exaggerating the details, and became actively involved in the theatrical community in New York City and upstate New York. She also made appearances in Boston, Buffalo, Indianapolis, Columbus, Philadelphia, Pittsburgh and Washington City.

Pauline was reunited with both her children after the war. Her son Charles Jr. died from illness in November of 1864, followed by her daughter Ida in late 1867.

In 1872 Pauline traveled to Los Angeles, California, where she fell in love with August Fichtner. They married on December 19, 1872, although Pauline knew it would mean the end of her $8.00 monthly widow's pension.

Sadly, Pauline was widowed less than a year after her second marriage. Moving to San Francisco, she spent the next five years living between the Bay Area and Santa Cruz, where she worked in the redwood logging camps.

In 1879, she met and married Jeremiah Fryer, a handsome

Cherokee man, many years her junior. They bought a hotel and livery stable in Casa Grande, Arizona Territory. The business thrived due to their hard work and the 1880 arrival of the Southern Pacific Railroad. Jeremiah later became Sheriff of Pinal County, but after a few more years together, they separated and Pauline returned to San Francisco.

Pauline's last years were spent at a boarding house on San Francisco's Market Street, working as a scrubwoman while battling arthritis and rheumatism. A doctor gave her morphine tablets for the pain, and on the morning of December 2, 1893, she was found unresponsive by her landlady. The official coroner's report stated that she died of a morphine overdose "taken without suicidal intent and to relieve pain." She was sixty years old.

In the days after her death, newspapers reported that the Major Cushman Fryer, who died in abject poverty, would be buried in potter's field. An uproar was led by the Grand Army of the Republic, an organization of war veterans, and donations poured in for a proper funeral. The Women Relief Corps (of the San Francisco Grand Army of the Republic) provided her a splendid funeral, with a large white coffin covered in thousands of white flowers.

She was venerated with full military honors—flags, honor guard and rifle salutes—on December 6, 1893. Her body was placed in the officers' circle at the National Cemetery in Presidio and her gravestone gives only her name and the title "Union Spy."

An excerpt from the *New York Times*, May 28, 1864, illustrates the high regard in which the Union held her. *"Among the women of America who have made themselves famous since the opening of the rebellion, few have suffered more or rendered more service to the Federal cause than Pauline Cushman, the female scout and spy."*

JOHN MORGAN was on a reconnaissance near Greenville, Tennessee on September 4, 1864. He stopped at the home of Mrs. Williams, whose husband was an officer on General Burnside's staff. During the night Mrs. Williams rode fifteen miles to a Union camp, and returned with a company of Union soldiers. When they surrounded the house Morgan awoke, drew his revolver, and attempted to escape, but was fired on and killed. He was thirty-nine years old.

GENERAL BRAGG'S army was routed by Maj. General Ulysses S. Grant in the Battles for Chattanooga. He was recalled in early 1864 to Richmond, where he became the military advisor to Confederate President Jefferson Davis. After the war General Bragg worked as the superintendent of the New Orleans waterworks, a supervisor of harbor improvements at Mobile, Alabama, and as a railroad engineer and inspector in Texas. He died in Galveston, Texas, while walking down the street with a friend. He collapsed and died of "paralysis of the brain" at the age of fifty-nine.

GENERAL ROSECRANS, in his role as an army commander, became one of the most popular generals in the Union Army, but his military career was effectively ended following a disastrous defeat at the Battle of Chickamauga in 1863. He was known to his men as "Old Rosy," not only because of his last name (the source for that nickname at West Point), but because of his large red nose, which was described as "intensified Roman". As a devout Catholic, he carried a crucifix on his watch chain and a rosary in his pocket, and he delighted in keeping his staff up half the night debating religious doctrine. He could swing swiftly from bristling anger to good-natured amusement, which endeared him to his men. He was briefly considered as a vice-presidential running mate for Abraham Lincoln in 1864. After the war, he served in diplomatic and appointed political positions and in 1881 was elected to Congress, representing California. He died at the age of seventy-eight.

GENERAL GRANGER'S success at Chickamauga earned him command of the newly formed IV Corps in the Army of the Cumberland. Under his command, this unit distinguished itself at the third Battle of Chattanooga, where Union forces broke through and forced the Confederates under General Braxton Bragg to retreat. After Chattanooga, Granger helped lift the siege at Knoxville, Tennessee. When the war ended, Granger remained in the Army, and was given command of the Department of Texas. On June 19, 1865, in the city of Galveston, Texas, he declared the institution of slavery dead in the state, setting off joyous demonstrations by freedmen and originating the annual "Juneteenth" celebration, which commemorates the freeing of the blacks in Texas. He died at age fifty-four.

GENERAL GARFIELD had opposed the Confederate secession while serving in the Union Army during the Civil War. He fought in the battles of Middle Creek, Shiloh and Chickamauga and was first elected to Congress in 1862 to represent Ohio's 19th District. Throughout Garfield's extended congressional service after the Civil War, he firmly supported the gold standard and gained a reputation as a skilled orator. In the 1880 presidential election, Garfield conducted a low-key, front-porch campaign and narrowly defeated Democrat Winfield Scott Hancock. Garfield advocated agricultural technology, an educated electorate, and civil rights for African Americans. He proposed substantial civil service reform in the Pendleton Civil Service Reform Act, which was passed by Congress in 1883. Despite his strong performance, Garfield is mostly remembered for being assassinated at age forty-nine. Having been shot twice on July 2, 1881, at the railroad passenger terminal in Washington City, he lived until September 19, 1881, finally succumbing to infection.

Antonia

A ntonia and Joseph Willard had three children: Joseph Edward, born on May 1, 1865; Charles F., born on April 13, 1867; and Archie F., born on February 9, 1871. Baby Charles lived almost four months. His brother Archie died at birth. Joseph Edward lived for fifty- nine years.

Antonia's brother Charlie Ford died on May 25, 1864 at the age of twenty-four, after the Battle of Hanover Courthouse. He fought to the end in the 2nd company of Stuart's Light Horse Artillery.

Clanie Ford married Mary McBride at the end of the war. They had one son, whom they named Clanie. Clanie Senior died in 1889 at the age of forty-four.

Pattie Ford married Lieutenant McKim Holliday Wells on February 25, 1874. They had four children. She died in 1888, only thirty-eight years old.

Frank R. Ford went to VMI in 1873 and graduated in the medical field. He married Barbara Bingham and they had five children. He died at age forty-seven on February 17, 1904.

Antonia's father, E.R. Ford, died suddenly of paralysis on November 26, 1871. He was fifty-eight years old. The Alexandria Gazette stated, "He had acquired a character for justice and integrity rarely equated."

James Ewell Brown (Jeb) Stuart was probably the most famous cavalryman of the Civil War. On May 11, 1864, during

General Grant's drive on Richmond, he stopped Sheridan's cavalry at Yellow Tavern, just north of Richmond. He was mortally wounded while fighting and died the next day. He was thirty-one years old and left behind his wife Flora and four children. Those who knew him well insisted that his love for Laura Ratcliffe never died, yet he never saw her again after 1863. General Lee gave him an epitaph worthy of a great spy: *"He never brought me a piece of false information."* That was due, in no small part, to the intelligence brought to him by Antonia Ford and Laura Ratcliffe. One of his closest friends, John Esten Cooke, described his last moments:

> *As his life had been one of earnest devotion to the cause in which he believed, so his last hours were tranquil, his confidence in the mercy of Heaven unfailing. When he was asked how he felt, he said, "Easy, but willing to die, if God and my country think I have done my duty." His last words were, "I am going fast now; I am resigned. God's will be done."*

John Mosby was promoted to Colonel of Mosby's Rangers, the 43rd Battalion of Virginia Cavalry, on December 7, 1864. He and his wife Pauline had four sons and four daughters. His son George died in 1873 and Pauline and an infant son Alfred died in 1876. General Ulysses S. Grant ordered Mosby "hanged without trial" if captured, but he was never caught. John Mosby died in 1916 at the age of eighty-three, after serving as Minister to Hong Kong under President Ulysses S. Grant.

Laura Ratcliffe became destitute after the war. In 1873, she inherited a comfortable home. In 1890, at the age of fifty-four, she married for the first time. Like her cousin Antonia, Laura married a Yankee soldier, Milton Hanna, her neighbor and long-time friend. Seven years after the wedding he was killed in a farming accident. This was another coincidence the cousins shared: seven years of marriage. She died at the age of eighty-seven on August 8, 1923 and was buried on her property, Merrybrook, in a family plot. Her house is listed on the National Register of Historic Places.

John Esten Cooke married Mary Francis Page on September 18, 1867. He wrote a number of Civil War novels after the war, based on his experiences and those of Antonia Ford. "Surry of Eagle's Nest" was the spy story of Antonia's wild ride to deliver intelligence to General Beauregard. John died in 1886 at the age of fifty-six.

Antonia and Joseph Willard enjoyed seven years of marriage together. They continued to tease each other about their disparate political backgrounds. When asked by a friend why she married a Yankee, Antonia laughed. "I knew I could not revenge myself on the nation, but I was fully capable of tormenting one Yankee to death, so I took the Major."

Five days after their third child, Archie F., died at birth, Antonia passed away from complications of childbirth. That was February 14, 1871. She was thirty-two years old. Her funeral was held at the historic New York Avenue Presbyterian Church in Washington, presided over by its pastor, Dr. Phineas Gurley—the same pastor who had married Antonia and Joseph. Pastor Gurley had also delivered President Lincoln's funeral sermon at the White House in 1865. Her obituary read: *"Whatever she thought to be right, she considered no sacrifice too great to accomplish it."*

Joseph Clapp Willard never remarried and spent the rest of his life mourning his beloved Antonia. He focused entirely on business and became a social recluse. In 1892 he purchased his brother Henry's interest and became sole owner of the Willard Hotel. He died in his home on January 17, 1897, at the age of seventy-seven. Present at the time of death were his son Joseph, brothers Henry A. and Caleb C., his nephew Henry K. Willard and their wives. At the time of his death, Joseph had amassed an estate valued at approximately seven million dollars, or two hundred million dollars today. Despite his great wealth, he left no will; his fortune went to his son Joseph. Joseph C. Willard was interred beside Antonia in the Oak Hill Cemetery in Washington D.C.

Joseph Edward Willard (Joe) was the only living son of Antonia and Joseph. After his mother's death, Joe was raised by his grandmother Julia and his Aunt Pattie. He served on the staff of General Fitzhugh Lee, Confederate General Robert E. Lee's nephew, during the Spanish-American War. At the time of his father's death Joe was a member of the Virginia House of Delegates. He married Belle Layton Wyatt and built her a sizable mansion called *Layton Hall*. Together they did a great deal of public service for the Fairfax Courthouse community. Joseph began renovating the Willard Hotel in 1902, finishing it in 1905. In 1902 he was elected Lt. Governor of Virginia and later served as Ambassador to Spain under President Woodrow Wilson. He died in 1924. He was fifty-eight years old.

Acknowledgments

No author works in a vacuum. Writing a novel is like rowing a boat into the wind. The writer often needs help, and when people come along at opportune moments with words of encouragement, new ideas, suggestions and a helping hand, the writer feels enormous gratitude.

My husband Michael and I were eating shrimp with our grandchildren at *The Raw Bar* on Jekyll Island when the idea for this book was suggested by three friends: Keith and Vicki McKenzie, and Vicki's brother Harry Paisley. During our conversation, Keith asked me what I knew about female Civil War spies. "Not much," I had to answer. He smiled, and the three of them (historians and re-enactors) delighted us with stories of several courageous women who worked as "scouts" during the Civil War.

Captivated, I hurried home to begin researching these women. I was astounded at how many females risked their lives because of strong loyalty to their country. I found myself especially drawn to the tales of two "lesser-known" heroines, whose stories deserved to be told. These women are Antonia Ford and Pauline Cushman.

Thank you, Vicki, Keith and Harry, for introducing me to this intriguing world of female spies.

I also would like to acknowledge and express my gratitude to my superb book team. Carey "Trip" Giudici and Pam Pollack, you deserve very special thanks for having worked with me for over fourteen years. As editors and authors, you are both exceptionally talented, hard-working and exceedingly patient. You never lost your wonderful senses of humor while dealing with my harried author's nerves. You constantly bring creativity and renewed energy to my writing.

Patty Osborne is another long-time team member: a gifted friend who takes my unadorned manuscripts and magically converts them into attractive books. Once again I stand humbly before you. Thank you for patiently dealing with my inconsistent behavior, which appears every time we put a book together. You're the best!

To my incredibly talented cover artist Gini Steele, a million thank yous! What a gorgeous image you've created for this book! I remain under your spell and totally appreciate your talent.

I am so indebted to Buddy Sullivan, Coastal Georgia historian, fellow author and a gentleman I am proud to call "friend." You have always been there for me, and so many others. I'm honored that you read the entire manuscript and provided me with a wonderful back cover blurb. Thank you Buddy!

They say it *"takes a village."* For this book, six incredibly talented proof readers read and untangled my manuscript, then offered wise critiques. They weeded out my errors and tightened up my writing. And often, it seemed their criticisms were tendered in a manner that was almost complimentary. What a pleasure to work with Cathy Drury, Diane Knight, Suzi Hassel, Scott Wells, Bob Whalen, and, for the first time ever, my 95-year-old mother, Phyllis Bauer. I thank each of you from the bottom of my heart!

A special thanks to three authors, whose books became my primary sources and opened up for me the worlds of Antonia and Pauline. Thank you William J. Christen, Karla Vernon, and Ferdinand L. Sarmiento. Their book titles are listed under *Resources.*

The title of this book changed several times, but my friends and family stuck with it until we all agreed on "The Dancing Delilahs." Thank you to my daughter Cassandra Coveney, my friend and book shop owner Nancy Thomason, and fellow role-players Chris Belis and Mike Earehart for coming up with such unique ideas.

The acknowledgments would be incomplete without a special mention to Elaine McHale, who met me at the Fairfax Museum in Virginia and answered my numerous questions about Antonia Ford. Then she sent me to the Fairfax Regional Library for even more resources. Thank you, Elaine, for your gracious assistance.

Lastly, I thank my husband Michael for his belief in me and his willingness to share this journey. Thank you for accompanying me to Virginia for the research. You never questioned my passion for this story. You have always supported me in ways that allowed me to follow the sources. Thank you, my love, for your constant encouragement, kind nature and validation.

Lord, thank you for walking with me every step of this journey. Thank you for the comfort of Your Spirit and Your grace to all mankind. I hope this book honors You.

BOOK GROUP DISCUSSION QUESTIONS

1. Why do you think the author chose to tell the story through the voices of two narrators? How are Pauline's observations and judgments different from Antonia's?

2. Which emotions, such as guilt, anger, pride, etc., motivate Antonia's and Pauline's decisions to risk their lives to become spies?

3. Were you, the reader, hoping that the women would meet during the war? How do you think they would have interacted?

4. Did you have a favorite protagonist? Did you identify with either one, or perhaps with them both?

5. This is a unique title. Did it fit the plot of the story?

6. Did Pauline or Antonia experience a religious conversion during the story? If so, how and when?

7. Did you feel there was a shift of balance as you moved through the story? Was one woman stronger at one time, and if so, did the other one also find her strength?

8. Did you get a sense the author had a strong vision of individual responsibility as a theme? What might have been her motivation to have chosen and recorded the stories of Antonia and Pauline?

9. Antonia's life dramatically changed from her comfortable upbringing to her terrifying imprisonment, and then to her unexpected love for her captor. How well did she deal with all of this?

10. Pauline seemed to struggle to survive throughout various periods of her life. Do you feel she was in bondage to maintain control—or to not be alone—or to find her personal truth?

11. Do you think the author intended to show that one woman was a stronger loyalist to her country than the other? Why or why not?

12. Acting is a prevalent theme in this story. How did it affect Pauline's experiences and her self-image? Would you also consider Antonia an actress?

RESOURCES

PRIMARY SOURCES

Christen, William J., *Pauline Cushman: Spy of the Cumberland*, Roseville, MN: Edinborough Press, 2000.

Sarmiento, Ferdinand L., *Life Of Pauline Cushman: The Celebrated Union Spy And Scout: Comprising Her Early History, Her Entry Into The Secret Service Of The Army Of The Cumberland, And Exciting Adventure With The Rebel Chieftains And Others While Within the Enemy's Lines,* Philadelphia, PA: John E. Potter and Company, 1865

Vernon, Karla, *The Spy in Crinoline: Antonia Ford's Civil War*, Westminster, MD: Fireside Fiction, 2006.

SECONDARY SOURCES

Alexander, John H., *Mosby's Men,* New York, NY: Neale Publishing Company, 1907.

Allardice, Bruce S., *Confederate Colonels: A Biographical Register*, MI: University of Missouri Press, 2008.

Bakeless, John, *Spies of the Confederacy,* Mineola, NY: Dover Publications, 2011.

Banks, Leo W., *Stalwart Women*, Phoenix, AZ: Arizona Department of Transportation, 1999.

Caravantes, Peggy, *Petticoat Spies: Six Women Spies of the Civil War,* Greensboro, NC: Morgan Reynolds Publishers, Inc., 2002.

Cooke, John Esten, *Surry of Eagle's Nest*, New York, NY: G.W. Dillingham Co, 1987.

Horan, James D., *Desperate Women,* New York, NY: G.P. Putnam's Sons, 1952.

Hunter, Ryan Ann, *In Disguise: Undercover With Real Women Spies,* New York, NY: Aladdin, 2013.

Jones, Virgil Carrington, *Gray Ghosts and Rebel Raiders*, Atlanta, GA: Mockingbird Books, 1956.

Kane, Harnett T., *Spies for the Blue and Gray,* New York, NY: Doubleday, 1954.

Markle, Donald E., *Spies and Spymasters of the Civil War*, New York, NY: Hippocrene Books, 2004.

Mosby, John Singleton, *Stuart's Cavalry in the Gettysburg Campaign*, MI: University of Michigan Library, 2009.

Moore, Frank, *Women of the War: True Stories of Brave Women in the Civil War,* Alexander, NC: Blue/Gray Books, 1997.

Neely, Mark E., *The Fate of Liberty: Abraham Lincoln and Civil Liberties*, New York, NY: Little, Brown, and Company, 1917.

Ramage, James A., *Rebel Raider: The Life of General John Hunt Morgan*, KY: University Press of Kentucky, 1986.

Ross, Ishbel, *Rebel Rose: Life of Rose O'Neal Greenhow, Confederate Spy*, New York, NY: Harper & Brothers, 1954.

Wellman, Manly Wade, *Rebel Boast*, Alexander, NC: Alexander Books, 1998.

Wert, Jeffery D., *Mosby's Rangers*, New York, NY: Simon & Schuster, 1990.

Winkler, H. Donald, *Stealing Secrets: How A Few Daring Women Deceived Generals, Impacted Battles, And Altered The Course Of The Civil War*, Naperville, IL: Cumberland House, 2010.

MANUSCRIPTS

"Antonia Ford, Letters from 1861 to 1863" (04/21/61, 10/07/61, 11/25/61, 04/13/63, 07/18/63, 06/26/63, 12/31/63) Library of Congress, Manuscript Division, Willard Papers, Boxes 1, 198, 201, 202, 203, 204.

Various documents, letters and notations from 1863 to 1864 of Antonia Ford Willard. (11/12/63, 11/30/63, 01/11/64, 01/12/64, 01/30/64, 02/01/64, 02/02/64) City of Fairfax Historic Collections, Fairfax, VA.

NEWSPAPER AND MAGAZINE ARTICLES

"Antonia Ford and Joseph Willard," *Morning Telegraph*, December 16, 1900.

Hunter, Ryan, "Pauline Cushman: Her Best Role," *History's Women Magazine*, 1955.

Johnson, William Page, "Joseph Willard's Decree of Divorce," *Evening Star*, March 2, 1864.

"Joseph Willard Dead: Long Identified with the Capital City's History," *The Washington Post,* January 18, 1897.

Moore, Frank, "Women of the War: Their Heroism and Self-Sacrifice," *The Savannah Republican.*

"Pauline Cushman"—4 part series of articles, *The Los Angeles Times* during the 1880s.

"Serenade to Miss Major Pauline Cushman," *The New York Times,*
June 3, 1864.

"Sesquicentennial Wedding Anniversary of the Spy Millionaire,"
The Fare Facs Gazette, 2014.

Wheeler, Linda, "A Confederate Spy, at Home in Virginia," *The
Washington Post*, April 15, 2007.

Whitehead, A.M, "Antonia Ford (1838-1871)," *Encyclopedia
Virginia,* Virginia Foundation for the Humanities, May 27, 2014.

INTERNET ARTICLES

"Antonia Ford," Encyclopedia Virginia, www.encyclopediavirginia.
org

"Antonia Ford," www.https.//en.wikipedia.org/wiki/Antonia_Ford

"Antonia Ford," Women's History, www.womenshistory.about.
com/od/civilwar/p/antonia_ford.htm

Careton, Eileen Metheny, "A Beautiful Spy," http://www.
virginialiving.com/virginia/history/a-beautiful-spy/

CasaMajor, George H., "The Secret Service of the Federal Armies,"
http://www.cililwarsignals.org/pages/spy/fedsecret/html

"Civil War Trust Biography of Mosby," http.www.civilwar.org/
education/history/biographies/john-singleton-mosby.html

"Clandestine Women: Spies in American History," National
Women's History Museum website: http://www.nwhm.org/
online-exhibits/spies/9.html

Drill, Christina, "The Actress Who Helped Lincoln Defect the
Confederary," http://www.salon.com/2014/05/19/the_actress_
who_helped_Abraham_Lincoln

"Female Soldiers in the Civil War," http://www.hallrichard.com/
civilwomen.htm

"History's Women," http://www.historyswomen.com/earlyamerica/
paulinecushman.htm

"How to Dress Like a Victorian Man from the 1860s," http//www.
vistoriana.com/men-clothing/

"Letter by John Mosby about Antonia Ford," http://digittool1.1va.
lib.va.us:8881/R/P1U9RLTH9MBK8MQVPUZCQXH5MXV
AM98I93TF22DK33IGK-01208?func=results-jump=full_set_
entry=000001

MacLean, Maggie, "Pauline Cushman—Civil War Spy and
Theatre Actress," www.civilwarwomenblog.com/Pauline-
Cushman/01/23/2008

"McArthur, John, Jr. (1823-1890)," https://www. philadelphiabuildings.org/pab/app/ar_display.cfm/27058

"Major Pauline Cushman," http://www.bklynlibrary.org/civilwar/ cwdoc071.html

"Mosby Heritage Area Association," http://www. mosbyyheritagearea.org

"Pauline Cushman-Biography," www.biography.com/people/ pauline-cushman

"Pauline Cushman," https://en.wikipedia.org/wiki/Pauline_ Cushman

"Pauline Cushman," National Park Service, www.nps.gov/ resources/person.htm?id=76

"Pauline Cushman Scrapbook-1863-1869, 1893," http://www.oac. cdlib.org/search?style=oac4;pInstitution=California History

"Pauline Wood Fryer (1833-1893)," Find A Grave Memorial, http:// www.findagrave.com/cgi-bin/fg.cgi?page=gr&GRID-6333443

"Photo of Antonia Ford in Military Style Costume," http://www. loc.gov/pictures/collections/civilwar/item/2010648711/loc.gov/ pictures/collections/civilwar/item/2010648711/

"Political Cartoon on Antonia Ford," http://www.loc.gov/pictures/ resource/cph.3c00253/?co=civilwar

"Portrait of Antonia Ford," http://www.loc.gov/pictures/resource/ cwpbh.02834/

Powell, Becky, "My Neighbor, the Spy," http://myneighborthe spy. com

"Scandalous Women: Pauline Cushman-Union Spy," http:// scandalouswoman.blogspot.com/2008/03/pauling-cushman-union-spy

"The Little Major," http://www.thewesternonline.com/ paulingcushman.html

"The Metropolitan, aka Brown's Marble Hotel," http://www. streetsofwashington.com/2009/12/metropolitan-aka-brow

"The Willard Hotel in the 19th Century/Streets of Washington," http://www.streetsofwashington.com/202/07/the-willard-hotel-in-19th-century

"Virginia Beauty or Confederate Spy," http://www. civilwarsummer.com/virginia-beauty-or-confederate-spy

"Women Soldiers, Spies & Vivandieres," www.uttyler.edu/vbelts/ women_soldiers_utm

ABOUT THE ARTIST

Combining her mutual love of photography and history, Gini Steele and her husband Richard have created an extensive collection of photographic images of times long gone by. Throughout their work with historical societies, archivists and researchers they realized that there was a need to restore and reproduce these historic images and make them available before they are lost forever.

Staying true to the genre Ms. Steele used traditional photographic processes to both restore and reproduce the collection of old glass plates, negatives and photographs. She enjoys the challenge of interpreting the old negatives in her darkroom and prints the silver gelatin photographs by hand one at a time. Once the photographs are printed , they are tinted by hand. Once the hand-tinting is accomplished, Gini uses digital technology to complete the image, creating a unique piece of art.

Gini resides in Beaufort, SC with her husband Richard and her two cats Bailey and Penelope Butterbeans.